THE DOCKLAND MURDER

MURDER

Mike Hollow

Allison & Busby Limited
11 Wardour Mews
London W1F 8AN
allisonandbusby.com

First published by Allison & Busby in 2021.
This paperback edition published by Allison & Busby in 2021.

A CIP catalogue record for this book is available from
the British Library.

10 9 8 7 6 5 4 3 2 1

ISBN 978-0-7490-2623-3

Typeset in 11/16 pt Sabon LT Pro by
Allison & Busby Ltd.

The paper used for this Allison & Busby publication
has been produced from trees that have been legally sourced
from well-managed and credibly certified forests.

Printed and bound by
CPI Group (UK) Ltd, Croydon, CR0 4YY

For Zoë, beloved child of a different London

CHAPTER ONE

The skeletal silhouettes of cranes stood watch over the Royal Albert Dock in the scant moonlight like mourners round a grave as a solitary man paced slowly along the south quay. Sharp gusts of wind blowing in off the Thames scoured his face, and the cold was like death in his bones, gnawing from the inside. He stamped his boots on the concrete, but it made no difference. It was always the same on nights: as the shift wore on, your body slowed down and the chill set in. No wonder they called it the dead of night.

He looked back to where spikes of orange flame leapt from the far end of the neighbouring Royal Victoria Dock. The bombers had hit something, but he couldn't see what. One of the transit sheds or warehouses that lined the quayside, perhaps, or maybe even a ship. Tonight, for once, on his own beat things hadn't been so bad: as far as he could tell, the planes had missed the Royal Albert. But behind him, beyond the dark, hulking buildings on the quay, the sky was bright with the glow of more fire. He couldn't see what was burning, but there was nothing between here and the river except the King George V Dock and the tightly packed streets of North Woolwich and Silvertown, where his own home was. Ever since the area had been pounded on the first night of the Blitz he'd been thankful he didn't have a family.

He walked on, listening to his own footsteps. The luminous hands on his wristwatch told him it was twenty past five. Still a couple of hours to go before the blackout ended, but only another forty minutes to work on his shift, if he got off on time. The noise of the men fighting the fires was too far away to be more than a faint backdrop, and the aircraft had gone. Where he was, all he could hear was the rats scurrying towards the sheds as he approached, and the lap, lap of inky-black water beside him. In normal times that was the way he liked it on a night shift: quiet. But these were not normal times. Now there was no knowing when Mr Goering's swarms of Heinkel and Dornier bombers would pay their next visit.

He'd been up in an aeroplane just the once himself: in 1932, when Sir Alan Cobham's Flying Circus came to do a display at the Low Hall Sports Ground in Walthamstow and he'd gone for a five-bob flip in the back seat of an Avro biplane left over from the Great War. He'd seen the Thames, his little house in Silvertown, and the three long rectangles of the Royal Docks glinting in the sunlight below. He didn't give it a second thought at the time, but now he was only too aware that if they glinted in sunlight they'd glint in a bit of moonlight too, and sometimes his spine shivered at the thought of standing in the middle of this unmistakable landmark. You could black out every house in London, every house in England, but you couldn't black out water, and when the moon shone its light on the river and these docks, there might just as well be a three-mile-long neon sign inviting the German air force to fly this way and do their worst.

It was Tuesday the fifth of November, 1940, which meant it was the last of his month of night shifts. It also meant the docks had been under attack from the air for two months now. It was a wonder anything was left standing.

This wasn't what Arthur Wilkinson had signed up for, nearly thirty years before. He'd joined the Port of London Authority Police in 1912, two years after it was set up, as a second-class constable on twenty-five shillings a week. His main reason for becoming a PLA copper was that it offered steady money, not the regular unemployment he'd known in the building trade before that, but he'd grown to enjoy the job. The Great War changed all that, of course. He'd policed the docks all the way through, and it was no laughing matter, especially when the Kaiser started bombing them. Keeping order in the peacetime years that followed was a merciful relief in comparison with that. But now it had started all over again, and with a savage intensity that the old Kaiser could only have dreamed of. Just a few weeks ago a PLA police sergeant and constable had been killed in this very dock when an unexploded bomb went off. Now, after nearly sixty nights of devastating air raids, he wasn't sure how much more his nerves could stand.

He pulled up short, noticing just in time by the moonlight that he was about to walk into a heap of discarded timber on the edge of the quay. The dockers called it dunnage, but to him it was simply lumps of old wood, just part of the junk they left lying around at night, ready to trip you up and send you plunging into the waters of the dock. Like all PLA policemen he was required to be able to swim fifty yards, but if you ended up in the water you had to have your stomach pumped. He'd had that done to him once and he never wanted to experience it again.

To say that the water was foul was an understatement. He had the smell of it in his nostrils now, and there was no denying it was pretty disgusting. He remembered some of the old-timers in the police saying that back in the days before oil-burning ships, the water in the docks was so clean they'd sometimes take a dip at the end of the day. Those days were long gone, of course, but in any case, he wondered, even without the oil, what about all the other stuff that got into the water? The ships' holds, for example: they were hosed out into the dock, no matter what noxious cargo they'd been carrying. And the toilets. It was against regulations for anyone to use these on the ships while in the dock, because they discharged directly into the water, but the lack of any alternative meant the regulation was ignored. And there were no toilets on barges, so barge hands often had no choice but to improvise as best they could – straight into the dock water. Then when you added the stench of rotting meat and vegetables, dead animals, chemicals, and anything else that fell or was dropped into the water, the dock was a thoroughly unsavoury place to work.

He moved away a little from the edge and tried to focus his thoughts on the end of his shift. Soon he'd be sitting down for a cup of tea and some breakfast, then having a welcome sleep and a bit of respite – if his house was still standing. He continued on his way, towards the next ship that lay at its mooring ahead of him. He could make out its name inscribed in big letters on the bow: *Magnolia*.

As he got closer, he heard the creak of a hawser on a barge moored beside the ship and looked down onto one of the many such craft that were left tied up around the ships in the dock overnight.

He had passed this point several times already during the night, but now there was just enough light to notice an odd outline at the near end of the barge. He pulled out his flashlight to check, and confident that there were no enemy planes overhead to see his light, he directed a brief beam downwards.

That was when he saw the man. He was wearing a dark civilian overcoat and a steel helmet. Just above his right elbow was an armlet bearing the words 'Home Guard'. He was lying on his back, draped awkwardly over the wooden coaming that framed the barge's hatch, and he wasn't moving. Wilkinson climbed down for a closer look and stopped: the man's eyes were wide open, staring at nothing. He knelt down beside him but could find no sign of injury. Then he slipped a hand beneath the man and felt something wet on his fingers. Using both hands, he lifted the body slightly at one side – enough to see the knife sticking out of the man's back.

CHAPTER TWO

The message from the station had been terse. Mr Soper wanted to see Detective Inspector Jago in his office at seven-fifteen. It was a common experience for Jago to be roused by duty from a sound sleep in his comfortable bed, or more recently from a fitful doze in his distinctly uncomfortable Anderson shelter in the back yard of his house, but it was less common for Divisional Detective Inspector Soper, his boss, to be in action at such an early hour. There must be something unusual going on, he thought, as he struggled into his clothes and grabbed a quick slice of bread and jam on his way to the car. Finding out precisely what that was, though, he was happy to leave until later: by then he might be awake enough to take it in.

At a quarter past seven precisely he knocked on the door of the DDI's office at West Ham police station, and a voice from inside bade him enter.

'Sir?' said Jago, presenting himself before Soper's desk.

'Ah, yes. Good morning, John. There's been an

incident in the docks – suspected murder. I want you to get down there straight away.'

'Which dock, sir?'

'The Royal Albert.'

'Right. I assume the PLA Police can't look after it themselves?'

'Unfortunately not. I've had a phone call from Divisional Inspector Grayson asking for assistance – he's their senior officer for the Royal Docks. Between you and me, I don't see why they have to call on the Metropolitan Police for help whenever they get something a bit out of the ordinary. It's not as though we're sitting around up here with nothing to do. I told him we're very stretched at the moment, especially what with having to run these new anti-looting squads.'

'Quite, sir.'

'Who'd have thought we'd need them? There's no morality these days. I can't begin to imagine what goes through the minds of villains like that who'll stoop to stealing decent people's possessions during air raids, but it's happening, and we've got to put a stop to it. I told Grayson we've had to double the number of officers working on it, not to mention getting extra detectives transferred to our division to take charge of them. I also pointed out that the PLA Police have their own CID and suggested they might like to deal with this suspected murder, but he said they only have one detective inspector to cover all the Royal Docks, so they want our help. We're stuck with it, I'm afraid.'

'Right, sir. So who's the victim?'

'I don't know his name, but it seems he was in the Home Guard.'

'Killed in the line of duty?'

'I don't know. But if you want my opinion, we're asking too much of those men. They're supposed to be our last line of defence against the Germans, and I understand they're being held in reserve to deal with any rioting that might break out too, but they're mostly boys and old age pensioners, as far as I can see.'

'Maybe they should be deployed to stop the looting.'

Soper sniffed contemptuously.

'Yes, maybe – but they've got a few slippery customers in their own ranks, haven't they? What about that case last week? Some seventeen-year-old lad in the Home Guard jailed for a month for stealing cigarettes from a bomb site. He admitted stealing them but said he didn't think it was looting. What's that supposed to mean? I worry about the youth of today, John. No backbone, no sense of right and wrong, that's the problem. How are we going to win the war with young people like that?'

Jago was beginning to feel his time would be better spent investigating a suspected murder in the Royal Albert Dock than on discussing the youth of today with DDI Soper, so he decided to take this question as rhetorical and make his exit.

'All right if I go down there now, sir? There's no point wasting time if it's our case.'

'Wasting time?' said Soper. 'Certainly not. Get started as soon as you can, and take young Cradock with you – I left instructions for him to be got out of bed. I've also called the hospital and told them to send that young medical chappie Dr Anderson down to take a look at the body. How's he shaping up, by the way?'

'Dr Anderson? He's doing very well, I think. Intelligent, thorough, and none of the airs and graces you get with some of those famous pathologists. Doesn't miss a thing, in my experience – it just goes to show some youngsters can teach the old dogs a trick or two.'

Soper made an indeterminate noise that sounded as though he accepted Jago's assessment but was reserving judgement nonetheless.

'Right,' he concluded. 'And when you get to the Royal Albert, you're to go to No. 20 Gate on Connaught Road and report to Detective Inspector Burton of the PLA Police.'

'Yes, sir.'

Jago left Soper and returned to the CID office, where he found Detective Constable Cradock waiting for him, munching a bacon sandwich from the canteen.

'Come along, Peter,' he said. 'We're taking a little trip down to the docks – the PLA Police have requested our assistance with a suspected murder. You can finish that on the way.'

'Very good, guv'nor,' said Cradock. He stuffed the rest of the sandwich into his mouth and chewed it vigorously as he followed Jago out to the yard at the back of the station. By the time they reached Jago's Riley Lynx he was able to speak again.

'I've never been in the docks,' he said. 'How does it work with us and the PLA Police – I mean, what's our jurisdiction?'

'It's simple – they're a separate force and deal with everything inside the docks, but they'll ask us for help with things like murder. Our jurisdiction's the same there as it is anywhere else in the borough, but theirs is just the docks and up to one mile outside them.'

Judging that this was sufficient information for Cradock to digest, Jago started the car and they set off.

It was about four miles' drive from West Ham police station to the Royal Docks, but the recent aid raids had made any kind of travel unpredictable. Jago took what should have been the most direct route, heading south down West Ham Lane to Plaistow Road and over the Northern Outfall Sewer, the great Victorian construction project that conveyed half of London's sewage through West Ham from the Abbey Mills pumping station in the west to the Beckton sewage works in the south-east. But a few minutes later, just past the East London Cemetery, they ran into a liquid obstruction of a different kind. The road ahead was flooded and closed.

'Look at that,' said Jago. 'Plaistow on Sea. One of those bombers last night must've hit a water main.'

'Yes,' said Cradock. 'Just as well they didn't blow up the sewer instead. Thankful for small mercies, eh, sir?'

'I suppose so,' Jago replied grudgingly. Hauling on the steering wheel, he performed a quick three-point turn in the blocked road and set off in search of an alternative route to the south of the borough. After more diversions in Canning Town they eventually arrived at Connaught Road and took the hydraulic swing bridge across the water channel linking the Royal Victoria Dock to their right and the Royal Albert to their left. Moments later they saw their destination: No. 20 gate, known as the Silvertown Gate, an entrance to the south side of the Royal Albert Dock.

Jago recognised the pathologist from Queen Mary's Hospital in Stratford standing by the gate and halted the car beside him.

'Dr Anderson,' he said. 'Good to see you. I hope you haven't been waiting too long. Hop in.'

As Anderson climbed into the back seat, the uniformed police constable guarding the gate came over to the car. Mindful that this would be an officer of the PLA Police and therefore might not recognise him, Jago identified himself to the constable.

'Thank you, sir,' the man replied, with a brief salute. 'Detective Inspector Burton's waiting for you down at No. 10 shed. Keep on this side of the dock and drive down Centre Road behind those big transit sheds – that's where the dockers store the cargo until the customers' lorries collect it. About two-thirds of the way down the road you'll come to the Customs and Excise Office, behind No. 14 shed. Park your car there, then walk through the gap between No. 14 and No. 12 sheds and carry on a bit further down the quay and you'll come to No. 10.'

They drove in through the gate. Passing the Royal Albert's two dry docks on their left, they continued down the road that ran between the long line of buildings on the south quay, much bigger than the name 'shed' would have suggested, and the corresponding row of structures on the north side of the King George V Dock, until they came to the gap the constable had described. They parked the car and completed their journey on foot along the quayside.

From here they could see the full expanse of the dock's placid water, with ships moored down both sides, their bows pointing to the west, clusters of barges around them, and here and there other barges to which the barrage balloons gleaming silver in the sky overhead were tethered. The sun was just rising in the east, the direction in which they were walking, and by its light they could see evidence of the destruction wrought by enemy aircraft undeterred and unhampered by the balloons. One of the big single-storey transit sheds was gutted, its steel-and-concrete framework still standing but the rest of it a desolate chaos of loose bricks and other debris, and the quayside crane outside it a mangled wreck. There was a chill in the air.

At No. 10 shed a man in an overcoat and trilby hat stepped forward to meet them.

'DI Burton,' he said to Jago. 'Jim Burton. I'm the CID inspector for the Royal Docks.'

He was a thin man, with a pinched nose and a mouth that looked permanently turned down. As they shook hands, Jago noticed that Burton's overcoat was frayed at the cuffs, and his tie crooked. He wondered whether his Port of London Authority Police opposite number had also been dragged out of bed before time this morning. He introduced Cradock and Anderson, and Burton responded with a nod and a half-hearted smile.

'If I can be of any assistance . . .' said Burton. He looked from Jago to Cradock and back again. 'But I don't suppose you'll need any from me.'

'I wouldn't say that,' Jago replied. 'We'll need any help you can give us.'

Burton gave a sort of shrug, said, 'Follow me,' and turned away in the direction of the nearest ship. Jago and Cradock followed, with Anderson bringing up the rear. Jago was looking to the left and right, taking in his surroundings, when something caught his eye. A taut mooring rope ran from the ship down to a steel bollard set into the quayside, and leaning against the rope was a rifle.

'Wait a minute,' he said. The other men stopped. 'Is this something to do with it?'

Burton glanced in the direction Jago's hand was pointing.

'Could be,' he said. 'I was going to mention it. The dead man's a Home Guard, and some of them have rifles, so it could be his. Don't worry, though, we haven't touched it. I thought we'd best leave it for you.'

Jago knelt down beside the firearm, thinking of the Lee-Enfield .303 he'd carried day and night as a soldier in the last war until he was given a commission and a pistol. This one wasn't a Lee-Enfield, but peering closely he could see the words 'Ross Rifle Co' engraved on the breech. He looked away, and as his eyes scanned the black expanse of the dock beyond, unbidden memories of sights and sounds from a quarter of a century earlier broke into his mind. The stench of the water recalled the unforgettable odour of rotting flesh, and for a moment he thought he could see a human face in the inky surface shimmering below him. The face of a man drowning.

He shuddered, and pushed the image out of his mind. When he was seventeen, nearly eighteen, and waiting to be called up for military service in the Great War, he'd reckoned it might be safer to join the navy than to fight in the trenches. But then he'd imagined having to go into action below decks in a warship, trapped behind watertight bulkhead doors and hearing the gunfire raging above until a shell or torpedo struck, with no escape from the inrushing water. The thought was unbearable. Anything on the land must be better than that – at least you'd have a chance. It was only later as a soldier at the front that he encountered a vicious irony of the war: seeing men who'd been gassed by the enemy, drowning on dry land as the evil chemicals did their work.

He snapped his eyes away from the water and checked that the rifle's safety catch was on before standing up and beckoning Cradock.

'Peter,' he said, 'get this checked for fingerprints. I assume it belonged to the dead man too, but I'd like to know who put it here, so we need to know whether anyone else has handled it.'

'Yes, guv'nor,' said Cradock, slipping his gloves on and carefully taking the rifle from him. He held it awkwardly, not used to handling such a weapon. Jago watched him, wishing that his own acquaintance with instruments of death like this had not been so intimate.

'DI Burton,' said Jago. 'Shall we take a look at the body now? I want to know what Dr Anderson makes of it too.'

'Certainly,' Burton replied. 'But I've got someone here you might like to have a quick word with first. He's called Danbury, and he's the dead man's commanding officer in the Home Guard. He seems in a bit of a hurry, but I told him you'd want to see him and asked him to wait. He's identified the body too – I thought it'd be useful to do that in case he had to run off before you got here.'

'Thank you. So who was the deceased?'

'Bloke by the name of Ray Lambert – lives locally, works in the docks.'

'Do you know him?'

'No, never seen him before.'

'Have you ever come across the name?'

'No. He hasn't come to our attention. But there's a lot of men working in here, you know.'

'Of course. Let's speak to Mr Danbury then.'

Burton brought Danbury over. He was a heavily built man but tall enough to offset the impression of portliness, and in his mid-fifties, possibly older, with a florid face and an overripe moustache. He wore Home Guard khaki overalls, with a single dark-blue stripe on the shoulder and a small row of medal ribbons over the left breast pocket, among which Jago noticed the purple-and-white of a Military Cross, the same as his own.

'Danbury,' said the man, extending his hand to shake Jago's. 'Major Danbury.'

'Detective Inspector Jago, West Ham CID. I'm afraid I'm not familiar with the Home Guard's rank insignia – what does that stripe signify?'

'Ah, yes. I don't suppose anyone knows what they mean outside the Home Guard. It means I'm a platoon commander, but in the army my rank was higher, so my name is Major Danbury.'

As a former soldier himself, Jago had a long-standing aversion to retired officers who insisted on retaining their rank in civilian life, but not wishing to give offence at their first meeting he decided to humour him.

'Well, Major Danbury, thank you for waiting. I understand you've identified the body as that of Mr Ray Lambert.'

'That's right, poor fellow.'

'And he was a member of your platoon?'

'Yes.'

'Were you on duty here in the dock overnight?'

'Yes, I was. But look, I'm rather keen to get away. It's just that my wife and daughter have been up all night too, working on the mobile canteen – voluntary work, you understand – and I need to get them home in the car. They're very tired – the weaker sex, you know. Could I possibly talk to you later?'

'Certainly – I'd like to find out more about Mr

Lambert. Do go, if you wish, but before you do, can you tell me who is Mr Lambert's next of kin? We'll need to inform them. An address would be useful too, if you have one.'

'Yes, of course.'

Danbury took a small notebook from his pocket and leafed through the pages.

'Here we are. He's got a wife – her name's Mrs Brenda Lambert. I don't know her, but she lives at 75 Saville Road, in Silvertown. Now, will that be all?'

'Yes. But may I have your address too?'

'I'm so sorry. You'll need that, won't you? It's in Forest Gate – The Cedars, Claremont Road. I'll be at home this afternoon.'

'Thank you, Major Danbury. I'll see you then.'

Danbury took his leave and set off at a brisk pace, not quite marching and yet not simply walking, in what seemed to Jago a semi-military style which aptly reflected the constitutional status of the Home Guard volunteers.

'Busy man,' said Cradock as Danbury receded from view.

'His sort always are,' said Jago. 'Right, you and I will have to go round and break the news to Lambert's widow when we've finished here.'

'Right.'

'And DI Burton, after we've done that I'd like to have a chat with you about how we're going to work together.'

'Fine,' said Burton. 'But as far as I'm concerned this is your case. If there's anything specific you want me to do, just ask, but I don't think there's any need for me to tag along with you all the time. I've got plenty on my plate already, and if my boss has called you in it can only be because he wants me to get on with that and not get distracted by a murder case.'

Jago wasn't sure how to interpret this, but at face value it sounded like an arrangement that would suit him.

'OK,' he replied. 'But I'd still like to talk to you as soon as we're back from Mrs Lambert's. I want to get some background.'

'By all means. How about a chat over a pint? I know one or two nice pubs round here.'

'It's a bit too early in the day for me, thanks. Besides, where I live the pubs aren't open this early in the morning.'

'Ah, well, it's different down here – the pubs near the dock gates have a special dispensation to open early in the morning so the lads can get a drink on their way in to work. We call them six o'clock houses. Very thirsty work, being a docker, you know.'

'Even so, I think I'd better decline, thank you.'

'OK. In that case, if you want me I'll be in the Albert Dock police office. But don't go to the old place – we moved last year, and now we're in the old Seamen's Hospital, right at the far end of the dock on the northern side, just inside No. 9 Gate.'

'Thanks. We should be with you by no later than ten o'clock, I would think. Now, let's see the body.'

'OK – it's on a lighter.' He threw a glance at Cradock,

half pitying, half scornful. 'And I don't mean a cigarette lighter, Constable, in case that's what you're thinking. You do know what a lighter is round here, don't you?'

Cradock pulled a non-committal face which he hoped suggested confidence rather than ignorance, but Burton seemed to recognise it as the latter. 'It's a barge, boy – a barge.'

Cradock nodded sagely.

'It's just down here,' said Burton, addressing Jago again. 'I've got PC Wilkinson there too. He's the man who found the body.'

Jago, Cradock and Anderson followed Burton a short distance along the quay to where the lighter was moored, with the dead man's body still sprawled face-up across it and the constable on guard on the quayside nearby.

'Good morning, PC Wilkinson,' said Jago. 'I understand you've been on duty here overnight.'

'That's right, sir,' Wilkinson replied.

'And what were you doing?'

'On the beat, sir. In the dock police there's always two types of duty – gate duty or beat duty. On gate duty you're manning the gates, and your job's to stop people nicking stuff, making sure they don't go out of the dock with anything they didn't bring in. Beat duty's patrolling the dock, of course. I've been on nights for a month, so all I do is walk round the dock all night.'

'On your own?'

'Yes, sir, it's just one man. A bit tricky sometimes, too. It's pitch-black in here at night now the war's on, because they've turned all the lights off, so unless there's a bit of moonlight you hardly know where you're going.'

'But there was some moon last night.'

'That's right – enough to see a bit, at least.'

'And what time did you find the body?'

'Five-thirty this morning, sir.'

'Did you see anything suspicious? Anyone else around?'

'No, sir. I just noticed the body lying on top of the lighter, and that was suspicious, of course. I had a bit of a look and saw a knife sticking out of the poor blighter's back. I left everything as I'd found it and reported back to the sergeant. That's all, really.'

'Right, thank you. We'll take a look.'

Jago and Cradock climbed down onto the barge, followed by Anderson. Burton joined them, but stood back.

'You first, Doctor,' said Jago to Anderson.

The young pathologist edged carefully past Cradock to get closer to the body. The deceased looked tall and lay with his arms spread out to either side and his face frozen as if in a moment of surprise. His right leg was bent back under him at the knee, like that of a man trying to get up.

'No external signs of injury to the front,' said Anderson, after examining it, 'so there's nothing to indicate that he landed face down. Now let's have a look at the other side.'

He rolled the body over carefully. The handle of a knife was protruding from the man's coat, about halfway up his back.

'There,' he said. 'Not much doubt about that.'

'What's your verdict, then?' asked Jago.

'My initial verdict is that it looks pretty straightforward – he's been stabbed in the back, and that's that. But I'll need to get him back to the mortuary and do a proper examination.'

'The PLA has its own mortuary, Doctor, if that would be more convenient for you,' Burton interjected, stepping forward. 'It's not far from here – just over on the north side of the Victoria Dock.'

'Thanks for the offer, Mr Burton,' said Anderson, 'but I think I'd rather get him back to my own post-mortem room at Queen Mary's, where I know where everything is. I'll arrange to have the body collected.'

Burton took a step back again, as if opting out of further discussion.

'We'll need to see if we can get some prints off that knife too before you do your post-mortem, Doctor,' said Jago. 'Take care of that, will you, Peter?'

'Yes, guv'nor,' said Cradock.

'Now, Doctor, if you're finished,' said Jago, 'we'll take a look in his pockets.'

He and Cradock poked into all the pockets they could find in Lambert's clothes. Jago came up with nothing but a grubby handkerchief and a front-door key, but Cradock's exploration was more productive.

'Here we are, guv'nor,' he said. 'A wallet.'

He opened it and emptied the contents into his hand.

'One identity card, a ten-bob note and a few shillings in loose change. Not planning to go out on a spree, then.'

'I don't imagine there's a lot to spend money on in the docks at midnight,' said Jago. 'And is the identity card in the name Danbury gave us?'

'Yes,' Cradock replied. 'Raymond Lambert. And the address is the one Danbury gave us for Mrs Lambert too.'

'Is that all? No photo of his beloved wife, no membership cards, driving licence? No letters?'

'No, sir. The only other thing is this.'

He handed Jago a crumpled scrap of paper that looked as though it had been torn from a notebook. Jago unfolded it and looked. It was blank except for two words pencilled in the middle of it: Dayabir Singh. He passed it back to Cradock.

'What do you make of that?'

'Looks foreign,' said Cradock, returning it.

'Yes,' said Jago. 'I think we can both be confident of that. But Singh's a name, isn't it? An Indian name.'

'The name of the bloke who killed him?'

'I suspect even Jesse Owens would find it too far to leap to that conclusion, although it'd be very convenient for us if you were right. But given that Mr Lambert was stabbed in the back and might not even have seen his killer, do you think he's likely to have had time to get a bit of paper and a pencil out and write the man's name on it?'

'Er, no, sir.'

'I agree. Still, it's something – we'll hang on to it.'

CHAPTER THREE

The narrow strip of soot-blackened shops and houses known as Silvertown had the feel of an island, squashed as it was between the Royal Docks to the north and the jumble of factories, chimneys, wharves and industrial premises that lined the River Thames to the south. It was just one of the areas of very poor housing hurriedly thrown up on marshland in Victorian times to accommodate first the construction workers who came to build the docks and then the tradesmen and labourers who worked in them. Silvertown had never been the most attractive of places, but now that the Luftwaffe had done their nightly work it was battered beyond recognition.

It was into this maze of bombed streets that Jago and Cradock now ventured in search of Mrs Lambert. Leaving the Albert Dock by the gate through which they had arrived, they turned left and headed south under the elevated Silvertown bypass onto Albert Road, passing the squat spire of St Mark's Church on their right.

'What's that?' said Cradock as a cloying smell assailed his nostrils.

'That'll be Tate & Lyle's sugar refinery, on the right there,' Jago explained. 'It runs right down to the river. Like Shirley Temple, isn't it? So sweet, it makes you feel a bit queasy.'

They reached the refinery and turned into Saville Road. The Lamberts' house was on the left-hand side of this narrow street, the end of which was cut off by the dock fence. Behind it loomed a huge ship, twice as high as the houses, in the King George V dry dock. It made the houses look like toys.

'Do you know why it's called Silvertown, sir?' said Cradock, surveying the gloomy surroundings as they came to a halt. 'I don't suppose it's because of all the silver mines.'

'Very observant of you,' said Jago. 'It's named after Samuel Silver, who I think built one of the first enormous factories along the river. He started the India rubber and gutta-percha works about half a mile west of here, getting on for a hundred years ago.'

'Gutta-percha? What on earth's that?'

'I don't know. Some kind of rubber, I think. It's what they made golf balls from, back in the old days. Ever heard of the Silvertown golf ball?'

'Er, no, sir. I don't play golf.'

'Neither do I, but they used to be famous, and they were made down the road in Mr Silver's factory.' He opened the car door with a sigh. 'Right, that's enough history. We need to go and tell poor Mrs Lambert that her husband's been killed.'

At number 75 a middle-aged woman opened the door to them. Her lined face suggested a lifetime of struggle, and Jago guessed she was probably younger than she looked. She was wearing the kind of cotton overall and turban that probably every woman in the street wore, and she had a duster in her hand.

Jago introduced himself and Cradock, and she let them in. The house was as humble on the inside as the exterior would have led them to expect, but it was clean and tidy.

'Mrs Lambert,' Jago began, 'I'm afraid we have some bad news for you. Would you like to sit down?'

She sat down on a chair without answering, but then held up a hand before Jago could go on.

'It's all right, Inspector. It's about Ray, isn't it?'

'Yes, it is.'

'Well, you needn't worry – I already know. He's dead, isn't he?'

'Yes. I'm very sorry.'

'Thank you,' she replied. Her voice was flat, and she sounded tired. 'One of his mates has already been round to tell me – Charlie Bell, one of his Home Guard pals.'

'I see. Can you tell me how he knew?'

'Yes – he was on duty with Ray last night at the dock. Not with him when he died, though.'

'And he was a friend of your husband's, you say?'

'Well, they worked together and they were in the Home

Guard together, so I suppose they were friends, yes.'

'I wonder if you could give me Mr Bell's address. We might want to speak to him.'

'Of course. I don't know the house number, but he told me he lives in Woodman Street. He's got lodgings on the corner with Dockland Street, just over the road from what's left of St John's Church since it was bombed.'

'Thank you. I'm very sorry about your husband's death, Mrs Lambert. Please accept my condolences.'

She raised her hand again wearily, as if to acknowledge his concern, or perhaps to dismiss it.

'You'll have to forgive me, Inspector – please don't think I'm heartless. It's just that I'm feeling a bit numb.'

'I understand.'

'It's come as a shock, you see. One minute you're waiting for your husband to come home, same as every other day, next minute they tell you he's dead. It knocks you sideways. But that's what life's like round here – just one shock after another. Mind you, it was bad enough before this rotten war started – men losing their jobs, families that never had two ha'pennies to rub together in the first place suddenly out on the street. And now what? You've seen it, haven't you? Half the factories bombed, and half the houses too – just ruins wherever you look.'

'I've seen some of it on the way down this morning. It's very bad.'

'We got bombed out of our place on that first night of the Blitz, back in September. It's just a pile of old bricks now – fell down like a house of cards. It was rented, of course, which I suppose is a mercy really, compared with losing a house you own, but just about everything we had went with it. Now we're in this little place with what bits of furniture we could scrape together, praying it won't happen again, but if this war carries on it probably will. And what's anyone doing to help? We haven't seen much of the government round here, nor the council. Mind you, if you live round these parts you get used to that. So I hope you can understand how I feel – don't get me wrong, I'm shocked to hear what's happened to Ray, but it just feels like I haven't got enough strength left to take it in. You know what it's like when a boxer's finished and he keeps taking the punches but doesn't have the sense to go down? That's how I feel.'

Brenda Lambert lapsed into silence, and Jago nodded sympathetically. She pulled a white handkerchief out from her sleeve and dabbed a tear that had appeared in her eye.

'I don't know how I'm going to manage now,' she continued. 'Ray had a bit of life insurance, but the company said he'd have to pay an extra couple of bob a week if he wanted it to cover getting killed on Home Guard duty, and I don't know whether he ever paid it.'

'What was your husband's job?'

'He worked in the docks, of course, like all the other men. I don't know much about it, though, so I'm not sure I can tell you a lot. I mean, I've never even been in the docks, have I? No one's allowed in unless they work there or they've got official permission, so people like me don't get in. I do know what Ray's job was, though. He was a tally clerk – he had to tally the cargoes.'

'What did that entail?'

'Well, he always used to say he was a counter – he said there were hundreds of men all over the docks, all counting different things in different places, on the ships, on the quays, in the transit sheds and warehouses. They counted how much cargo went onto the ships when they were being loaded, how much came off when they were being discharged, how much went into the sheds, how much came out. You name it, they counted it, and it all had to tally up with what the ships reckoned they were carrying and what the customers were expecting to receive, as well as all the stuff that was lost or damaged on the way.'

'Had he done that job for long?'

'Oh, yes. He was a tally clerk when I first met him, and before that I think he was an ordinary docker. The job was just casual, of course, getting work from day to day with nothing guaranteed for tomorrow, but that's the way he liked it. There was a time when people said he ought to get a regular office job on the PLA staff – he was good with numbers, see – but he was always a bit of a restless soul, and I don't think that appealed to him.'

Jago took a scrap of paper from his pocket and showed it to her.

'Can you tell me – have you seen this before?'

She examined it and gave him a blank look.

'No. Should I have?'

'Not necessarily. We found it on your husband – we think it's a name.'

'Really? Well, I'm sorry, but if it is it's no one I know.'

'Thank you.' He folded the paper and put it back in his pocket. 'Now, I'm sorry to have to ask you this, but can you think of anyone who might've wanted to harm your husband?'

'Harm Ray? No – I can't imagine anyone'd want to do that.'

'And can you tell us where you were overnight?'

'Yes, I was in the public shelter down the street, waiting to get blown to pieces. Stinking little hole, it is. You have to go out every twenty minutes just to get some air.'

'Can anyone else corroborate that you were there?'

'Well, we're new here, like I said, so most of the neighbours probably don't know who I am yet, but I expect I can find someone.' She paused for a moment's thought. 'Here, you don't think I done him in, do you?'

'It's just a routine question, Mrs Lambert.'

'I see. Well, that's all right then. I don't want anyone thinking I could do a terrible thing like that. It's all upsetting enough as it is.'

She wiped her eyes with her handkerchief and gave a little sniff. Jago moved towards the door.

'Once again, Mrs Lambert, I'm very sorry about what's happened. We may need to talk to you again, but we'll say goodbye now for the time being.'

She looked at him and forced a weak smile.

'Yes, of course, dear. Bye bye.'

'Goodbye,' said Jago, 'and thank you.'

Jago and Cradock left the house, shut the front door quietly behind them and returned to the car.

'Must be awful to get news like that out of the blue,' said Cradock. 'She seemed to be coping well, though, didn't she?'

'Yes,' Jago replied. 'But the women round here are tough – they have to be. They're used to coping with the worst life can throw at them, and it's the way their mothers brought them up. Nothing comes easy when you live in a place like this.'

'And I suppose there's no telling what she might be thinking and feeling inside. She might just be doing her best to put a brave face on it.'

'Exactly.'

CHAPTER FOUR

Spots of rain spattered onto the car's fabric roof as Jago settled in behind the wheel and started the engine. The sweltering days of September, when the bombs had begun to pound this area to rubble, were long gone, and the chances of driving with the roof down again before next summer looked slim.

'Right,' he said, as the car pulled away from the kerb, 'we can get back to DI Burton now.'

He retraced their journey back to the Royal Albert Dock, this time entering a little farther up the Connaught Road through No. 9 Gate, which led onto the northern side of the dock. The police office was just inside the gate, and they found Burton at his desk. To Jago's eye he didn't look busy.

'Ah,' said Burton, looking up. 'You're back. That didn't take you too long, then. Anything I can do for you?'

'Yes,' said Jago. 'I'd like to talk to whoever's in charge on that ship, the *Magnolia*, the one that's moored next to where the body was found. Is it all right if I just go on board and introduce myself?'

'Don't see why not,' said Burton. 'But I'll come with you, just in case you need a hand.'

He got up from his desk and took his hat from a hook near the door. The three men left the office and walked round to the southern side of the dock, where the ship still lay at its mooring.

'How do we get on it?' said Cradock, as they stood beside the ship. 'Shouldn't there be one of those gangplank things to walk up?'

'It says *Magnolia* on the side, not *Mauretania*,' said Burton. 'Liners have gangplanks, but not little things like that. You go up there.'

Cradock followed the direction in which Burton was pointing and saw only a rope ladder dangling from the ship down to the quay.

'After you,' said Burton.

Cradock had never climbed a rope ladder onto a ship before. He turned to Jago with a helpless expression on his face, but Jago, who had, merely echoed Burton's invitation with a casual wave of his hand in the direction of the problem.

Fortunately, at least the shower had abated. Cradock put a foot on the first wooden tread and gingerly hauled himself up, clinging to the ladder for dear life, but he was soon in trouble.

'This is killing my arms, sir,' he called down.

'Hold the ropes, Peter, not the treads, and lean back a bit,' Jago replied. 'This is a useful skill for you to learn.'

'Thank you, sir,' Cradock replied, gritting his teeth.

He followed the instruction and with some difficulty made it to the top, then with equal difficulty managed to pull himself over the ship's rail and onto the deck. To his annoyance he then watched Jago and Burton make their way up the offending contraption with apparent ease.

As Burton joined them on the deck a man of about fifty wearing an old duffle coat and sea boots appeared, heading from the stern end of the ship to intercept them. He was a little on the short side, but his stocky build suggested they would go no farther without his say-so.

'And who would you be?' he said, in what sounded to Jago like a Scottish accent.

'Police officers,' said Burton. 'These men need to talk to you about the man found dead down there this morning.'

He jerked his thumb over his shoulder in a vague indication of where the body had been found. The seaman followed the direction of Burton's gesture with his eyes and nodded.

'Welcome aboard, gentlemen,' he said with a kind of cautious growl, and stepped back.

'Detective Inspector Jago, West Ham CID,' said Jago, shaking his hand. 'And this is Detective Constable Cradock.'

'Duncan Carlisle. I'm the mate,' the man replied. He glanced at Cradock. 'That means I'm the second in command of this vessel, sonny. The master's in charge, but he's not here just now. Come this way.'

He led them to a small cabin and sat them at a table. Taking a pipe and a tobacco pouch from his pocket, he filled the pipe, lit it and started puffing.

'Would you like a drink?' he said, seeming a little more relaxed now.

'No, thank you,' said Jago. 'We shouldn't be long.'

'As you please. So what can I do for you?'

'Well, at the moment we're trying to work out exactly what happened. So first of all, can you tell me whether you were on board overnight?'

'Aye, I was.'

'And the master too?'

'No, he's been ashore since early yesterday evening, before the blackout. I think he's got a lady friend somewhere nearby.' He gave Jago a broad wink and a knowing smile. 'That's why I was aboard, otherwise I'd have been away having a bit of fun myself. One of us has to be here, so that there's an officer responsible for the ship. Just in case anything goes wrong, you know, and that can happen in dock too, not just at sea, especially when there's bombs flying about.'

'Of course. Now, did you see anything that might have some connection to that man's death?'

Carlisle thought for a moment and shook his head.

'No, I don't think so. It was a pretty ordinary sort of night as far as I was concerned.'

'How long have you been here in the Royal Albert?'

'We got in two days ago – managed to get a berth that was relatively undamaged, and we'll be here for about a week before we sail again. We came down from Scotland, and I can tell you that trip was even less fun than it was in the last war.'

'The Germans, you mean?'

'That's right. Very active, they are, and a little old tub like this isn't the most reassuring place to be when they turn up. We have to run the gauntlet down the coast to get here – we've got E-boats trying to torpedo us, planes dropping bombs and strafing us, and mines everywhere. It's as bad as the Atlantic convoys, except we've got our own mine barrage running all the way up the coast from the Thames Estuary to the Moray Firth. That usually keeps the enemy submarines out, but those E-boats are light enough and small enough to get through. That's why we call it E-Boat Alley. And all we've got to protect us is Harry Tate's Navy.'

He chuckled to himself, with the pipe still gripped between his teeth, then pulled it out sharply as he began to cough.

'Harry Tate?' said Jago. 'The old comedian with the car that used to fall to bits? I don't understand.'

'You would if you'd been in the navy. It's what they used to call the Auxiliary Patrol in the Great War – it was mainly trawlers requisitioned by the Admiralty and manned by fishermen. Now we've got the same thing again, only they've changed the name to the Royal Naval Patrol Service. New name, same old tubs.'

'Ah, yes, I've seen it mentioned in the papers.'

'Right, well, if you could see what it's got to defend us with you'll realise why everyone still calls it Harry Tate's Navy – liable to fall to pieces at any moment. Brave men, though, to take on U-boats and E-boats and the Luftwaffe at eight knots maximum. A fisherman told me we've already lost more than a hundred of those trawlers on minesweeping duties. Anyway, however many are left, we need them more than ever now that France has thrown in the towel.'

'Why's that?'

'Because now the Germans have put big guns in on the French coast just the other side of the Channel, and they can shell our merchant shipping as it sails past.'

He leant forward and jabbed the stem of his pipe towards them.

'This time last year more than a third of the country's trade was coming through the Port of London. You just imagine what a state we'd be in if that was all trying to get through the Channel now. Even the government could work out that might be a problem if war broke out, so they decided to divert some of the shipping to what they reckoned were safer ports, further away from the bombers, and that's why we're so busy up and down the east coast. Most of the imported food comes into places like the Clyde, and then they send it down south by train or by coasters like the *Magnolia* to storage facilities here at the Royals or the West India Docks. Clever, eh?'

'Yes. So you've been carrying food?'

'That's right. Canadian bacon and canned fish – herring, mackerel and salmon. It came over on a convoy from Nova Scotia to the Clyde and then it was transferred to us to bring down to London.'

'I see. Now, I'd like to ask you a bit about last night. What kind of crew do you have on this ship?'

'Just the usual. There's twelve of us altogether – the master, chief engineer, second engineer, bosun and three sailors, three firemen, a cook and me.'

'And apart from yourself, was anyone else on the ship during the night?'

'No, just me. When we're in dock there's often only me or the master on board. We let the rest go on shore leave – most of them aren't due back till Friday night.'

'So just you, and nobody else.'

'Well, there was a lascar, but he was down in the boiler room.'

Jago could see a puzzled frown forming on Cradock's face.

'Perhaps you could explain to my colleague what a lascar is,' he said to Carlisle.

'An Indian seaman,' the mate replied. 'You'll find them on a lot of British merchant vessels. They're cheap, you see – the ship owners only pay them a quarter of what a European seaman gets. They do the dirty work too – they're usually taken on as firemen or trimmers.' He looked at Cradock as a teacher would at a slow pupil. 'And when I say fireman, I don't mean he puts fires out. He does the opposite – his job's stoking the boiler with coal, to make steam. And before you ask, a trimmer doesn't do the ship's haircuts. He keeps the fireman supplied with coal, so the fire doesn't go out while he's looking for it.'

Jago thought Carlisle was being unduly patronising to Cradock, but assumed this was part of the price youth had to pay on a ship if they wanted to learn.

'Is this man on board now?' he asked.

'Aye,' said Carlisle, 'he is.'

'I'd like to speak to him, if I may.'

'Of course. I'll go and fetch him.'

The mate examined his pipe with a disapproving scowl, knocked it out into a saucer on the table and left it there.

'Watch your step, though,' he cautioned as he left the cabin. 'You know what foreigners are like – they'll tell you a pack of lies without turning a hair. Personally, I don't trust them – too many of them want to jump ship as soon as they get here.'

Burton snorted when he heard this, and as the door closed behind the departing mate he voiced his agreement to Jago and Cradock.

'That doesn't surprise me. Some of these foreigners, they're good workers, but in the end they're only in it for themselves – they just do it for the money, and when they've got enough, they're off.'

'Is that any different to British workers?' said Jago.

Burton gave him a look that seemed both dismissive and pitying.

'Have you ever worked with natives? I could tell you a story or two – I was in India with the army during the war. When it finished, the Indian Imperial Police Service was taking on some ex-army types, so I joined and did three years as a sub-inspector. I had Indians serving under me and I got to know the way they think. When it came to the point, they didn't want us there. You couldn't rely on them.'

'Well, I suppose when it comes to the point we've tended to expect them to give their own compatriots a sound thrashing on our behalf to keep them in order. Maybe they don't like that.'

Burton scowled at Jago.

'You sound like you're on their side. I didn't take sides – I just did my job.'

Jago wasn't seeking an argument and was relieved when the mate arrived with an Asian man of about forty dressed in loose, pyjama-like clothes streaked black all over with coal dust and with a small pillbox-style hat on his head.

'Just stand there,' Carlisle told him. 'There's nothing to worry about. This gentleman's a police officer and he wants to ask you some questions. Understood?'

The seaman nodded.

'May I ask your name?' Jago began.

The man looked at him suspiciously.

'You want to know my name?' he said. 'No one wants to know my name. British people never bother to use my name – they always just call me a "lascar".'

'Well, I'm a policeman and I like to know the name of everyone I speak to, so I'd be obliged if you'd give me your name.'

'All right. It's Abdul Jamal.'

'Thank you. And you're from India, Mr Jamal?'

'Yes, from Bengal.'

'I see. And I understand you were on board the ship last night. Is that correct?'

'Yes. I'm always on the ship.'

'No shore leave?'

'No. But I don't care – I've seen London once and I don't know anyone here, so I don't need to see it again. Anyway, I prefer to stay on board and save my money, take it home

45

for my family. I was here on the ship all night, on duty.'

'What duty was that?'

'In the boiler room – we have to keep the boiler going even when we're in port, to generate electricity. I'm a fireman and trimmer, you see.'

'Ah, yes. Mr Carlisle has explained to us what firemen and trimmers do, but I thought they were two different jobs.'

'On a big ship perhaps they are, but on a little one like this there is just me. I am the fireman and the trimmer, and I have to do it all by myself. I may not be an important man on this ship, but without me it cannot move.'

'Very good, Mr Jamal. Now tell me, please, did you come up on deck at any point during the night?'

'Yes. At about four o'clock I came up for some fresh air.'

'Did you see anyone on the quay when you came up?'

'Yes. I saw two people, but not clearly – there was only the moonlight to see by.'

'What were they doing?'

'They were facing each other, so I thought they were talking.'

'Could you hear what they were saying?'

'No. They were too far away.'

'What did they look like?'

'I could see that one was taller than the other, but I could not tell you how tall they were. The bigger one looked like he was carrying a rifle, so I assumed it must be one of the sentries.'

'Could you see what they were wearing?'

'Just ordinary clothes – overcoats and trousers.'

'And hats?'

'It looked as though one of them was wearing a metal helmet, like the air-raid wardens do, and the other one just had a hat.'

'What kind of hat?'

'I don't know what your English hats are called – they're all just hats to me. And anyway, it was too dark to see clearly. It was just a round hat.'

'Did you see them do anything else?'

'No. When I looked round later they had both gone.'

'Is there anything else you can tell me?'

'No, that was it. I've told you everything I saw.'

'Just one last question, then.'

Jago took the piece of paper from his pocket and showed it to Jamal.

'Does this mean anything to you? Dayabir Singh? It's an Indian name, isn't it?'

'That is correct. Any man whose name is Singh is a Sikh, and the Sikhs are Indian. They are a religious minority in India – except in the Punjab, where they are the majority.'

'And Dayabir? What does that mean?'

'I don't know what it means, but I believe it is also a name used by the Sikhs.'

'Do you know anyone by that name?'

'No, I do not.'

'And do you have any idea why the man who was murdered might've had this name in his pocket?'

'Certainly not, sir. It is just a name to me.'

'Right. That'll do for the time being – you can go now.'

The seaman gave a silent nod and left the cabin.

'All done here, then?' said Carlisle when the door had closed.

'Yes, thank you,' said Jago. 'We'll leave you in peace.'

Jago, Cradock and Burton said goodbye to Carlisle and made their way back down to the quay.

'Could we have a chat?' Jago asked Burton. 'Perhaps in your office?'

'Of course,' said Burton.

The three men returned to the Royal Albert Dock police office, where DI Burton led them to his room.

'Come in,' he said. 'Make yourselves comfortable, if you can.'

The office was furnished in spartan style: Jago and Cradock managed to find a couple of chairs, but they seemed to have been designed to prevent anyone spending too long sitting around.

'Sorry about the facilities,' said Burton. 'As they say, there's a war on – an excuse for anything, isn't it? This building went out of use when they opened the new Albert Dock Hospital a couple of years ago over in Alnwick Road, and some bright spark reckoned it'd make a good home for the police office. All very nice, except the reason why the hospital moved out was because the foundations were collapsing – subsidence, apparently – so all I can say is watch out in case the whole lot comes down round our ears. The Germans'll probably thank us for saving them a job.'

He laughed at his own joke, but without much conviction, then opened the bottom drawer of his desk and pulled out a bottle of Scotch and three glasses.

'If the thought of that worries you, perhaps a drop of Dutch courage would help. I may not be a docker, but I certainly find a drink helps to start the day, so if we can't go to the pub we'll have one here. Sorry it's only a blend – all the pure malts seem to have gone for vital exports to keep the British economy afloat. Scotch is our biggest single export to the USA, apparently.'

He uncorked the bottle and held it over the first glass, looking at Jago expectantly.

'No, not for us, thank you,' said Jago.

'Drop of rum instead? Not so easy to come by since the war started, is it? I've got a bit put by here for these cold mornings.'

'No, thank you.'

'Oh well, suit yourself.'

Burton poured himself a whisky and swirled it in the glass appreciatively before taking a mouthful.

'So,' he continued, 'what can I tell you? You wanted some background, you said.'

'Yes, I'd like to know a bit more about how things work down here in the docks, if you don't mind. Most of us on the outside don't know much about what goes on inside – it's a bit shut off.'

'Too true, mate. It's like a little world of its own in here. This side of the fence everything's got its own rules, its own traditions, people with jobs you've never heard of, all handed down from father to son. That's why we have a separate Port of London police force. We're specialists – unique skills, you might say. I know this place like the back of my hand – I've been working in the docks for the last eighteen years, ever since I came back from India, so there's not much I don't know about them. It's not a job in here, you know, it's a way of life – it takes over all your time and doesn't leave much room for anything else. You a married man?'

'No,' said Jago, caught off-balance by this sudden change of tack. *But at least I manage to put a clean collar on my shirt every day*, he thought, catching sight of the grubby edge of Burton's.

'Me neither,' said Burton. 'Married to the job, that's me. Mind you, there's plenty of fish in the sea, that's what I say – no point wasting all your time on one, is there?' he added, with a theatrical wink.

Greeted with silence on Jago's part, Burton hastily got back to his original subject.

'Not that it's some sort of quiet little backwater here, mind. Do you know how big these docks are?' He didn't wait for an answer. 'The three Royal Docks make up the biggest continuous stretch of dock water in the world. Impressive, eh?'

Jago nodded dutifully.

'There's no end of cargo passing through here every day, and it's our job to make sure it's all safe and above board. If you think your boys are overworked, you should try a few shifts down here – we've got all our usual work, we're getting the worst of the bombing seven nights a week and we're still expected to keep everything neat and tidy. On top of that we've had the government getting all jittery about German agents being smuggled ashore, so they expect us to keep a constant beady eye on the little ships like that *Magnolia* in case they're dropping off spies on the coast or in the docks.'

'I didn't know that.'

'Well, there you are, see? People say we're just the PLA flatties, not proper police, no use for anything except the docks. Not like the Metropolitan Police Service – you're the glamour boys, aren't you, catching all the murderers and master criminals, Inspector this and that of the Yard, all over the newspapers? Well, there's a lot we do that people don't even notice.'

'So when you say your usual work, what kind of thing is that?'

'Well, a lot of it's maintaining security – everything from stopping local kids trying to sneak in for a lark to making sure dockers don't try to sneak something out for themselves. We had a shed man from East Ham up before the magistrate only last week for stealing a half-pint bottle of whisky from the King George V Dock. We caught him at the gate with the bottle down his coat sleeve. The temptation's too much for some of them, you see.'

'So pilfering's a problem?'

'There's a bit, but we keep it under control. What you have to understand is the work's hard and physical in the docks, and so are the men. You'll always get a few questionable characters, but when we catch them we come down on them like a ton of bricks.'

'Talking of questionable characters, can you tell me something? Who can get into the docks at night? I don't mean people like the police, the Home Guard, the tea ladies, the ships' crew members – they're all in here legitimately. I'm talking about other people – people who shouldn't be in here, and if they do get in are likely to be up to no good.'

'The answer's simple – no one. It's a well-known fact. We've got men on every gate, and that's the only way in or out of the docks.'

'But what if someone offers, let's say, an inducement to one of your officers to let them in?'

'Impossible. We don't tolerate corruption in the PLA Police, and it doesn't happen.'

'So you're confident no outsider could've got in here and killed that man?'

'Yes, I am.'

'That makes our job a bit easier then, doesn't it?'

'I suppose it does, yes.'

Jago paused to reflect on Burton's answer.

'Now, just one more thing. Where I work we're seeing crime increasing because of the blackout, but you say you've got pilfering under control. Does that mean generally you're not seeing a significant rise in crime?'

'I think that's right, yes. I suppose the difference is that we've got a big fence all round these docks, and police officers on all the gates, like I said, so blackout or no blackout, it's just the same. The only difference would be if a bomb made a big hole in the fence, I suppose, but we'd soon get that fixed. Mind you, I'm not saying it couldn't change – I reckon there could be a lot more trouble coming our way.'

'Why's that?'

'Well, you heard that bloke Carlisle on the ship – he said the government's diverted a lot of the shipping away from London.'

'Yes.'

'That meant last year, when war broke out, we only had about half as many ships coming here as we'd had the year before, and since these big air raids started, trade in the Port of London's down to about a quarter of what it used to be. That's bad for business, of course, but it's bad for jobs too – loads of dockers have lost their jobs since the war started, and if men aren't getting a wage, they have to find other ways of putting food on the table.'

'You mean criminal ways?'

'It happens.'

'I see.'

Jago glanced at his watch.

'Look,' he said, 'we'd better be going – I want to see how the pathologist's getting on. Thanks for your help.'

'You're welcome,' said Burton. 'And next time we'll have that drink, eh?'

'Maybe.'

Jago grabbed his hat and coat and headed for the door, followed by Cradock. He was keen to know the results of the post-mortem examination, but more than that he wanted to get his visit to the hospital mortuary out of the way as quickly as possible. Standing in a cold room discussing a dead body freshly cut up by a pathologist, even one as competent and agreeable as Dr Anderson, was an experience he never enjoyed. He wondered whether he should have taken up DI Burton's offer of a shot of Dutch courage after all.

CHAPTER FIVE

When the two detectives joined Dr Anderson in the mortuary at Queen Mary's Hospital, Jago was pleased and relieved to find that the pathologist had completed the more gruesome parts of his examination and that the body was covered with a sheet. The bare, white-tiled room seemed even colder than the street they had just left, and he pulled his coat more tightly around him.

'Right,' he said, 'let's get this over and done with. I expect you've got a busy day ahead of you, and I don't want to take any more of your time than necessary. What can you tell me?'

'Well,' Anderson replied, 'at the risk of stating what may seem to you the obvious, the first thing I can say is that there's no doubt about the nature of the murder weapon, because there's only one wound and the dagger was still in place when the body was found.'

He showed Jago the knife, which was lying on a steel tray next to the post-mortem table.

'It looks rather exotic, doesn't it?'

Jago took a close look at the weapon that had cut short the life of the man laid out before him. It had a bone handle and a blade about eight inches long which curved to a point, and was engraved with a curious symbol that he didn't recognise.

'Certainly looks foreign,' he replied. 'Does that marking mean anything to you?'

'I'm afraid not,' said Anderson. 'Engravings on foreign knives are somewhat outside my field of competence.'

'Mine too. When you're done with it I'll take it with me and see if I can find someone who can tell me what it means, if anything.'

'Oh, I've finished with it. It's all yours.' He wrapped the knife in a clean cloth and handed it to Jago, who passed it to Cradock for safe keeping.

'Shall I proceed now to the nature of the wound?' Anderson continued.

'Yes, please.'

'Very well. Now, with stab wounds it's not difficult to establish the injuries that've been caused, because by dissection we can see the damage. Do you want to have a look? I have of course removed the damaged internal organs, and I've also removed the skin and its wound and preserved them in formalin for future reference, so you can always examine them separately if you wish.'

'Of course,' said Jago, beginning to feel a little light-headed. 'I think your explanation of the wound will suffice for me. I don't need to hear all the details of your dissection either, but just tell me this, please – am I right to assume we're looking at a case of murder?'

'Well, I think we can rule out suicide – there's no way he could've reached round and stabbed himself in the back like that. As for accidental death, that would be for you to find out. What I can tell you is that it was certainly the stab that killed him. The blade entered the body just beneath the scapula and penetrated the left ventricle.'

'So he was stabbed in the heart, yes?'

'That's right. The victim would've been unconscious before he hit the ground.'

'And how long before he was dead?'

'Oh, seconds. Once the heart stops pumping, you've had it.'

'Quite. So would that explain why there's only the one wound?'

'I'm not sure one could go so far as to say that. In a homicidal attack I'd normally expect to see several wounds, but I suppose if the victim collapsed immediately his attacker might've assumed he was dead and been more concerned to get away than to try a second wound. But on that I can only speculate, and that's your job, not mine.'

'Could the fact that there's only one wound suggest the killer was someone who knew what he was doing, knew where to stab?'

'I'm afraid it's not possible for me to deduce from the wound itself what kind of person inflicted it. It could've been an expert job or a random strike by an amateur – the effect on the body would be the same.'

'Should I expect there to be blood on whoever stabbed him?'

'Possibly, but with wounds like this there's comparatively little external haemorrhaging, as a rule. I'd expect most of the blood to stay within the victim's chest cavity, and I certainly found plenty there.'

'Right. So can you tell me anything else about the murderer? Male, female? Left-handed, right-handed? Tall, short?'

Anderson shook his head sympathetically.

'Not really. The only slightly odd thing about this wound is that the knife appears to have entered from below, in an upward direction, whereas normally with a stabbing I'd expect it to be from slightly above, with a downward thrust. In the latter case, it's quite difficult for the knife to get in between the ribs, whereas a thrust from below would penetrate more easily. It could be purely accidental, or it could be that the assailant had enough basic medical or anatomical knowledge to direct the blade that way. As for who did it, however, this wound could've been inflicted by just about anybody. I'm sorry not to be of more help with this, but I can only go by the evidence.'

'But he was definitely attacked from behind?'

'All I can say is that the blade of the weapon entered this man's back and penetrated his left ventricle, causing death by cardiac arrest.'

'Was he killed in the barge, where he was found?'

'Possibly, but not necessarily.'

'So could he have been killed on the quay and then

fallen down onto the barge, or been pushed?'

'That would also be possible, I think. As I said when we saw him in the dock, there were no external signs of injury to the front of his body, and I found nothing else internally, but I did find some signs of bruising on his right arm, so he may have landed on that side and then rolled onto his back.'

'But you just said he would've been dead within seconds. Would there have been time for bruises to develop? I thought bruises can't form after death.'

'Well, that's not actually true. However, it's difficult to be hard and fast on whether any given bruise occurred just before death or not, so all I can say is that this bruising took place at about the time of death.'

'And what time did death occur?'

Anderson nodded slowly and pursed his lips, as if mentally reviewing his own evidence.

'Judging by the temperature of the body,' he said, 'and taking into account that it was found outside on a rather chilly November night, I'd say he died sometime between half past two and half past four this morning.'

Jago was pleased at last to have something concrete to work with, but before he could express his appreciation Anderson added a further comment.

'Of course, it's impossible to give an accurate timetable, much as I'm sure you'd like one. I'm afraid that's the best I can do.'

'I would've expected no less of you, Doctor,' said Jago. 'Between two-thirty and four-thirty's good enough for me.'

CHAPTER SIX

Back in the car, Jago unfolded the cloth in which the dagger was wrapped and studied the blade carefully.

'This curved shape looks a bit eastern, don't you think, Peter?'

'Yes. It reminds me of the daggers those Arab sheikhs wear in their belt in the films, like that *Beau Geste* last year.'

'I'm not sure if we'll find any Arab sheikhs around the docks – and in any case I think they were Algerian tribesmen in the film, not Arabs – but I'm wondering whether it might be Indian. I'd like to see whether that lascar, Mr Jamal, can make anything of it. Come on, let's go and find him before he gets another job or decides to go home.'

Jago and Cradock returned to the SS *Magnolia*, where they spotted Carlisle, the ship's mate, on the foredeck.

'Can we come aboard?' said Jago, calling to him from the quay.

'Be my guests,' Carlisle shouted down to them.

They climbed up the ladder, Cradock trying to improve his performance this time, and found Carlisle inspecting a winch on the deck.

'Sorry to disturb you, Mr Carlisle,' said Jago, 'but I'd like your help with a small question – one that your lascar Mr Jamal may be able to help me with too. Is he on board?'

'Yes, I'll send for him.'

Carlisle walked over to a nearby sailor who was trimming a rope and dispatched him below to find Jamal. While they were waiting for the man to return, Jago showed Carlisle the knife.

'Do you recognise this, Mr Carlisle?'

'No, can't say I do,' Carlisle replied. 'It's not the kind of knife I'd use. I prefer a straight one.'

'What about your foreign crewmen? Is it the sort of thing they might use? Lascars, for example?'

'Maybe, I suppose. But here he comes now – you can ask him yourself.'

Jago turned to see Jamal approaching.

'Ah, Mr Jamal,' said Jago. 'You might be able to help me.' He held the knife forward. 'Have you seen this knife before?'

Jamal looked at it for a couple of seconds, then glanced towards Carlisle as if seeking his permission to speak.

'Mr Carlisle,' said Jago. 'I wonder whether we might speak to Mr Jamal in private.'

Carlisle shrugged.

'Please yourself – I'll leave you to it. I'll be on the bridge if you need me.'

When Carlisle had gone, Jago repeated his question to Jamal.

'This knife – have you seen it before?'

'No, sir,' said Jamal.

'Have you seen one like it?'

'Yes, I have.'

'I'd like to know more about it. Is it Indian?'

'It looks like some knives I have seen in India, yes.'

'What can you tell me about it?'

'If it is what I think it is, it's what they call a *kirpan*. That's a Punjabi word. I don't speak Punjabi, because Punjab is in the west of India, and Bengal, where I come from, is in the east, but I believe the word means something to do with honour and mercy.'

'You say you've seen knives like this before, but have you seen this one?'

'I have seen many of these knives, but I do not know whether I have ever seen this particular one before – many people in my country have such knives.'

'Do you have one?'

'No. There would be no reason for me to have a knife like this. The *kirpan* is carried by followers of the Sikh religion, and I am not a Sikh. I am a Muslim, sir.'

'Do all the Sikhs carry a weapon like this?'

'All the men do, because their faith requires it. But I believe it is a ceremonial dagger, and they are only supposed to use it in self-defence or to protect someone else who's in danger. They are not supposed to use it in anger.'

'I see. Now tell me, are there any other crewmen from India on this ship?'

'No. I am the only one. There was an Indian before me, but he left the ship in Scotland. They needed someone to replace him, and I had no job because my previous ship was hit by a mine off the coast and badly damaged, so they hired me.'

'What can you tell me about this man?'

'Nothing. I never met him.'

'Well, thank you, Mr Jamal.'

Jamal nodded in acknowledgement.

'And now, sir, if you will excuse me, I must return to my duties, otherwise I may be in trouble.'

'Of course, Mr Jamal. Thank you for your help.'

Jamal left them.

'Right, Peter, it's time we got going,' said Jago. 'I have to report to Mr Soper.' Looking up, he saw Carlisle standing on the open bridge and waved a farewell to him as they made their way back down the ladder to the quay.

Jago set off at a brisk pace.

'Any chance of getting a bite to eat on the way, sir?' said Cradock, hurrying to keep up. 'It feels like days since I had breakfast.'

'No. You can find yourself something in the station canteen while I'm with the DDI. And you can get me a sandwich too.'

'Very good, sir,' Cradock sighed.

'And then we'll go and see Major Danbury. I want another word with him.'

'Yes, sir.'

'So,' Jago continued, glancing back over his shoulder at the *Magnolia*, 'what do you make of all that?'

'Well, the lascar fellow was interesting. I suppose we know a bit more about the murder weapon now – at least, we know it's Indian. But if it's only meant to be used for self-defence, how did it end up in a Home Guard's back?'

'I think he meant the Sikhs aren't supposed to use it in anger, but that doesn't mean someone else can't. And who knows? Perhaps Sikhs sometimes make exceptions too.'

'So it could be anyone.'

'Exactly. Now, I want you to get the uniform men to take photos of that knife into all the local pawnshops, bric-a-brac shops and junk shops in the area to see if anyone's sold one like it, and if they have, who they sold it to.'

'Will do, sir,' said Cradock. His stomach rumbled as Jago started the car.

CHAPTER SEVEN

Jago entered Divisional Detective Inspector Soper's office for the second time that day. He found the DDI in his chair behind the desk, just as when he'd left him that morning, but there was something a little slumped about Soper that suggested to Jago the air of a man asleep – or even, he thought with a sudden twinge of alarm, that of a man recently deceased. To his relief he saw Soper twitch and look up at him.

'Ah, John,' he said. 'Sit down, sit down.'

Jago took a seat on the nearer side of the desk.

'I've been chained to this desk all day,' Soper continued. 'Not a moment's rest. But that's war for you, I suppose.'

Jago wondered what form Soper's war had taken in his absence, other than perhaps the unwinnable war against sleep that seemed the fate of all men once they reached a certain age. An age that, if Jago's eyes had not deceived him, was already more than certain in his superior officer's case.

Soper pulled himself up in his seat and leant forward on his elbows across the desk.

'And you, I imagine, have been scampering about all over the docks. How's your investigation going?'

'Early days, sir, but the post-mortem confirms it was definitely murder, and we have the murder weapon, which I'm hoping will provide some leads in the direction of the killer. But no suspects yet, of course. We're still trying to establish exactly what happened, but we're working on it as hard as we can.'

'All haste, John, all haste.' Soper's words now seemed infused with more energy. 'If a Home Guard's been murdered, someone needs to hang for it. The seaways are vital arteries, bringing the lifeblood of the Empire back to London, its heart, and the docks are the, er . . .' Barely had his oratory begun to take wing, however, than his ability to extend the metaphor farther seemed to have failed him.

'Ventricles, sir?' said Jago in a helpful voice.

'I don't know,' said Soper impatiently. 'What I mean is the docks are very important, because they ship our exports out and bring all our supplies in, and the Home Guard are doing a very important job defending them.'

'Yes, sir.'

'What witnesses have you got?'

'Only one so far, a lascar – you know, an Indian seaman – from Bengal. He's a crewman on the freighter next to where the body was found.'

'Hmm, a foreigner then.'

'Yes, sir, but Bengal is part of the Empire, so he's not entirely foreign, or at least not as foreign as some foreigners.'

'That's as may be, but all foreigners are unreliable, and I don't like the idea of having a foreigner as the only witness. See if you can find someone more dependable, someone a jury will take more seriously, if it ever comes to court.'

Jago was beginning to think Soper would find a soulmate in Detective Inspector Burton if ever they met.

'I'll do my best, sir, but beggars can't be choosers, and if he's the only witness I have, there's not much I can do about it. Besides, I see no reason why an Indian seaman can't be as honest and reliable as a British one.'

'As a British seaman? That's not saying much. If you ask me, sailors are a shifty lot, and they all drink like fish.'

'Well, this one won't drink, sir – he says he's a Muslim.'

'Even so, unreliable. All the inferior races are unreliable. You only have to look at the French.'

Jago caught his eye, and Soper made a half-swallowed harrumphing noise.

'Er, not your mother, of course. She must've been British by marriage, surely? Anyway, French people who live here are different, not like the French people in France. I'm talking about proper foreigners. Unreliable. And the further east you go, the worse they get.'

Jago wondered how far the writ of Soper's conviction ran. Assuming the DDI believed in a round world rather than a flat one, this precept might certainly extend as far as India, and quite possibly China. It might even include Americans, and if his mind roamed further across the Atlantic, there was every likelihood that he would include the Irish within this global category of unreliable races. Jago imagined Soper's notion of such peoples extending right up to the three-mile limit of Britain's territorial waters.

'When I was fighting in France, sir, people who'd been out there before me, in 1914 and 1915, seemed to think the Indian Army had played a key part in holding the line against the German advance and had fought very bravely. An Indian soldier won the VC at Ypres within a couple of months of the war starting. And they were all volunteers, not conscripts like me.'

'Yes, well, under military discipline and British command perhaps they are reliable, but this fellow of yours in the Albert Dock is under neither, so I think my point remains valid.'

'Yes, sir,' said Jago, sensing there was little to be gained from pointing out to his senior that the *Magnolia* had a British master.

'Now,' Soper continued, 'there's something else I need to mention, John.'

'Sir?'

'While you were out I heard from Divisional Inspector Grayson again. He says there's a suspected racket going on with whisky at the docks in Scotland, and they're wondering whether there might be a connection with the London docks, for some reason. He'd like you to look into it while you're down there, if you can spare the time. Has DI Burton mentioned it?'

'No, sir.'

'Well, I told Grayson you'd follow it up, so have a word with Burton next time you see him, right?'

'Yes, sir.'

'Speaking of which, how are you getting on with Burton?'

'I think he's trying to be helpful, sir.'

'Trying?'

'Well, I'm not sure his heart's in it – he doesn't seem too happy to have us there. Encroaching on his territory, I suppose. He seems to think we're the glamour boys from the Metropolitan Police who come down and take all the best cases out of their hands. A touch of jealousy, perhaps?'

'I expect your turning up like that has put his nose out of joint. His type are all right for sorting out any minor dirty business down in the docks, but when it comes to capital crimes it's only right that we should investigate them, not him. Surely he must understand that. It can't be the first time he's had to accept that in his career.'

Jago thought that was perhaps precisely why Burton felt the way he did, whether he was jealous or simply disgruntled at being obliged to give way to a Metropolitan Police officer. It might also explain why Burton hadn't rushed to involve him in investigating whatever the whisky racket was. Since it was Soper who'd sent him down to the docks in the first place, however, he doubted whether his boss would welcome this insight, and kept it to himself.

Their conversation seemed to have stalled. Soper cleared his throat as if to signal that he was restarting it.

'Have you seen anything of that American woman recently?' he said. 'The journalist?'

'You mean Miss Dorothy Appleton, sir?'

'Yes, that's the one. I was just wondering. I've, er, heard it said that you seem to be getting quite friendly with her.'

'Really, sir?' said Jago, with an air of naive innocence that mirrored the tone in which Soper had asked the question. 'Well, we do seem to get on all right – but then that's what that man from the Ministry of Information wanted, wasn't it? He wanted me to show her round and keep her informed of things from our point of view, and generally be a point of contact for her with the police, didn't he?'

'That's right,' Soper replied hesitantly. 'As long as you don't take it too far. She may be sympathetic to our cause, and so may her newspaper, but remember she's still a foreigner.'

'And therefore not to be trusted?'

'I didn't say that. But she's still not one of us. I had a phone call from that man Mitchell at the Ministry this morning, and he wanted to know how things were going, so I just need to know the assurance I gave him was valid.'

'And what was that assurance, sir?'

'That you were doing what you'd been told to do, and everything was under control. Is that true?'

'Everything under control? I think so, sir.'

'When are you seeing her next?'

'I've arranged to have lunch with her tomorrow, sir, as a matter of fact. She's coming over here and we're eating just down the road.'

'Very cosy. Just the two of you?'

'No, sir, I was planning to take Detective Constable Cradock with me. And we won't be long. I can't spare any time with this murder investigation, but it was her request that we meet, and I didn't want to cancel at the last moment if I could possibly avoid it. I've said I'll call her this evening, so I'll explain to her that I'm very busy – is it all right to tell her I'm investigating the murder of a Home Guard volunteer?'

'Certainly. If a man's been murdered in the docks, we can't hope to hide it from the press. I actually asked Mr Mitchell that very question when he phoned this morning, and he agreed. He did make one point, though, and on this I agree with him. The government's making a lot of these Local Defence Volunteers, or Home Guard, or whatever they call themselves. More than a million and a half men volunteering since May makes it a good story from their point of view, something positive they can talk about after France falling and Dunkirk. That whole catalogue of errors and failure is something they want to leave in the past as quickly as possible, and the idea of ordinary British men in their hundreds of thousands standing up to face the enemy and shoot down parachutists or whatever it is they're supposed to be doing is a heroic tale of courage and determination to fight on till Victory. They're everyday heroes.'

'I see, sir. But then if one of them gets knifed in the back for reasons unknown in the Royal Albert Dock it might take some of the shine off the government's optimistic outlook, mightn't it?'

This idea seemed to give Soper cause to reflect.

'I imagine so, yes,' he concluded, then paused. 'I say, you don't suppose he was murdered by a fifth columnist, do you?'

'At this stage, sir, I'd say no lines of enquiry are being ruled out.'

'It could've been an enemy agent spying on the ships in the dock, couldn't it, or planning some sabotage?'

'It could, sir, yes.'

'In that case, your Home Guard fellow would be a hero. They'd like that, I'm sure. Yes, that'd make it a much more positive story.' He paused again, perhaps noticing the quizzical way in which Jago was looking at him. 'But you must do your duty as you see fit, John, and serve your country to the best of your ability. I know I can rely on you to do that.'

Jago wasn't sure whether this was a hint from Soper

regarding the direction his enquiries should take, but he decided the appropriate response would be not to seek clarification.

'You can, sir.'

'So you can tell Miss Appleton about the case – the press still seem to be free to report murders without being censored.'

'Indeed, sir. I've even seen one or two reports of overzealous Home Guards shooting motorists who declined to stop at their roadblocks – there was something in the paper recently about a Special Constable out in the country somewhere getting shot dead because he failed to observe a challenge, which would suggest the censors aren't totally committed to protecting the volunteers' shiny reputation.'

'That's as may be, but I'd like you to do what you can to influence Miss Appleton in the direction of seeing these brave volunteers for what they are and depicting them accordingly.'

'I think I can do that, sir. She's a very perceptive woman.'

For a moment Soper looked uncertain whether Jago had just run a ring round him, but he left his uncertainty unspoken.

'Very well, that will be all, John. Remember – everyday heroes.'

CHAPTER EIGHT

By the time he left Soper, even Jago was feeling hungry. On returning to the CID office he found that Cradock had obtained a sandwich for him: it was waiting on a plate on his desk. He lifted a corner of the bread to see what was inside and was pleased to find a generously thick slice of cheddar accompanied by some form of pickle. Cheese had been getting a bit short in the shops of late, and he wondered how long it would be before the government added it to the list of rationed foods.

'Thank you, Peter,' he said to Cradock. 'I trust you managed to find something left in the canteen for yourself too?'

'Oh, yes, thank you, sir,' Cradock beamed. 'Fried egg and chips, bread and butter, and a mug of tea – set me up a treat, it did.'

'Very good. We don't want you to starve.'

'Shall I get you a cup of tea too, sir?'

'No, thank you. I'd like to go and see Major Danbury.'

He picked up the sandwich. 'I'll eat this on the way – you can drive.'

The afternoon traffic was light, and Jago settled back in the Riley's front passenger seat to eat his sandwich. DDI Soper's questions about Dorothy were still in his mind, and as they passed St John's Church on its island site in the middle of Stratford Broadway he thought of their visit to the Martyrs' Memorial some weeks before. Standing before this monument to the cruelty of centuries past, Dorothy had talked about the suffering and death she'd witnessed in Poland and Spain in the last three years. It was like discovering a new side to her. And then, when she told him what she'd seen at first hand in the front-line trenches of the Spanish Civil War, even if only briefly as a war correspondent, he'd begun to feel that perhaps she had some real understanding of his own past and the experiences that had shaped him.

His mind drifted to a more recent conversation, and he winced at the memory of his own awkwardness when she'd begun to push gently at the feelings he had locked away inside himself: his desire not just to pass through his allotted life and on into oblivion but to matter enough to someone for them to remember him. When she spoke about letting another person know us as we really are it had seemed like a challenge, but he wasn't sure it was one he could meet. He wondered whether she knew.

The car gave a sudden lurch, snapping him out of his reflective state. He was relieved to see it was only because Cradock had forgotten what gear he was in: his young colleague was still having the occasional difficulty in mastering the Riley's pre-selector gearbox. Judging by Cradock's anxious glance towards him, Jago concluded it would be superfluous to point out his error.

They continued eastwards along Romford Road without further incident and turned left at the Princess Alice pub into Woodgrange Road, then took the second road on the right. Forest Gate was a striking contrast to the area of Silvertown they had seen when visiting Mrs Lambert, and Claremont Road was a quiet, leafy avenue of mainly detached Victorian villas which seemed to have escaped bomb damage so far. The only sound came from a gang of dustmen who were hauling the local residents' steel dustbins onto their shoulders and tipping the contents into the back of a council dustcart before returning the bins with a clatter to the houses they belonged to. Cradock drove carefully round the men and stopped when they found The Cedars, about one-third of the way down the road.

It was a grand-looking, old-fashioned house, with a wide bay window to each side of a front door protected by a brick porch. It looked as though it had probably seen Queen Victoria's Golden Jubilee, but had more recently acquired to one side a twentieth-century addition, a modest garage which, to Jago's eye, was not big enough to accommodate the stately motor car which was parked in front of its double wooden doors. The car was a good twenty years old and the size of a truck.

Jago rang the front-door bell and waited. Eventually

the door creaked open to reveal the Home Guard platoon commander he had met earlier that day, only now wearing not his uniform denims but a baggy tweed suit. Beside him was a woman Jago had not seen before: an upright, commanding figure with penetrating blue eyes and tightly crimped steely-grey hair. Like Mrs Churchill but without the smile, he thought.

The man looked down at Jago from the doorway as though not recognising him.

'Yes?' he said.

'Detective Inspector Jago and Detective Constable Cradock, West Ham CID. We met earlier this morning, sir.'

'Ah, yes, of course,' said Danbury in a brusque tone that reminded Jago of some of the less sufferable privately educated and Sandhurst-trained officers he'd encountered during his time in the army. 'Come in.'

He stood back and motioned them into the hall, then closed the door behind them.

'My wife,' he added, with a wave of his hand towards the woman beside him. Jago assumed he would learn her first name in due course, but apparently not from her husband. She smiled primly at him and offered a limp hand.

'Louise Danbury,' she said. 'Named after the late princess, Duchess of Argyll, Queen Victoria's daughter.'

Before Jago could think of a suitable reply to this information, Danbury interrupted.

'Come along, let's go into the drawing room.'

He showed them into a large, somewhat overfurnished

room and gestured vaguely towards a sofa.

'Do take a seat,' he said. 'And please excuse the mess – our maid's left. Says she can get better-paid work in a war factory, and we haven't found a replacement yet. We've managed to get a cleaner to come in, but it's not the same. Still, you know what it's like trying to get staff these days.'

Jago didn't. Nor could he identify exactly what mess the major was referring to. He sat on the sofa, followed by Cradock.

'We manage, though, don't we, dear?' said Mrs Danbury with the patient smile of the long-suffering as she turned to Jago and Cradock. 'Do let me get you a cup of tea, gentlemen – it's what I do these days. It feels as though I've done nothing but make tea and coffee for the last few months.'

'Please don't trouble yourself for us,' said Jago.

'No, no, I insist,' she replied, in the tone of one accustomed more to issuing instructions than to complying with those of others.

'I think I mentioned that my wife does voluntary work with a mobile canteen,' said Danbury.

'Ah, yes,' said Jago. 'Have you been doing that for long, Mrs Danbury?'

'A few months,' she replied. 'When my husband was asked to command a Local Defence Volunteers platoon in the Royal Docks I decided I would make my contribution too. We all have to do our bit, don't we? Women aren't allowed to join the Home Guard, of course, but I do believe it's my wifely duty to support my husband, so I chose to offer my services with the mobile canteen in the docks and support him and the men he commands as closely as possible. My daughter helps too, and I'm proud that as a family we're helping to keep the docks working in these difficult days. She's studying law at London University, you know.'

'Really?' said Jago, assuming she intended to tell him more of her daughter's accomplishments, but Mrs Danbury was already moving towards the door.

'Before you go, Mrs Danbury,' he added, 'your husband mentioned this morning that you'd been on duty with the mobile canteen in the docks last night. Was that in the Royal Albert?'

She stopped and turned to face him.

'Yes, it was, as it happens. I assume you're here because of the unfortunate death of that man in the docks last night?'

'That's right,' said Jago. 'Mr Lambert.'

'Yes. My husband told me what had happened.'

'I just wondered whether you knew Mr Lambert, since he was a member of your husband's Home Guard platoon.'

She gave him another patient smile.

'No. I may have seen him, of course, but I don't actually know any of the men my husband commands.'

'And just one more question, if you don't mind. Did you see anything unusual last night, anything out of the ordinary?'

'No, nothing particularly unusual, I would have

said. When I'm there I'm fully occupied in the vehicle, serving food and drink, so I don't notice much of what's happening outside. You'd be better off asking my daughter – she seems to be more observant than I am. But now, if you'll excuse me, I must return to the kitchen and resume duty as my own housemaid.'

With that she swept out of the room. Once she had gone, her husband sat down in a plush armchair. Jago took in the tasteful and expensive-looking surroundings.

'Very nice house you have here, Major Danbury,' he said. 'And I noticed a fine-looking car outside when we arrived.'

'Ah, that old beast. I picked it up years ago – bought it from a friend. It's an Armstrong Siddeley. Something of a relic now, I suppose, and not as reliable as one might wish, but still very comfortable.'

Yes, thought Jago, *just like the English upper classes*, but he kept the observation to himself.

'So how can I help you?' said Danbury.

'Well,' Jago replied, 'as I said, I'd like to know what more you can tell me about Mr Lambert. Had he been in your Home Guard platoon for long?'

'Pretty much since it was set up, as far as I can recall. It was certainly when we were still called the Local Defence Volunteers, so it would have been between the middle of May and the middle of July, when our name was changed.'

'What would his duties have been on the night he died?'

'He'd have been patrolling the dock. These docks

are a strategic objective, and our role is to protect them against attack. That could mean anything from sabotage by fifth columnists or enemy agents to the Germans parachuting troops in, as they did in Holland, to put them out of action or even capture them. In general, you could say it's our job to defend the docks and keep them working – a job we could no doubt do more effectively if we were adequately equipped.'

'Ah, yes. I assume you're referring to the question of weapons. There's been a lot of talk about that.'

'Yes, and it's not just weapons, either. We're supposed to be creating a credible fighting force, but there aren't enough greatcoats or steel helmets to go round and we don't even have proper battledress yet, just what the army call denims – cheap surplus overalls for us to wear over our everyday clothes. And not all the men even have them. At least when we started I had my old uniform from the last war, so at first I wore that, but now the Secretary of State for War has said we can't, so I have to wear those confounded denims too.'

'I assume some of your men are armed, though. We found a rifle on the quay not far from Mr Lambert's body. It was a Ross.'

'Ah, yes, the Ross. The Canadians had them in the war – very good for bagging moose, I dare say, but too long and heavy for the trenches. Most Canadians I knew would happily have thrown their Ross away if they could get their hands on a British Army Lee-Enfield. But better than nothing, and at least some of our men have something to shoot with now. I expect you saw what Churchill said the other day – a million Home Guards equipped with rifles or machine guns, but by my reckoning that still leaves seven hundred thousand with nothing but pikes and broomsticks to fight with. However, I don't suppose we'd even have those second-rate Ross weapons if it weren't for the fact that the docks are such a major target for the Germans.'

'Quite. Now, the men in your platoon, are they all dock workers?'

'Yes, that's right. Decent chaps, for the most part – salt of the earth, you know.'

'For the most part?'

'Yes, well, you know how it is with men like that. Always a few bad eggs among them.'

'Men like what?'

'Well, uneducated, working-class men. You must know what I mean. Trouble is, one doesn't always know who the bad eggs are. I should watch my step if I were you with those dockers – too many lazy, indolent types, always trying to pull the wool over the management's eyes, pilfering and so on. They need a firm hand. Fortunately I've plenty of experience of dealing with that type of fellow – met a few when I was in the army, and I worked in the docks myself for a while.'

'Did you? In what capacity?'

'Management, of course – in the Royal Docks, after I came out of the army. I retired from the army with a pension, but my daughter's education has been expensive, so a little extra income has been both necessary and useful. I'm retired from the docks too now, since the end of 1938, but when the LDVs started I offered to serve, and the higher command obviously believed that as an experienced officer I was the best person to lead this platoon.'

He glanced at the door as his wife came in, bearing a tray from which she distributed cups of tea to the three men.

'If you'll excuse me,' she said, 'I'll leave you gentlemen to your conversation. I have things to do.'

Jago thanked her as she deposited a sugar bowl and a small jug of milk on a side table and left.

'Do carry on, Inspector,' said Danbury.

'Thank you,' Jago replied. 'Now, you said Mr Lambert would've been patrolling the docks last night, so can you just tell me what that would've involved? What sort of area would he have had to cover?'

'Well, the Royal Albert Dock has a good three miles of quay, so we divide it up. Lambert would have been patrolling the whole of the southern side – the quayside itself, and all the buildings along it. The men are already very familiar with the site, of course, since they work here, but we train them in the military approach – to maintain silence, especially on a still night, keep to the shadows, vary their route and so on.'

'Would he have been alone?'

'No. The men had instructions to patrol in pairs.'

'So who was Lambert patrolling with?'

'He was with Bell.'

'Is that Charlie Bell? His name's been mentioned.'

'That's right.'

'And what does he do when he's not on Home Guard duty?'

'He's a stevedore – he gets cargo on and off the ships. Bit of a hothead, by all accounts, from Scotland. The men call him Bonnie, and I think that's something he brought down from Scotland with him. After Bonnie Prince Charlie, you see. Fighting for a hopeless cause and ending up living in exile in a foreign country.'

'A hopeless cause?'

'Just one of nature's fighters, I suppose. I don't know much about his background, but my impression is he hates bosses and Nazis, in that order. Chip on the shoulder sort of chap, you know, but very keen. He's one of my section leaders – that's what we'd call a corporal in the army.'

'Would you say he and Mr Lambert were friends?'

'Oh, yes. Lambert was just an ordinary volunteer, the equivalent of a private, so there was a difference in rank, but they seemed very close – always chatting together, laughing behind people's backs, as if they were enjoying some kind of private joke.'

'Close friends, then, you'd say?'

'Oh, yes, thick as thieves, those two. But volunteers nonetheless, willing to do their duty and put their lives at risk while some of our civilians don't seem to care about anything other than saving their own skin. As raw material these chaps may be rough, but we're turning them into men of dedication, initiative and courage, just as we did in the last war.'

'Can you think of anyone who might've wanted to harm Mr Lambert?'

'Harm him? No,' Danbury replied without hesitation. 'This has come as a complete surprise to me. I can't imagine why anyone would want to kill him. I'm sure it can't have been any of my men, though – they're a disciplined fighting force, ready to lay down their lives for each other and for their country.'

'Just one more thing,' said Jago, pulling a piece of paper from his pocket. 'Do you recognise this name?'

Danbury took the paper and scrutinised it briefly.

'Dayabir Singh?' he said. 'Some sort of foreigner, presumably.' He shook his head disdainfully. 'The answer's no, it means nothing to me. Should it?'

'No, not necessarily. Well, thank you, Major Danbury, that'll be all. You've been most helpful.'

'My pleasure,' said Danbury. 'But before you go there's a small matter I'd like to raise with you.'

'By all means. What is it?'

'Well, it's just that I had occasion to speak to one of your men recently, and I have to say, if you ask me, they could do with exercising a bit more of that initiative that mine are starting to show. Then we might all sleep a little safer in our beds – even if those beds are in our Anderson shelters.'

'What makes you say that?'

'The response I got from one of your officers when we were the victims of a crime.'

'When was that?'

'It was just a week or so ago.'

'Do you remember the precise date?'

'Yes, it was the Sunday before last – the twenty-seventh of October.'

'Would you mind telling me what happened?'

'By all means. It was during the night. I was on Home Guard duty down in the docks, and my wife and daughter were helping with the mobile canteen, so the house was empty. When we got home the next morning I discovered we'd been burgled.'

'How could you tell?'

'One of the windows was smashed.'

'And not just the usual blast damage, presumably?'

'No,' said Danbury. 'This was just one small window at the side of the house, where it's sheltered from blast by the brick wall between us and our neighbours. And besides, none of the windows at the front or back of the house had been damaged.'

'Did you lose anything?'

'Yes, but nothing of value, I'm glad to say – just a few odds and ends, the sort of things a fellow can stuff into his pockets and make off with. I don't keep large amounts of cash in the house.'

'Very sensible, sir. Burglars have been doing nicely out of the war – the blackout makes their work easier and ours harder, and as for looting, well, that's one of the worst things about these air raids. We're finding that "odds and ends" are just the kind of thing the thieves are going for – cash, jewellery, cameras, portable wireless sets, bits of clothing.'

'Well, fortunately we didn't lose anything as valuable as a portable wireless, so I suppose we should be grateful. But it's still a disgraceful thing to do.'

'And you say you reported it to the police, yes?'

'I told the first constable I saw. He had "WR" on his helmet, so I assume he was one of those temporary War Reserve ones. I said I wanted to speak to a real policeman, but he insisted he was a real one. He wrote something down in his notebook but didn't sound hopeful about catching whoever did it, so I told him not to bother. As I say, I wasn't worried about getting anything back, but it left me thinking that things have come to a pretty pass when someone will break into a man's house during an air raid to steal his property – and all the more so when I know my platoon are out every night ready to fight to the death if the Germans land.'

'Well, I'm very sorry to hear that, sir. Would you like me to pursue the matter?'

'No, there's no need. I'm sure you have more important things to do. But I hope you'll be putting rather greater effort into finding out who killed a member of my platoon.'

'I can assure you of that, Major Danbury. We shall.'

CHAPTER NINE

'So,' said Cradock as he and Jago emerged from Danbury's house, 'if Lambert and Bell were meant to be patrolling together, how did someone manage to creep up on Lambert and kill him?'

'Exactly the question I was asking myself, Peter,' Jago replied, 'and one which I think we need to put to Mr Bell. We'll go down to Woodman Street and see if we can find his lodgings on the corner, like Mrs Lambert said. If he's not there we'll have to try the docks, but I reckon he'll have finished work by the time we get there. Either way, we should be able to get back before the blackout starts if we don't run into any trouble. I'll drive – we'll go down Manor Road, then we can slip round the other side of the Royal Victoria, and I'll show you that gutta-percha place on the way.'

'Thank you, sir,' said Cradock, struggling to disguise his lack of interest in the factory.

Manor Road was clear of obstacles, and soon they were on the new Silvertown Way flyover. The road had been open for six years, but it still felt odd to be driving up in the air, looking down on the surrounding area. Jago wondered how George Bidder had imagined it would end up when he'd bought all this land a hundred years ago. Then it was just the Plaistow Marshes, sparsely populated pasturage and at one time home to the notorious highwayman Dick Turpin. Bidder had acquired all the marshland between Bow Creek and Gallions Reach and built the railway, beginning the transformation into what was now Silvertown, North Woolwich and the Royal Docks.

Glancing to his left, Jago noticed Cradock was trying to hold his nose discreetly, but as they crossed the bridge over the western entrance to the Royal Victoria Dock from the river it seemed his young colleague could contain himself no longer.

'Oh, sir,' said Cradock in disgust, 'what's that horrible pong? Is that what gutta-percha smells like?'

'I don't think so,' said Jago. 'That's further down the road. The war's put a stop to some of the businesses down here, and a lot of the factories have been knocked about in the air raids, so I don't know which ones are still working and which aren't. I suspect what you can smell is just one of the many distinctive odours of Silvertown.' He pointed ahead with his right hand. 'Just down there you can see one of the most important local industries – the Peruvian guano works.'

'Guano? What's guano? One of those things foreigners eat?'

Jago smiled to himself.

'You mean things like guava or avocado that we used to get from South Africa before the war?'

'That's right.'

'I'm afraid not. Guano's more like what Lord Nelson gets from those pigeons in Trafalgar Square, all over his hat.'

'What, you mean—'

'Yes. Apparently if you go to the coast of Peru you can find islands where seabirds have been leaving similar deposits on the ground for thousands of years, more than a hundred feet deep, and someone's discovered it's excellent manure. Ever since Victorian times they've been digging it up by the shipload and sending it to Silvertown to make it into fertiliser for our gardens. But I don't suppose you're much of a gardener, are you?'

'No, sir,' Cradock replied, his voice distorted by the fact that he was still holding his nose.

'A bit too exotic for you round here, is it?'

'No, sir, it's just that it stinks a bit.'

'Indeed it does, and it's hardly surprising. On our left we've got the docks, and on our right not just the guano works but Knight's Silvertown soap works too, where they make Primrose soap.'

'At least fancy soap smells nice, though.'

'Not when they're making it, it doesn't. You do know it's made out of old animal fat and bones, don't you?'

'Oh, no – that's disgusting.'

'Just imagine what it's like if you have to live here. Mix in a few of the other local smells and it's enough to turn anyone's stomach.'

By the time they reached Woodman Street the stench had faded a little, screened perhaps by the sweeter smell from the Thames sugar refinery which they passed again on the way. Cradock was breathing more freely as he and Jago approached the corner house where they'd been told Charlie Bell had his lodgings.

The front door at which they knocked looked as though it had once been smartly finished in dark green paint, but now it was chipped, scuffed and tired-looking. A few seconds later it opened on creaking hinges to reveal a strong-looking, sinewy man with ginger hair and a pencil moustache.

'And who would you be?' he said, eyeing the visitors suspiciously while wiping his nose on a greying white handkerchief. His accent seemed to Jago to bear out his reported Scottish origins.

'Detective Inspector Jago and Detective Constable Cradock, West Ham CID. Mr Bell?'

'That's right. What do you want?'

'We'd like a word with you, if you don't mind.'

'Aye, well, you're welcome to come in, as long as you don't mind catching a cold.'

'That's all right, Mr Bell. We won't be long.'

Bell stepped back to let them in, and they edged past him into the narrow hall. The air was soggy with the smell of damp laundry.

'This way,' said Bell, leading them to the back of the house.

They entered the kitchen in time to see a short, thin woman with tired eyes and straggling hair emerge from the scullery. She was wearing a dark, shabby dress in some heavy fabric and was wiping her hands on an old towel. A saucepan full of handkerchiefs was boiling steadily on the range behind her.

'This is Mrs Higgs, my landlady,' said Bell.

'Pleased to meet you,' she said, her voice cautious. Jago thought she looked about forty, although she might have been younger than her care-worn appearance suggested. He gave a nod in acknowledgement of her greeting.

'You'll have to excuse the mess,' she continued. 'I know it's not Monday, but I've got the copper going all day. I take washing in, you see, to make ends meet. You know what it's like – soul-destroying work, but that and a bit of charring in the morning brings in ten bob in a good week, which is very helpful. Can I get you gents a cup of tea?'

'No, thank you, Mrs Higgs. I can see you're very busy, and it's Mr Bell we've come to see, so perhaps we could talk to him in your front room and leave you to get on with your work.'

'You're welcome. That's his room anyway.'

Bell took Jago and Cradock into the front room. With a bed, a table, a chair and a single wardrobe squashed into the small space there wasn't much room left for the three men.

'Probably best if you two sit on the bed, if you don't mind,' said Bell. 'I'll take the wee chair.'

'That's fine,' said Jago. The bed sagged with a creak as he and Cradock sat down.

'That was Mavis,' Bell continued. 'She's an exceptional woman. Always working, always got washing on the go, stuff drying on the pulley and in front of the range, piles of ironing. I've known some women in my time, but never anyone like her. She had a good-for-nothing waster of a husband who ran off years ago and left her up to her ears in debts, but she never complains, just gets on with it.'

He leant forward on the chair and peered intensely into Jago's eyes.

'Some people just don't understand what life's like here in Silvertown. We're all jammed in like sardines, in terrible housing that was already falling down years before the war started, and now what's left is being blown apart by bombs. It's the same old story – you're born with nothing and you die with nothing, and you're supposed to just put up with it in between. If you ask me, it's about time the government started taking money off the rich and giving it to the poor.'

'Like Robin Hood?' said Cradock.

Bell shifted his gaze to one side and glared at Cradock. 'Aye, well,' he said, 'maybe he wasn't so far off the mark – and how many hundreds of years ago was that? Maybe we could do with a few more like him today.' He sat back on his chair and wiped the handkerchief across his nose again. 'Anyway, I don't suppose you've come here to find out how the poor of Silvertown are suffering. What is it you want to know?'

Jago adjusted his position on the bed, which was already proving notably lumpy.

'We're investigating the death of Mr Ray Lambert last night. I understand you reported what had happened to Mrs Lambert. Is that correct?'

'Yes, it is. I'd met her, you see, been to their home, so it seemed the least I could do – break the bad news to her, I mean. I dropped in on my way home from duty.'

'How did she take it?'

'Well, she's a strong woman, I'll give her that. Took it very bravely, although it was obviously a terrible shock for her.'

'I understand you were friends with Mr Lambert.'

'Aye, I suppose so. We got on all right – but then you've got to watch each other's back when you're serving in the Home Guard.'

'And you were patrolling with him last night?'

'Er, yes, I was.'

'Did you see the attack?'

'No.'

'Did you hear the attack?'

'No.'

'So in what sense were you watching his back?'

'What is this? The third degree?'

'No, Mr Bell, but if you didn't see or hear him being attacked, it doesn't sound as though you were keeping a close eye on him.'

'All right, but that's not my fault. It was just a terrible coincidence. There was only a short time when I wasn't with him, and that must've been when it happened.'

'So where were you?'

Bell appeared to be calming his ruffled feathers.

'Well, it's like this, you see,' he continued. 'I was going down with a cold, as you can probably tell. I dare say I should never have gone on duty at all, but you can't let your unit down, can you? We were passing this ship, the *Magnolia*, and bumped into the mate. He'd come down onto the quay to stretch his legs, you see.'

'That would be Mr Carlisle?'

'That's right.'

'Were you friends with him too?'

'No. Ray and I had just been chatting with him the previous night, on the quay, so he said hello as we were passing. I happened to mention I'd got this cold, so he said he'd fix me a hot toddy. Well, that always works for me when I've got a cold coming on, so when he invited me on board for it I asked Ray if it was all right by him, and Ray said sure, go ahead. He said it wouldn't do for both of us to abandon our patrol, so he'd go down to the end of the dock and back while I had the drink.'

'What time was this?'

'Hmm . . . Difficult to say, really. I didn't check the time. I reckon it was about four in the morning, but that's the time of night when my body's telling me it ought to be asleep, so I'm not at my brightest then. I'm sorry I can't be more precise.'

'How long did you stay on the ship?'

'Half an hour? An hour? I'm not sure. But then when Ray didn't come back to meet me I went down onto the quay – but I couldn't see him anywhere.'

'And you didn't raise the alarm?'

'No. I thought he'd probably gone off to obey the call of nature, as they say, and he'd find me when he'd finished, or I'd find him, so I decided to carry on patrolling on my own,

I had a look round for him before I went, but of course in the dark that wasn't very easy. Then as the drink worked its way through I thought I needed to go and spend a penny myself, so I went to look for some suitable spot. By the time I got back to the ship, there was one of your boys there. He told me to keep clear and go about my business, so I carried on patrolling on my own, hoping to come across Ray.'

'But you didn't.'

'No, I didn't. And the next thing I heard was that he'd been killed. I felt terrible – I mean, if I'd been with him I probably could've saved his life, couldn't I? In fact, whoever it was probably wouldn't even have attacked if he'd seen two of us. Ray was a good pal of mine, Inspector.'

'Yes, I see. Did you know Mr Lambert before you joined the Home Guard?'

'No.'

'But you work in the docks, don't you? I've been told you're a stevedore.'

'Who told you that?'

'Your platoon commander, Major Danbury.'

'Right, then. I might've seen Ray before we both joined the Home Guard, but I didn't know him. I suppose we never ran into each other. There's a lot of men in these docks, you know.'

'Yes, indeed. So tell me, what does being a stevedore entail? Am I right in understanding you get the cargo on and off the ships?'

'That's right. The ordinary dockers who cart the stuff off into the sheds, they're just labour – porters, basically. They don't need to know anything about ships or the sea, but we do. We're the downholders – we get down into the hold and bring the cargo out. We pack it in when the ship's being loaded, too, so we need to know what happens when a ship's at sea, how to get everything in so it won't move. If whatever's in the hold shifts in heavy seas it can get damaged and even put the ship at risk. We know how to stow the cargo in all the awkward little nooks and crannies on the ship, to get it as full as possible and keep it all safe.'

'And tell me, how long have you been in the Home Guard?'

'Since it started, when it was the Local Defence Volunteers – in May.'

'Why did you join?'

'Well, I missed out on the last war, because I was building warships. I was a riveter – did a five-year apprenticeship at the Beardmore yard on Clydebank when I left school. Now I'm too old for the forces in this war, and in any case stevedoring's a reserved occupation, so the Home Guard's the closest I can get to fighting.'

'I see. Now, I may need to speak to you again, so if I want to get hold of you in the daytime, will someone at the docks be able to tell me where to find you?'

'Aye, probably. I'm most likely to be working a ship or loading a barge in the Albert Dock – ask around the stevedores in there, and someone'll be able to point you in the right direction.'

'Thank you. You've been most helpful – and if you remember anything else about Mr Lambert that you think might be of interest, do let me know.'

'Aye, I'll be sure to do that.'

CHAPTER TEN

'Morning, sir,' said Frank Tompkins, the station sergeant, as Jago arrived for work the next day. 'I trust Bonfire Night didn't keep you awake last night.'

Jago laughed.

'Morning, Frank. I don't suppose anyone was giving much thought to Guy Fawkes' Day this year. It's not the same, is it? Not when you get bonfires and firework displays every night of the week, all laid on for free by the Luftwaffe. But at least the blackout's saved those dads all the trouble of trying to light rockets that don't work and Catherine wheels that fall off the fence post as soon as they get going.'

'No great loss as far as I'm concerned,' Tompkins replied. 'I've not been too keen on fireworks ever since the last war – heard enough explosions then to last me a lifetime, I reckon. And with no crackers or bangers going off it meant we could all get a good night's sleep, didn't it?'

'Very amusing, I'm sure.'

The door clattered behind Jago as DC Cradock entered the station.

'Morning, sir. Morning, sarge,' he said cheerily. 'Sorry I'm late.'

'I've only been here about two minutes myself,' said Jago, 'so I think you can be excused. It was a long day yesterday.'

'Ah, yes,' said Tompkins. 'I was off yesterday, but I heard you had a bit of an early start. Did you have a pleasant time down at the docks?'

'Kind of you to ask, Frank.'

'Well, when I heard you were looking into a spot of bother down there I thought it might've proved challenging, sir. Those dockers can be a right bolshie bunch. I mean, when we had that General Strike in 1926 it seemed like every man jack of them in West Ham walked out. No end of trouble, that was – I was glad to see the back of it. Do you remember? We had every plain-clothes officer back in uniform and on the beat, and then we had all those amateur special constables too.'

'Ah, yes. Who could forget them?'

'You should've seen it,' Tompkins said to Cradock. 'It was a sight to behold. Young toffs, most of 'em, issued with an armband and a warrant card and thrown out onto the streets without the faintest idea about policing. And some of them still wearing their plus-fours, too – they must've been mad. People round the docks hated them.'

'Water under the bridge, now, though, Frank,' said Jago.

'You think so? I'm not so sure. There's still plenty of people with a chip on their shoulder from those days – wouldn't lift a finger to help a copper.'

'I've had no problems so far.'

'Well, you watch your step, sir, that's my advice. People say it's like Ali Baba down in those docks, wherever you look – the amount of nicking that goes on is nobody's business. If there's one thing everyone in West Ham knows about the dockers, it's that they always seem to have stuff other people can't get their hands on. It's a world of its own down there, and no one on the outside really knows what goes on inside. Mind you, time was when some of the coppers in the docks weren't much better themselves.'

'You're talking about the good old days, I suppose?'

'That's right, sir. When I was a young constable and you were just a nipper. The PLA Police hadn't been set up yet, so there was only the dock police, run by the companies that owned the docks. By all accounts those boys weren't the cream of the crop, and there weren't many of them. The pay was poor, even worse than ours, and you know what they say – you get what you pay for. The shippers wanted the Metropolitan Police to take over, but that wasn't on, because the docks were all private property. So that's how we ended up with the PLA force, and if I recall correctly, once that got going, some of those coppers from the good old days got sacked for being drunk on duty. One or two even got caught sneaking stuff out of the docks without a proper pass themselves.'

'Stop, Frank. You're shocking me.'

'Yes, well, I'm sure they've weeded out all the rogues

long since. I'm talking about what it was like thirty or forty years ago.'

'Still, I'll watch my step, Frank.'

'Very good, sir. And by the way, talking of thieving, have you had a look in the occurrence book yet?'

'Not yet, no.'

'Well, someone's reported a burglary, so I expect you'll want to take a look. Gentleman phoned in this morning to say he'd had a break-in overnight. Lost a bike and a few other bits and pieces, it seems.'

'Where?'

'128 Clova Road.'

'That's interesting. We heard about another break-in not far from there yesterday – seems the Home Guard platoon commander from the docks had some uninvited visitors in the night recently. Quite put out by it, he was, but then he's another old soldier like you and me – on a better pension, though, by the looks of it. You should've seen his car – a huge old Armstrong Siddeley, the sort of thing you'd expect to see dropping off a Gaumont starlet outside a premiere in Leicester Square, not parked on the street in West Ham.'

'Sounds like someone's doing the rounds and helping themselves during the blackout, doesn't it?'

'It does, yes. Who's the victim this time?'

'It was reported by a Mr Alfred Whitton.'

'OK, we'll pay him a visit. Could you give him a call and tell him we'll come round after lunch, if that's all right with him?'

'Ah, yes. Speaking of which, would I be correct in

thinking you won't be lunching in the canteen today, sir?'

'That's right, but so what?'

'I suppose you've had a better offer, eh, sir?'

He gave Jago an enquiring look, as if expecting some kind of confession. Jago's face gave nothing away, but he wondered how Frank came to know about his dining plans.

'What if I have?' he replied. 'Sometimes a man might want a change from police canteen beef stew and dumplings on a Wednesday.'

'Something like a nice bowl of clam chowder, perhaps?'

'Clam chowder? What on earth are you talking about?'

'Nothing, sir. I just thought perhaps if you fancied something different it might be an American dish you had in mind.'

'I see. There's little mystery where your mind's concerned, is there?'

'Just thinking, sir. Just thinking.'

'And what sparked off this particular train of thought in your mind today, may I ask?'

'Nothing, really. It's just that I took a call about half an hour ago from that American lady friend of yours. She said she was just ringing to confirm she'll be arriving for lunch at one o'clock, as you suggested, and would I tell you.'

'Ah, now it all begins to fall into place. With powers of deduction like that you should've been a detective.'

'Maybe I should, but they never asked. Passed over, I was. And when I look at some of the young detective constables we get these days, I don't know whether to laugh or cry. Which reminds me, will DC Cradock be with you for lunch too?'

Cradock gave Tompkins the most withering look he could manage.

'Yes, he will, as a matter of fact,' said Jago. 'We'll be down the road at Rita's cafe. Why do you ask?'

'It's only because the American lady said she hopes you won't mind if someone else joins you for lunch too. She's getting a lift here from a friend, and this friend's interested in meeting you.'

'Did she say why?'

'No, that was all she said – she had to dash off to a meeting or something, so that was it.'

'Well, thank you for passing on the message. Now, will that be all?'

'Actually, there is just one other thing I ought to pass on. The thing is, I've got a case for you – just the sort of thing you like to get your teeth into, I'd say.'

'Oh, yes? And what's that?'

'Well, my missus was down the butcher's yesterday, and she said she saw him fish something out from under the counter and pass it to this woman in the queue in front of her. The woman slipped it into her bag, quick as a flash, but the missus says she reckons it was a bit of extra bacon – and that's been rationed since January, hasn't it? And the woman didn't give him her ration book either.'

'He wouldn't be the first shopkeeper to slip his favourite customers a bit more than the ration, and he won't be the first to be fined a few quid for his trouble. But it's a matter for the Ministry of Food inspectors, not us. Tell her to report it to them.'

'I did, but then she said the butcher gave this woman something else – it was a packet of something, with printing on it, and you don't get packets like that in butchers' shops, do you? My missus reckons it was a packet of sugar – she said she could see part of the label, and she was sure it said Tate & Lyle. Now, if he's a butcher he won't be licensed by the local Food Control Committee to sell groceries, so I reckon that sugar was black market – knocked off from somewhere.'

'Same applies to sugar,' said Jago. 'Tell the food inspectors and let them look into it. If they find evidence and want to get us involved they can let us know.'

Cradock appeared to have been thinking.

'There's a lot of it about, isn't there, sir?' he said. 'Nicking, I mean, not sugar. And shopkeepers profiteering and making a fortune from under-the-counter stuff. That ship we were on yesterday was carrying bacon, wasn't it? Do you reckon someone's been nicking that?'

'I dare say someone somewhere has stolen bacon since January, but there must be a lot of ships bringing it into the country, and I imagine one piece of bacon's the same as any other. How would you be able to tell? Anyway, there was no report that any was missing from the SS *Magnolia*. And before you ask, she wasn't carrying sugar, either.'

'Yes, well, there's still too much of that sort of thing going on.'

'Indeed there is, Peter. But that's what keeps us in a job, isn't it?'

CHAPTER ELEVEN

Cradock was still in what seemed to Jago an enviably cheery mood when they reached the CID office.

'So, what's the plan for today then, guv'nor?' he said. 'Do we need to do anything about what Mrs Tompkins said – that business with her butcher?'

'Not today, certainly,' Jago replied. 'Not when we've got a murder on our hands. I think we can let that particular sleeping dog lie for the time being, and wait for the food inspectors to wake it up if they want to. We need to see this Mr Whitton who's been burgled after lunch, but this morning there's one or two points I'd like to clarify with Carlisle on that ship of his. Anything else you can think of?'

'Yes, sir. Mrs Danbury said she didn't see anything unusual happening in the dock when she was working the canteen, but she said her daughter was more observant and we'd be better off asking her. So do you think we should do that?'

'You mean should we go and have a little chat with the young student daughter? I wonder what made you think of her.'

'Only the fact that she's a potential witness,' said Cradock defensively.

The shyness in his eyes was touching, and Jago decided not to tease him further.

'Quite right, Peter. We'll try her first, then go and see Carlisle.'

When they arrived at the Danburys' home, the door was opened by a slim, confident-looking young woman with short dark hair, wearing a jumper, slacks and flat shoes. She stood with her feet apart in the doorway and looked both of them in the eye.

'Good morning?' she said, as if expecting them to account for why they had knocked on her door. 'If you've come to see my father, I'm afraid he's out. I'm not sure what he's doing, but it'll probably be something to do with the golf club or the Home Guard. He's always busy with something.'

'I'm Detective Inspector Jago, and this is my colleague Detective Constable Cradock. And you are?'

'My name is Evelyn Danbury. As you'll have inferred from what I just said, I'm Major Danbury's daughter.'

'Indeed, and if you're his only daughter, then it's actually you we've come to see.'

'Really? Well, in that case you'd better come in.'

She took them into the drawing room they had visited the previous day and offered them a seat, then sat down on a chair opposite them and faced them with her head to one side, eyebrows raised as if still waiting for them to explain themselves.

'We won't be long, Miss Danbury,' said Jago. 'There's

just a small matter you might be able to help us with.'

'I see. Well, I'm always happy to help the police. I'm in my final year studying law, actually.'

'Yes, so your mother told us. At London University, I believe.'

'That's right,' she replied with a smile, her expression now more relaxed. 'You must excuse my mother – I expect she told you all about it.'

'Not at all. In fact, I was wondering how the university's managing to operate in the present circumstances.'

'Well, these dreadful air raids are disrupting everything, of course, so it's not easy to keep up with lectures and studies, but we're all doing our best. I'm hoping to graduate next summer, and then I want to train to be a barrister. There's no reason why a woman shouldn't be, these days.'

'Indeed not – the world's changed since I was your age,' said Jago. 'We may see each other in court one day, then,' he added with a smile.

'Perhaps we shall. I was born in 1919, you see, the year that the Sex Disqualification (Removal) Act was passed, so that means I'm part of the first generation to grow up in a world where it's possible for a woman to be a barrister. Do you know who Helena Normanton is?'

'Yes – the first woman in England to practise as a barrister.'

'Well done – that's right. She's my heroine – I've written to her. And she was born in Stratford, right here in West Ham, so if she can do it, why shouldn't I? My mother worries, of course, about whether I'm doing the right thing. She believes a well-bred Englishwoman's first duty is to bear children, to

106

produce the stock this country needs if it's to avoid sliding into degeneracy. I must admit, a few hours in court observing the kind of people who come before judges and magistrates are enough to convince me she has a point, but for her that means my only ambition should be to find a man of breeding and quality and marry him, as it was hers. There we differ. I don't see why I shouldn't have a professional career and a husband too. I'm going to be a barrister, and nothing's going to stop me – and certainly no man is.'

'It's quite an ambition.'

'Yes. I don't expect it to be easy – the odds are still very much stacked against us women, you know. The real power's in the hands of the judges, and they're all men, and they tried hard to stop the first women who wanted to be barristers. What we really need, of course, is not just women barristers but women judges. That's the only way we'll get real justice in this country – when women are in a position to judge men. My aim is to be the first woman judge in England, and for that I need to become a barrister.'

'Well, I wish you every success.'

'Thank you, that's very kind of you. I don't imagine you've come to consult me on a point of law, though. What is it you wanted to see me about?'

'It's to do with the unfortunate death of a man in the Royal Albert Dock.'

'Ah, yes, I've heard about that. Shocking business. By the way, can I get you a drink?'

'No, thank you very much.'

'As you please. Actually, I seem to do nothing

107

but make tea these days.'

'So I gather – at least, I understand from your parents you do some voluntary work of that nature in the docks.'

'That's right. I do two nights a week in a mobile canteen with my mother, making tea and slices of bread and dripping for the men, and sometimes driving the van. I volunteered because I wanted to do my bit, but also because my father has Home Guard duties in the docks, as you know, and his eyes aren't too good for night driving. I know there's that new regulation now that says we can keep a masked headlamp on during an air raid, but even so, I prefer to drive him if I can. Mummy can't drive, you see – I don't think many women of her generation can – and I feel I need to look after them. My parents have made a lot of financial sacrifices for my education, and it hasn't been easy for them.'

'I see. So this mobile canteen – is it run by the Women's Voluntary Service?'

'No, it's run by the PLA, actually. Just as well, really – if it'd been the WVS my mother would've had to shell out quite a lot of money for the uniform, but with the PLA we can just wear overalls over our oldest and most comfortable ordinary clothes and stick a little turban on to keep our hair out of the way instead of having to spend seven and eleven for a WVS hat. Apparently if you want to wear the WVS uniform you have to buy the whole lot yourself and it costs you more than nine pounds. I don't imagine men would put up with that.'

Jago thought she was probably right, but now was not the time to discuss it.

'So,' he said, 'your work involves taking the mobile

canteen round the docks and serving cups of tea to anyone who's working there at night?'

'Yes. I've even served tea to my own father. He's pretty particular about how his tea's brewed, a bit of a stickler all round really – he likes it strong enough to stand the spoon up.'

'That all sounds a far cry from your legal studies.'

'Not so far as you might think, actually. For example, this might sound trivial to a man like you, but we're down there risking our lives all night making tea, and drinking the odd mug or two ourselves, yet there are no women's lavatories for us to use. I went to complain to the dock superintendent, and he said it's because there are no women employees in the docks. Imagine that! It seems the only facilities they have are for men, and I've been told those are just buckets, or a communal plank over a big metal tank. How disgusting – can you imagine it?'

'I was a soldier in the last war, so I'm afraid I can, yes.'

'Well, I wasn't prepared to accept it. "What do you do if the Lady Mayoress of West Ham visits?" I said. "Show her to the nearest plank?" He insisted there was nothing he could do about it, so I quoted the Factories Act 1937 to him, and what it says about providing lavatories for women at their place of work. That only applied to women who were employed there, he said, and since no women worked in the docks it was irrelevant. I wasn't going to let him get away with that. I said I was working, and so were my fellow canteen volunteers, and the Act put him under a legal obligation to afford proper separate accommodation for persons of each sex. All nonsense, of course – I wasn't employed by the docks, so I don't suppose I had a leg to stand on legally, but as soon as I started invoking the law his attitude changed. Anything for a quiet life, I suppose. He said we could have a key to his own personal lavatory at his office and use it, and he handed one over to me on the spot.'

She sat back and smiled at the recollection of her own success.

'A small victory, Inspector, but an important one for the lady volunteers on the mobile canteen. Now, what is your particular interest in our work?'

'I understand you were on duty with your mother from Monday night to yesterday morning, when the man's body was found. Is that correct?'

'Yes, that's right.'

'When you were in the Royal Albert Dock, do you remember seeing a ship called the SS *Magnolia*?'

'*Magnolia*? I'm afraid I don't take much notice of the names. Where was it?'

'On the south side of the dock, towards the eastern end. Where was your van parked?'

'We were on that side, about halfway down, by No. 16 shed. That's our usual spot.'

'Did you see anything unusual happening towards the eastern end?'

'I didn't see much of that end at all. The van was parked at right angles to the water, with the counter dropped down on the left-hand side to shelter it from the wind, so when we were serving we were facing in the opposite direction – towards the western end, I suppose. There was one thing, though . . .'

'Yes? What was that?'

'Well, things had quietened down – we didn't have any customers, and even the anti-aircraft guns hadn't fired for a while – so I decided to take a quick break. Stretch my legs and have a cigarette. My mother doesn't like me smoking in the van – she says I'll get ash in the sandwiches, and she's probably right. So I slipped outside and lit up on the quayside. That's when I heard it.'

'Heard what?'

'Just a noise, not loud. If I'd been in the van I might not have heard it, but being out on the quay I did. I wondered what it was, so I popped round to the other side of the van to see where it was coming from. It was down towards the end where you said that ship was. It sounded like there was a bit of an argument going on.'

'How many people?'

'Just two. As far as I could tell, they were having what people in that part of the world call a bit of a ding-dong. Quite animated, in fact. One of them had his back to the water and the other was facing him.'

'Can you describe them?'

'Not really. Both looked as though they had heavy coats on, but there was only the moonlight to see by, so I couldn't make out their faces or anything.'

'Could you hear what they were saying?'

'No, they were too far away. I was intrigued, though, and started walking down the quay towards them to try to see what was happening. I still couldn't tell what they were saying. The only thing I caught was one of them calling the other a rude name – you know, questioning his parentage. But I imagine that sort of thing's quite common in the docks. Anyway, by then I'd begun to think better of getting any closer, and in any case I'd finished my cigarette, so I turned round and went back to the van and thought no more about it.'

'Did you notice anyone else nearby who might've witnessed what was happening?'

'No. Not a soul.'

'What about your mother?'

'She stayed in the van – wouldn't have seen anything.'

'Just one more question. Do you remember what time it was when you witnessed the argument?'

'Yes. When I got back in the van I looked at my watch. It was a quarter past four.'

'Thank you, Miss Danbury, that's most helpful.'

'You're very welcome. Now, are you sure you won't have something to drink?'

'Quite sure, thank you. We need to be getting along.'

Evelyn seemed distracted for a moment. She glanced down at the table beside her and tutted.

'Look at that,' she sighed. 'A horrible stain where someone's put a wet cup down and taken the polish off. What does that cleaner do all day? She's supposed to dust and polish, but she doesn't see the most obvious things that need doing. I don't know why my mother pays her.'

CHAPTER TWELVE

The door closed behind them and they walked down the Danburys' garden path to the front gate. Cradock opened it for Jago and stood back for him to go through first.

'Well,' said Jago. 'What did you make of Miss Danbury? A very capable young lady, but would she displace that girlfriend of yours, Emily, in your affections?'

'Emily's not my girlfriend, sir. We've been to the pictures together a couple of times, that's all.'

'But even so?'

'Even so, I think if I had an evening spare I'd rather spend it with Emily than with her. A bit too high-powered for me – university and all that. And not what you'd call a looker, is she?'

'So Emily is what you'd call a looker, is she?'

'She's very nice.'

'I'm glad to hear it. I just wanted to check whether it'll be safe to take you for lunch today at Rita's cafe. I wouldn't like to be in the room if you were going to tell Rita you'd gone off her daughter. Far too dangerous.'

'I don't think I'll be discussing Emily with her mum if I can help it, sir. It'll be nice to see Miss Appleton again, though. And this lunch – is it business, sir, or pleasure?'

'Oh, strictly business, Peter – as always – and no doubt she'll be as delighted by your company as I am.'

The response that ran through Cradock's mind might, he thought, be interpreted as sarcasm, so he left it unspoken.

'Thank you, sir,' he said, and took his seat beside Jago in the car hoping to change the subject.

'So,' he said, 'what are those points you want to clarify with Carlisle?'

'Just two things,' said Jago. 'I want to see if he can tell us anything about that other Indian who was a crewman on the *Magnolia* before Jamal joined the ship, and I also want to know whether he can substantiate what Charlie Bell said about that drink Lambert had with him.'

At the Albert Dock they found Carlisle on his ship. He was standing on the deck, looking over the rail, dressed as before in duffle coat and sea boots, but now with the addition of a dark knitted hat pulled low over his ears. He looked surprised to see them. Jago and Cradock went on board and exchanged greetings. On this occasion Carlisle did not invite them to his cabin, so they stood with him by the rail.

'This won't take a moment, Mr Carlisle,' Jago began.

'There's just a couple of things I'd like to ask you.'

'Oh aye, and what's that?'

'I understand Mr Jamal joined your ship in Scotland for this latest run of yours down the coast. Is that correct?'

'It is.'

'I wondered if you could tell me about his predecessor. Was he Indian too?'

'Aye, he was. He left the ship when we were in Clydebank, taking on the cargo we've just brought down here.'

'Can you tell me why he left?'

'No, I can't.'

'Why's that?'

'Because unfortunately I'm not a mind-reader, that's why. He just decided to jump ship one night, and men who jump ship don't generally leave you a note explaining where they've gone and why. This fellow was the same – he just went off. He could be anywhere in the world by now.'

'Do you know which part of India he came from?'

'From the Punjab, I think he said.'

'Was he a Sikh?'

'They're the ones who wear the turbans, aren't they?'

'I believe they are, yes.'

'Well, he wore one of those, so if that makes him a Sikh, he was a Sikh.'

'Do you remember his name?'

'It was Singh.'

'I'm told that all Sikh men are called Singh. Did he have a first name?'

'I dare say he did, but I cannot remember it just now.'

'Was it Dayabir?'

'I told you I don't remember.'

'Could you find out for us?'

'All right. You two wait here and I'll go and check.'

Carlisle strode off and disappeared through a door in the ship's superstructure. Within minutes he came back out onto the deck and rejoined them.

'I looked it up. His name was Amrit – Amrit Singh.'

Jago concealed his disappointment that the man's name was not what he had hoped it would be.

'Do you know whether he had a knife like the one I showed you yesterday?' he continued.

'I noticed him wearing a knife once or twice,' Carlisle replied, 'but it was in a sheath, you know, so I couldn't see the blade. It was the same curved shape, though, I can tell you that.'

'And you haven't seen him or the knife since he went missing from your ship?'

'That's correct. Easy come, easy go – that's the way it is with some of those fellows. And that reminds me – did that Jamal try to sell you some silk?'

'No. Why do you ask?'

'Oh, nothing – it's just that a lot of these lascars do. They try to flog a silk shawl to anyone who'll listen to their patter. It's usually cheap stuff, and it's just so they can make a bit of extra money and save it up, then when they give up the seafaring and go back home to India they might have enough to start a wee shop or something. In some cases it's just a little private enterprise to help them provide for their future – I doubt whether they can do that on what we pay them – but sometimes it's more organised, and there can be crooks involved, so it's as well to watch out.'

'Well, thanks for the advice, Mr Carlisle.'

'You're welcome. Will that be all, then? I'm sorry I cannot be more helpful to you.'

'That's all right. There's something else you might be able to help us with, though, which should be simpler. We've been talking to a stevedore called Charlie Bell, who's a volunteer in the Home Guard. He was on duty in the early hours of yesterday morning, patrolling the dock, and he says he stopped off to have a drink with you. I just wondered whether you could confirm that for us. Is it correct?'

Carlisle hesitated. Unlike when he was talking about the missing Indian crewman, he seemed uncomfortable, as if unsure what to say.

'A simple yes or no will do, Mr Carlisle,' said Jago.

'I know, I know. It's just that . . . Well, I don't want to get the man into trouble, you see. Are these Home Guard fellows allowed to drink on duty?'

'I've no idea, Mr Carlisle. I don't know what their regulations are, but I'm not here to get him into trouble. I just need to know whether you can corroborate what he said.'

Carlisle's expression relaxed.

'I see. In that case, yes, he did. He mentioned that he was suffering from a cold, so as one Scot to another I offered him a wee dram to help fight it off. A hot toddy can work wonders when you've got a cold, you know, even though these days you can't get a lemon for love nor money.'

'Indeed. Can you tell me what time this was?'

'What time? No, I'm afraid I can't. It wasn't something we'd arranged, you see. I just happened to bump into him and another Home Guard, and offered the drink on the spur of the moment. I didn't look at my watch to check what time it was. I was up all night keeping an eye on the ship, so it was a bit of light relief to have someone to chat to, especially someone from my own part of the world, that's all.'

'Can you remember how long he was with you?'

'Well, we got chatting about this and that, so it may've been half an hour or so, but I can't be sure. I'm very sorry, but it was just a drink, and at times like these it's maybe not such a bad thing to drown our sorrows.'

'You mean the war?'

'I mean everything, Inspector. The whole world's a bit depressing, isn't it? To be honest with you, I think I've been in this game too long. I was in the last war, as I told you – in the mercantile marine, same as now. It was a bigger ship than this, so at least they stuck a gun on her for protection – not that that was much help against a U-boat, any more than it is now. But the *Magnolia* isn't

118

armed at all – we're like sitting ducks, just waiting for the next passing German ship or plane to take a pop at us. And if we're sunk and lucky enough to survive, the owners stop our pay. What kind of life is that? Still, I don't suppose a policeman's life is a bed of roses, is it? We all just have to make the best of it we can.'

Jago felt disinclined to enter into a discussion of a police officer's woes, so he limited himself to what he hoped was a sympathetic shrug of the shoulders.

'Well, don't let me keep you,' said Carlisle.

'Thank you,' said Jago. 'That's all I wanted to ask, but if you happen to remember those times more accurately, please let me know.'

'I'll be sure to,' Carlisle replied. 'But don't hold your breath.'

CHAPTER THIRTEEN

'It must be funny living on a ship like that,' said Cradock as they made their way along the quay, away from the SS *Magnolia*. 'I mean, being thrown around on the sea in a little old tub all day and all night. I don't think I'd fancy it.'

'You don't see yourself as a future Nelson, then?'

'Certainly not, sir. Not even a future Carlisle. I can't think of anything worse – out in all the bad weather, probably being seasick half the time, and now they've got the German navy and air force out there doing everything they can to sink them too. It must be terrible.'

'I think you're right – it's certainly not my idea of fun. I prefer having my feet on something a bit more solid.'

'Me too – give me concrete or cobblestones any day.' Cradock stamped his booted foot on the quay as if to test his assertion. 'So anyway, now we're back on dry land, what's next, sir? Anything else we can do while we're here?'

'That's just what I've been wondering. I think

perhaps while we're in the area we should drop in on Mrs Lambert to see how she's doing. She might've remembered something after a night's sleep.'

'If she slept, that is.'

'Indeed. The chances must be slim where she lives.'

The first thing Jago noticed, to his relief, when they arrived in Brenda Lambert's street in Silvertown was that her house was still standing, although there were signs of fresh bomb damage round the corner. He could also see that she was outside the house with a bucket of water, scrubbing the front doorstep. She rose awkwardly to her feet as they approached, and stood with her scrubbing brush in one hand and her other hand pressed into the small of her back. She was wearing an old, discoloured cotton overall, with a similarly worn-looking cotton scarf tied round her head.

'Morning, Inspector,' she said. 'You'll have to excuse me – my knees aren't what they used to be.'

'Good morning, Mrs Lambert. I'm sorry to disturb you.'

'Oh, don't you worry. You must think I'm daft, scrubbing my step when there's all this dust and soot around everywhere from the bombs, but I had to do something, otherwise I'd just be sat in the house thinking.'

'I understand. I just thought I'd drop by and see how you are.'

'That's very kind of you. I'm not too bad, all things considered. My son's home on leave, so he's looking after me.'

'I'm glad to hear it. You didn't mention that you

had a son when we spoke yesterday.'

'No. Silly of me, I suppose, but I didn't think.'

'Do you and your husband have any other children, or is he your only one?'

'Only him – and Tom's my son, not Ray's. Actually, that doesn't sound very good, does it? What I mean is, he's my son from before I married Ray, so Ray was his stepfather. Tom's got embarkation leave.'

'I see. So he's in the forces?'

'That's right. He's a corporal in the Royal Marines. He's going back at the weekend.'

'Could you tell me his full name, please?'

'Yes, it's Harold Thomas Lightfoot, but everyone calls him Tom. He's not in any trouble, is he?'

'No, but I'd like to have a word with him. When do you think I might be able to catch him?'

'Not today, probably. He's gone out for the day and didn't say where. Your best bet's to come back tomorrow morning, but not too early – he said he'll be out late tonight and having a lie-in.'

'Very good, we'll do that. Thank you.'

'You're welcome. So, is that all? Only I've got a little cleaning job a couple of days a week, and they don't like me to be late – or early, for that matter. They're a bit particular.'

'There are just a few more things I'd like to ask you about before you go, if that's all right.'

'Of course. What do you want to know?'

'First of all, I want to check that I understood you correctly. Mr Lambert was your second husband, yes?'

'That's right.'

'And how long have you been married?'

'Nine years – we got spliced in 1931. Nothing fancy, you know – just the basics. We were both thirty-seven by then, so old enough to know what we were doing and wise enough not to spend a load of money on a wedding.'

'May I ask what became of your first husband?'

'Ah, I suppose you're wondering whether he died or we got divorced, but we weren't properly married actually, with a certificate and everything. I was what they call his common-law wife. My fault really, I suppose, I shouldn't have stood for it, but I was young and I loved him, and he said it'd cost too much to have a wedding, and what difference did a bit of paper make if we loved each other? Still, we live and learn, don't we? I didn't want to do the same with Ray. We got married properly, all fair and square. Mind you, now I've got the certificate but I haven't got Ray. And I won't get a pension either.'

'I'm sorry to hear that.'

'Yes, well, that's what comes of being a casual. Ray was always a casual, same as his mate Len. There were times when I thought he might be able to move onto the PLA staff, become a proper employee with a pension and everything, but to be honest, I don't think he ever wanted to. The thing was, he loved the freedom of it – being casual, I mean. There's no guarantee of a job, but on the other hand you're free to work or not work as the fancy takes you. Ray seemed to make more than enough without working every day, so it gave him time to do other things.'

'What kind of things?'

'I don't know. He never told me much about what he got up to, and I learnt not to ask – hanging about with his mates mostly, I expect.'

'And this Len that you mentioned, was he a close friend?'

'Certainly. Ray's oldest pal, I'd say. They go back years.'

'Is he a tally clerk, the same as your husband?'

'No, Len's a docker – I think he moves the cargo round when it comes off the ships, puts it in the sheds, that sort of thing. The tally clerks reckon they're a cut above the ordinary dockers – I think that's why they wear proper hats instead of flat caps – but they're all casuals, fighting for work. The only difference is the tally clerks get paid more. Mind you, I think Ray earned it – he said he had to stand in the same place all day, whatever the weather, counting everything going on or off the ship and marking it down on his tally cards with a pencil. Making sure it all tallied, see? And he had to keep his eyes peeled, because if his record didn't tally with what it was supposed to be there'd be hell to pay – and all the time there'd be the dockers trying to claim extra payment or distracting his attention so they could cheat with the loading and nick some of the cargo, and the cargo owners trying to claim for damage, with the poor tally clerks caught in the middle.'

'So the dockers like Len and the tally clerks like your husband aren't on the same side.'

'What do you mean?'

'You seemed to be saying the dockers might be

working a swindle, and men like your husband would be there to prevent them doing that.'

'Well, I suppose you could say that, but I don't really know enough about it.'

'Can you tell me Len's surname?'

'It's Potter – Len Potter.'

'And which dock does he work in?'

'The Royal Albert, same as Ray.'

'Could you tell me where he lives, please?'

'Yes, it's in North Woolwich – Barge House Road, the one with the causeway at the end.'

'Thank you. Which number?'

'I'm not sure what number it is, but it's the second house on the left, with a blue door – you can't miss it.' She paused before hastily adding what sounded like an explanation. 'I know his wife, you see – we're friends.'

'Quite. I'm sure it's a help to have friends around you at a time like this.'

'Yes. It still doesn't seem real, Ray going like that. I don't know what I'm going to do – with what I earn I can pay the rent or eat, but I can't do both. I'll have to find some more work, but I don't know where. If you'd asked me a few months ago I'd have said I'll try to get in at Keiller's jam factory down at Tay Wharf – I knew a girl who worked there – but I've heard it got blown up in that first big air raid in September, so I don't know if it's still working. I'll have to try and find something in one of the other factories down by the river – if they're still standing. But still, Tom's very good – he says he'll make sure I don't go short.'

'That reminds me, Mrs Lambert. When I asked you earlier what became of Tom's father, I don't think you actually told me.'

'Oh, I'm sorry. I don't seem to be concentrating too well at the moment.' She gave a light frown as if to focus her thoughts before continuing. 'We were together from 1915, but then he ended up in France for nearly two years, in the trenches. I think that's what did for me, you know – everyone talks about what it was like to get the telegram, but for me it wasn't that, it was getting up every day and thinking is he already dead? He might be lying there, shot in the head or blown up, and I wouldn't know until maybe a week later when the telegram came, telling me he'd been killed in action or died of wounds.'

She paused, the memory seeming to affect her.

'Did he make it through?' Jago asked gently.

She nodded, wiping her eyes.

'He came home in August 1918, but by then my nerves were shot to pieces. He was in a state too. He'd been wounded – he was half-lame, so he couldn't go back to work in the docks. He got a little job in a shop eventually, but he hated it. The real wound, though, that was in his mind. He wasn't the man I'd known before the war, not the man I'd loved. I couldn't cope, nor could he. He ended up in the chronic block at the West Ham Mental Hospital in Goodmayes, and we sort of drifted apart. In the end I wrote to him and said I couldn't go on. I got a letter back saying he understood. Then I married Ray.'

'I'm sorry, Mrs Lambert. There's just one more thing I'd like to ask before I go, if you don't mind. It's a delicate matter, but to put it bluntly, were you and Mr Lambert happily married?'

She reflected on his question for a while before answering.

'Happy enough, I suppose. Happy enough.'

CHAPTER FOURTEEN

Jago drove as quickly as the law and the state of the roads allowed in order not to be late for his lunch appointment. The breeze was still chilly, but the clouds had parted to reveal patches of blue sky, and whether it was that or the prospect of seeing Dorothy he could not tell, but something caused his spirits to lift the closer they got to West Ham police station. Following his conversation with DDI Soper the previous day, he had told her on the telephone that their lunch would have to be quick because he was investigating the murder of a Home Guard, but the thought of even a brief meeting with her – even one with young Cradock and Dorothy's unnamed friend present – was enough to take his mind off the misery of violent death for a while.

As they arrived, a saloon car parked on West Ham Lane almost directly outside the police station caught his eye. It was clearly American, looked about twice as big as Jago's Riley, and had a conspicuously long bonnet, no doubt concealing an engine four times as big as the Lynx's to haul its weight. Curiously, however, it was painted in drab military camouflage and looked like an army staff car.

They went into the station and were met by Sergeant Frank Tompkins, who gave Jago a conspiratorial nod and in a somewhat exaggerated manner swivelled his eyes towards two figures seated across the lobby.

'Your friends are here, sir. I told them you'd be along any minute.'

Jago looked round and saw Dorothy rising to greet him, and beside her a man he did not recognise. As the stranger got up, Jago could see that he was slim, with a muscular frame, and was a few inches taller than himself.

'Hello, John,' said Dorothy. 'May I introduce you? This is Philip Eliot – he's a colleague of mine.'

Eliot extended a hand and clasped Jago's in a hearty and painful shake, then repeated the action with Cradock.

'When Philip heard that I was visiting a police station in West Ham and knew a detective inspector, he begged me to let him come along too,' Dorothy continued. 'He's a journalist, you see, like me, and he can't resist an opportunity to meet interesting people doing interesting work in unusual places.'

'Mr Eliot,' said Jago by way of acknowledgement. 'No relation to T. S. Eliot, I suppose?'

'We're cousins, actually,' Eliot smiled. 'But distant ones.'

I might've known, thought Jago. *And an American*

accent: he's probably pals with the Roosevelts too.

'Ah, yes,' he replied. 'He was originally American, wasn't he?'

'That's right. He's a British subject now, but he was born in St Louis, Missouri.'

'You sound American yourself.'

'Yes. I'm with the *New York Times* and based here in London at the Savoy, covering the war, the same as Dorothy.'

'So I imagine that must be your car parked outside – I couldn't miss it as I was coming in. It's an impressive-looking beast. What is it?'

'It's called a Buick Special – 1938 model – but it's nothing special, really, just a regular sedan.'

'But it looks like a military car – why that paintwork?'

'Maybe I could tell you about that over lunch, Inspector. I think Dorothy's quite eager to eat.'

Jago felt an unexpected twinge of annoyance at being implicitly criticised for neglecting Dorothy, but his face betrayed no sign of it.

'Come along, Dorothy,' he said, turning to her with a smile. 'We'd better go and see what Rita has to offer. Have you told your friend Mr Eliot that we're eating at her place?'

'Oh, yes,' she replied. 'He was very pleased when I told him we'd be having lunch at Rita's cafe. You know – interesting people, unusual places.'

She added a conspiratorial wink so fleeting that he wasn't entirely sure he'd seen it.

'I hope it lives up to his expectations,' he said. 'Now, shall we all go and get something to eat?'

They walked together down West Ham Lane to the cafe, where Rita welcomed them and showed them to a table. The large front window was still patched with plyboard after being shattered by a bomb blast, but the table was positioned by one of the small panels of glass that she'd managed to get fitted into the board to admit a minimal ration of daylight.

'Best seats in the house,' she said. 'At least you can just about see what you're eating here. Mind you, some of my customers say they prefer not to.' She followed this with a throaty laugh which degenerated into a cough. 'Excuse me,' she said, recovering her composure. 'Only joking, of course.'

'Of course, Rita,' said Jago. 'No one with a sense of taste would ever think that of your food. Now, allow me to introduce you. This is Mr Eliot, who's a friend of Miss Appleton. He's American.'

Rita eyed her new guest up and down as though the mere fact of being American placed him in the same category as Clark Gable or Gary Cooper.

'Oo,' she said. 'Pleased to meet you, I'm sure.'

Jago feared she might curtsey but was relieved to see her take the man's hand and give it a limp shake. He was further relieved to see that Eliot's grip seemed not to be as crippling as the one he'd received himself a few minutes earlier at the station. He and his guests took their seats as Rita produced her notepad and pencil to take their orders.

'I think America's lovely,' said Rita, still gazing at Eliot. 'I've seen it in the films.'

'It's not all lovely, Rita,' said Dorothy. 'Not everything's the way it seems in the movies. We have our share of undesirable places and people, just like anywhere else.'

'Well, I'm sure Mr Eliot's a very nice gentleman. You're very welcome, sir. Now, what would you all like to eat? We're doing a special today – sausage and mash.'

'That sounds delicious,' said Jago, looking round the table with an expression that invited agreement. 'Sausage and mash all round?'

There was a general nodding of consent.

'Mr Eliot's car is the sort you might've seen in the films, Rita,' said Jago. 'It's a proper American car, huge, like you see racing through the streets of Chicago in those gangster films, with Jimmy Cagney standing on the running board firing a sub-machine gun.'

Rita looked a little concerned, Jago thought, perhaps at the idea of Chicago-style violence coming to the streets of West Ham.

Eliot gave a loud laugh.

'Well, I'm no gangster, Inspector, I assure you of that. Mind you, I did experience something a week or so ago that was a bit like the old days in Chicago, and right here in London.'

'Really?'

'Yes, I had a brush with some of your colleagues in the Metropolitan Police. I was having a drink at a club in Regent Street – one of those places they call "night resorts". It was after the pubs had closed, and a few of us had gone on there, all feeling very brave because the bombing had only just died down for a bit. Someone had said you could still get a drink there, and we did, but what we didn't know was that it was apparently an illegal party. It got to about midnight, and everybody was having a good time, when suddenly there was a raid – and I don't mean an air raid. This was a police raid.'

Rita's face suggested that this American man's life sounded a bit too racy for her, and she made her exit in the direction of the kitchen.

'Ah, yes,' said Jago. 'We call them bottle parties, because they're unlicensed clubs that only sell liquor by the bottle after all the pubs and restaurants have closed for the night – and at outrageous prices too. And yes, they are illegal. The government decided to crack down on them in July, and the Home Office gave the police powers to close premises where there's evidence of drunkenness or disorderly conduct at night. So my colleagues in the West End have been doing exactly that.'

'The management didn't seem too pleased to see the police turn up in the middle of their party,' Eliot replied.

'I'm not surprised. Running a club like that without a licence can get you into a lot of trouble these days. Mind you, some people say it won't work and most of the bottle parties will carry on just as before.'

'Well, I wouldn't say it was a lot of trouble. Not like it was in the States during Prohibition, anyway – if you were caught in a raid then, you were likely to find a Prohibition agent pulling a gun on you. When your police raided us, all they did was tell us it was illegal, take our names and addresses and send us home.'

'I'm glad to hear that. I think the real problem is that some of these clubs have connections with the more unsavoury aspects of London life, including what the law regards as "entertainment of a demoralising character". That's why the courts come down hard on them.'

'Unless the judge is a customer, I guess.'

'I'm afraid that's always a possibility. Actually, only this morning I was talking to a young woman who's studying law and has already made up her mind she wants to be the first woman judge in England. She said we'll only get real justice when women are in a position to judge men. An interesting thought, isn't it? Do you have female judges in America?'

'We do have them, yes, but not many. In some states, women can't even serve on a state jury, let alone be a judge – even my own highly respectable mother isn't allowed to in Massachusetts, where I come from.'

'It's different here with juries,' said Jago. 'We've had women serving on juries for a few years, but not many married women. The problem is there's still a property qualification, and a married woman's house is usually in her husband's name, so she's not eligible. And believe it or not, man or woman, if you live in a rented house with less than fifteen windows you can't sit on a jury either – so that rules out just about everyone in an area like this.'

Rita returned with four plates of sausage and mash and set them on the table before her customers.

'Thank you, Rita,' said Jago.

'Yes, thank you,' added Dorothy. 'You know, Rita, I'm going to write something for my paper about eating out in Britain now that there's a war on. I'll tell them about sausage and mash and everything else you have on your menu. And maybe I could come back with a photographer and get a picture of you. Would that be OK?'

'Oo, yes. That would be lovely.' Rita beamed at the thought of her image gracing the American press, then headed back to the kitchen.

Eliot, meanwhile, was still poking at his lunch uncertainly.

'Don't worry,' said Jago. 'Go ahead and try it. You might find it's less dangerous than it looks.'

Without waiting for him, Jago tucked into his own meal.

'So,' he continued, 'you've had one exciting brush with the Mectropolitan Police, Mr Eliot. What is it that so interests you that you wanted to come over here today and meet us?'

'Look, please call me Philip. It makes me feel like a suspect when you say "Mr Eliot".'

'Very well. What is it that interests you in West Ham, Philip? It's not exactly on the tourist route at the best of times, and right now it's pretty wrecked.'

Eliot cast a look in Dorothy's direction, as if appealing for help.

'Philip cares about what's happening here, John,'

she said. 'You remember when we first met, I told you I'd visited Silvertown just after that terrible night in September when they had the first big air raid?'

'I do.'

'Well, Philip has been there too – in fact, he came with me on that same visit. So he knows how terrible it is, and he's reported it, like me.'

'That's right,' said Eliot. 'I guess you know that area really well.'

'Reasonably well. I was down there today.'

'On a case?'

'Yes, as it happens.'

'Can you tell me anything about it?'

'I can tell you that a member of the Home Guard has been found dead there, in suspicious circumstances, and that we suspect murder, but that's all.'

'Not just a little bit more?'

'No.'

'Nothing at all?'

'No.'

'OK. You'll have to excuse me. I guess journalists are like police officers – never off duty. It's just that I'm very interested in the Home Guard.'

'Why's that?'

'Because I think they're brave men doing what'll be a deadly dangerous job if the Germans invade. And because I'm one myself.'

Jago looked at him, trying to judge from his expression whether the American was joking. Before he could speak, Eliot continued.

'That's why the car's painted the way it is. You're speaking to Volunteer Eliot of the First American Mechanised Squadron, Home Guard. I'm hoping someday soon it'll be Private Eliot, but the Home Guard's not allowed to use proper army ranks yet. Some units have sergeants and corporals, but it just depends on what the platoon commander decides. The regulations don't even say whether we're supposed to salute our commanders, so some battalions do and some don't. Still, we're hoping that some of those small problems will be fixed soon.'

'Isn't the fact that you're presumably not a British subject a slightly bigger problem?'

'It was – when we started the unit we were, strictly speaking, illegal, but then your king issued an order in council that made it all OK, and now we've been recognised by your government. There's about seventy-five of us – all American citizens living in London, including, I might add, almost all the press correspondents like myself. Our ambassador, Mr Kennedy, doesn't approve, but we don't want to be just spectators, watching you fight for your lives here. If Britain goes down, we all go down with you – this is a fight for democracy, and we'd feel ashamed if we didn't help out in some small way.'

Cradock, who had been silent throughout this conversation, was the first to finish his food.

'So did you paint the car yourself?' he asked.

'That's right. They're our own cars, so they're mostly American, but we've had them camouflaged at our own expense and put them at the disposal of the squadron.'

'I bet some of our Home Guard blokes wouldn't mind having a few cars like that.'

Eliot laughed.

'Sure – some of them have told us that.'

'And you're all trained, like ours?'

'Yes, we train three nights a week in Westminster. Of course, I'm not as fit as I used to be.' He patted his left leg with his hand. 'Got hit by some shrapnel in Madrid, 1937 – I was covering the Spanish Civil War and got in the way of one of Franco's shells. I can't complain, though – at least I got out alive. Like Dorothy here, I've been through a few adventures around the world since we were both youngsters in Boston. Remember how prim those tea dances were, Dorothy?'

Jago scanned Dorothy's face quickly, and it seemed to him that she looked a little embarrassed by this reference to what appeared to be their shared past, but he couldn't be sure. The rest of the meal passed in small talk, and all too soon for Jago's liking it was time for them to go. He felt a vague sense of irritation and frustration that this lunchtime with Dorothy had not been as pleasurable as he'd expected. He paid Rita for the meal and joined his three companions, who were waiting for him by the door. Cradock and Eliot left first, deep in conversation – probably about American cars, Jago guessed. He stepped aside for Dorothy to pass, but instead she held him back until the other two were out of earshot.

'John, I got the impression you didn't like Philip trying to get information out of you about your case in Silvertown.'

'That's right.'

'But he's only doing his job, just like me – and you sometimes tell me about your investigations.'

'Yes, but with him it's different.'

'Why's that?'

'I'll give you two reasons. The first is that in your case I've been asked by the Ministry of Information to assist you in your work, so it's official and above board. They haven't asked me to do that for him. The second is that you don't press me for information, but that's what he was doing. And if you want a third reason, it's that I trust you, but I don't have any reason to trust him.'

'Except that he's a friend and colleague of mine.'

'Yes.'

'I see.'

There was an awkward silence between them. Jago feared that Dorothy might take his antipathy towards Eliot as a criticism of herself, but he didn't know what to say to correct or forestall that impression, or whether saying anything more would only make matters worse. He was still wrestling with this question as Dorothy said goodbye and walked out into the street, where Eliot was waiting to take her away.

CHAPTER FIFTEEN

Danbury's house in Forest Gate had been large, but when Jago and Cradock arrived at Mr Whitton's residence in Clova Road they could see that, if anything, it was slightly bigger. Like Claremont Road, this street ran parallel to the busier Romford Road, on its more expensive northern side, and consisted mainly of comfortable-looking Victorian villas.

The last Jago had seen of Dorothy was Eliot showing her into his car and closing the door behind her, then striding confidently round to the driver's side and getting in. The engine gave an equally self-assured, low-pitched growl and bore them away, back towards central London. Jago's mood was both annoyed and frustrated, but as he knocked on Whitton's door he tried to shake off his feelings and focus his attention on the job in hand.

The man who opened the door was solidly built, with a confident bearing and dressed in a business suit that suggested bespoke tailoring. The lines on his face were those of a man in his fifties, but his neatly groomed dark hair – possibly dyed, Jago thought – gave the impression of a younger man. He introduced himself as Alfred Whitton.

'Good morning, gentlemen,' he said. 'I've been expecting you – come in. I hope this won't take long – I have to get to my office this afternoon and must leave shortly. Time and tide wait for no man, and neither does my job.'

'Thank you, sir,' said Jago, stepping over the threshold, followed by Cradock. 'What kind of work would that be, may I ask?'

'I'm a company director,' Whitton replied. He halted in the middle of the spacious hallway and turned to face them, clearly intending to take them no farther.

'Well, this shouldn't take a moment,' said Jago. 'We understand you've reported a burglary.'

'Yes. It's an outrage.'

'And it happened last night?'

'That's correct. My wife and I were in the Anderson shelter overnight. We didn't hear anything, but when the all-clear went and we came back into the house I could feel a draught. I had a look round and found a window broken. It looks to me as though someone forced open the wooden gate at the side of the house and broke the window, then unclipped the sash and pushed it up. If they closed the gate after them, it would've been very easy for them to climb in and out without being seen or heard.'

'I see. I'll take a look at the window in a moment.

Can you tell us what they took?'

'Yes – my daughter's bicycle. It was inside the gate, under a sort of lean-to to keep the rain off it.'

'Would that be a child's bicycle, sir?'

'No. My daughter's eighteen.'

'So she was in the shelter with you too, overnight, was she?'

'Yes, she was, but she didn't hear anything either.'

'And what kind of bicycle was it?'

'A Rudge-Whitworth ladies' bicycle, black, with a basket on the front. We bought it last year.'

'Do you by any chance happen to know the frame number?'

'No, I'm afraid I don't, but my wife may have a note of it.'

He strode to the bottom of the stairs and shouted up them.

'Marjorie! The inspector wants the frame number for Anne's bike. Do you have it?'

A woman's voice sounded faintly from above.

'Yes, dear. I'll bring it down in a moment.'

Shortly afterwards Mrs Whitton came down the stairs and joined them. She greeted the two detectives with a smile and, since Jago was the older of the two, addressed him.

'Inspector?'

'Yes, Mrs Whitton. Detective Inspector Jago, West Ham CID.'

'I'm terribly sorry, Inspector, but I couldn't quite put

my hand on that number. I know I've got it somewhere, but it wasn't where I thought it should be. I'll have to search around for it.'

Whitton let out a short breath which sounded to Jago like exasperation.

'As soon as we find it,' he said, 'my wife or I will drop it in to you at the police station. I assume that won't prevent you making an immediate start to your enquiries.'

'Thank you, sir,' Jago replied. 'That'll be most helpful. It always makes our job a lot easier if we've got a number to identify the machine. Now, did they take anything else?'

'Oh, yes – he or they clearly had a look round to see what else they could find in the house. As far as we can tell, the other things missing are a carriage clock, a cigarette case, a necklace, a bottle of perfume that I gave my wife for Christmas and my wife's handbag, plus about seven pounds in cash.'

'Was there anything of value in the handbag, Mrs Whitton?'

'No, I don't think so. Just the usual things – lipstick, powder compact, hairbrush and my purse, but that probably only had a pound or so in it.'

'Can you describe the missing items?'

'Yes,' said Marjorie. 'The perfume was Yardley's Lavender Water, unopened.' She flashed a smile at her husband which Jago thought looked a little forced. 'I was going to try it, dear, but what with one thing and another I, er, just hadn't quite got round to it.'

'And the other items?'

'Oh, yes. The carriage clock was the usual thing – small, brass, roman numerals – but quite attractive. The necklace was four rows of stones, but only diamanté, not real. The cigarette case was chrome, although a thief might think it was silver, with a faint stripe pattern. The handbag was brown leather, and the compact was square, with a picture of a ship on the front. I don't suppose you need to know what shade the lipstick was.'

'No, that won't be necessary,' said Jago. 'Thank you.'

'If you ask me,' Whitton interjected, 'the blighters took what they could fit into the basket on that bicycle and made off with it in the dark.'

'Very possibly, sir. Most of the items you've mentioned are things they could probably sell without too much trouble.'

'Yes, and I want them back. Especially my daughter's bicycle – she uses it a lot, and we bought it for her eighteenth birthday, so apart from anything else it has sentimental value.'

'Of course, sir. We'll do everything we can to retrieve your property, although I have to say the chances are slim – these kind of people tend to get rid of their stolen goods as quickly as they can, and not necessarily locally. This is the second report we've had of a burglary during the blackout in this vicinity, so it may be what you might call professionals at work. Unfortunately the blackout makes their work easier and ours harder, as I was saying to the other gentleman.'

'The other gentleman?'

'The other gentleman who was burgled. It was a week or so ago, in Claremont Road. Name of Danbury – do you know him?'

'Yes, I do, but only slightly, through the Rotary Club. My daughter plays tennis with his daughter – Wanstead Tennis Club, you know.'

Not being a tennis player, Jago did not, but he'd heard of the club and nodded his head.

'That's one of the things she uses her bicycle for,' Whitton continued. 'Getting to and from the club, you see, although now the weather's getting colder it's more for social events than for matches, I believe. There's not a lot for young people to do these days, and I don't want her volunteering for any of those ghastly things like the Land Army, digging up potatoes all day.'

'Quite. Now, the house was locked, I assume.'

'Of course. We always leave the house locked when we're in the Anderson shelter, precisely because we don't want any Tom, Dick or Harry to wander in and steal things. I can't believe anyone would have the gall to deliberately take advantage of an air raid to break in. Respect for private property is the bedrock of English society. People like that are nothing but scum.'

'Yes, sir. Some of these burglars are very callous.'

'Callous? They're vermin. In the old days we used to cut people's hands off for stealing. I sometimes think that wouldn't be such a bad idea today.'

'That was a long time ago, sir. Now, do you mind if I just take a look at the window you think they broke to gain access?'

Whitton showed them the window in question and Jago and Cradock duly examined it. Only one pane was smashed, and the fragments of glass were on the inside of the room, so Whitton's inference seemed reasonable.

'All right if we close it now you've seen it?' said Whitton. 'I'd like to get a man in to patch it up.'

'Yes, that'll be fine, sir. I think that's all we need to know, so we'll leave you to get away to your office.'

'And if I understood you correctly, I shouldn't be too hopeful of you catching whoever did it.'

'I wouldn't say that, sir. We'll make every effort to find the culprit. We take a dim view of people who break into other people's houses during air raids.'

'Well, I just hope for his sake you find him before I do.'

'We also take a dim view of people who take the law into their own hands, Mr Whitton. I advise you not to consider doing that. We'll do everything we possibly can.'

Whitton thrust his face a little closer to Jago's.

'I judge a man by his results, Inspector, not by his good intentions. I pay my rates and I expect results.'

CHAPTER SIXTEEN

'Crusty sort of bloke, wasn't he, guv'nor, that Mr Whitton?' said Cradock as he and Jago returned to the car. 'Don't think I'd enjoy working for him.'

'Do I take it that means you don't find me too crusty?' Jago replied.

'Course not, sir – always a pleasure working for you.'

Jago was touched by this unexpected commendation from his subordinate. He hoped DDI Soper never asked him the same question, however: he might struggle to respond with the same enthusiasm. He rewarded Cradock with a hint of a smile.

'Thank you, Peter, I'm glad to hear that. But that doesn't mean I don't expect results too, you know.'

'Oh, yes, sir, definitely. I just didn't like the way he made his point, that's all.'

'Neither did I. I expect he's never read *How to Win Friends and Influence People*.'

'What's that?'

'It's a book written a few years ago by an American gentleman called Dale Carnegie.'

'Is he anything to do with the Carnegie Library in Prince Regent Lane?'

'No, the library's named after an American philanthropist who gave the money to build it back at the start of the century. He made hundreds of millions of dollars out of steel and gave most of it away – even to benefit people here in West Ham. He was called Andrew Carnegie. The one who wrote the book's a very rich man too, I gather, but he's made his money out of teaching people how to make other people like them so that they can succeed in business.'

'You haven't read the book, have you, sir?'

Jago looked askance at him, but it was difficult to tell whether Cradock was speaking ironically, or even whether he was capable of doing so.

'Of course not,' he said as he unlocked the car door. 'I don't have time for that kind of thing. But I'm just wondering whether it might be a good idea to slip a copy into Mr Whitton's Christmas stocking.'

They got into the car, and Jago started the engine.

'Now,' he said, 'speaking of friends, I think we need to meet this Len Potter that Mrs Lambert told us about – her husband's friend. I'd like to know what he can tell us about Ray Lambert.'

They set off, driving through East Ham and Beckton to the eastern end of the Royal Docks and then down the

Woolwich Manor Way. By Jago's reckoning this would be the fastest route to Potter's house, as long as the barges weren't being shifted earlier than usual – sometimes up to a hundred of them would be moved through the King George V Dock entrance lock to the river to catch the tide, in which case the bascule bridge over the lock would be raised and the road traffic held up. They made good time, however; when they got there the bridge was down and the traffic was light. Once across the bridge, they were into the narrow stretch of land between the King George V Dock and the Thames.

'Not far now,' he said, pointing to the sprawling buildings on their left. 'There's Harland & Wolff's North Woolwich works.'

'Is that shipbuilding? They built the Titanic, didn't they?' said Cradock.

'Yes, but that was in Belfast. Here it's mainly barges, I think, but it's the biggest yard in London.'

'And why's it called North Woolwich? Woolwich is on the other side of the river, in Kent.'

'I'm not sure – I think it goes way back into history, but as far as I know there's always been two bits on this side of the river that are part of Kent, not Essex. It's all jumbled up round here – one end of the Albert Dock's in West Ham and the other end's in East Ham, and the borough boundary runs through the George too. Where we were this morning, at Brenda Lambert's house in Silvertown, that's in West Ham, but when you come over this way it turns into North Woolwich. Then it's East

Ham for a bit, and then it's North Woolwich again.'

'I see – I think. So now we're definitely in North Woolwich, right?'

'Yes, from here round to the far end of Beckton gasworks.'

Cradock's face crumpled with concentration as he digested this brief geography lesson. Meanwhile, Jago turned left into Barge House Road, which led down to the Thames foreshore. Both sides of the street were lined by long terraces of small, red-brick houses built at the turn of the century, whose front doors opened directly onto the pavement. Jago guessed that they were probably only two-up, two-down homes, but there was something charming about their style, which was different to that of most other housing in the area. He parked the car outside the second house on the left-hand side and they got out.

It was Len Potter who opened the door. He had a long, lean face and thinning dark hair with greying patches, and he stood with a slight stoop. He looked suspiciously at Jago and Cradock, but once they had identified themselves he let them in.

'We're here in connection with the death of Mr Ray Lambert,' said Jago.

'Yes,' said Potter, 'I've been expecting you – Brenda told me about it. Shocking news, it was. I can't believe it's happened to such a nice bloke.'

'I'd like to learn a bit more about Mr Lambert, so I'm glad we've found you at home, Mr Potter.'

'Yes, well, I wish I wasn't. I had some work this

morning, but when I went back just before one o'clock for the afternoon call I couldn't get anything, so I came home.'

'The call?'

'That's how we get our work – I'm a docker, see, and the work's casual. We all turn up on the pavement first thing in the morning inside No. 9 Gate at the Royal Albert – that's the Connaught Road gate – then at a quarter to eight the foreman comes out and stands in the middle of the road and picks the ones he wants to work for a day or half a day. We call it the call-on. Everyone's trying to stand near the front so they can catch the foreman's eye, pushing and shoving and shouting out. We all want to work in the docks, because you can earn twelve bob for a full day – a few bob more if you get piecework rates. But if you don't get picked, you don't work, simple as that. Trouble is nowadays there's never enough work to go round all the men who want it, so you have to fight for it. It's getting like it used to be in the old days, ten years ago, when you'd see hundreds of men scrapping over a dozen jobs. People were so poor, little kids would try and steal a bit of food from the carts bringing it out of the docks. It's a right mess.'

'Is it the same system for the tally clerks too?'

'For the casuals it is, I think, except they have their call-on outside Barclays Bank. Don't ask me why, though. And sometimes they get taken on for a week, which we don't.'

'I see. Now, I understand you and Mr Lambert were friends.'

'Yes, ever since we were kids. My dad was a docker before me, so when I was a nipper and times were hard my mum had to work too, to try and make ends meet. Ray's family lived just round the corner, so his mum used to look after me. Ray and I used to play together, then we went to school together.' He chuckled to himself. 'He was a rough lad in those days . . . yes, very rough sometimes.'

'You mean he was violent?'

'Yes, but only in a kid's kind of way. He was a bit older than me and used to bully me – for instance, if I had sweets he had most of them, and he'd kick me in the shins and punch me, then just laugh. I never told anyone, of course. But when we grew up we became mates.'

'You also ended up in different jobs, didn't you? You a docker and Ray a tally clerk.'

'That's right. He'd be ticking off how many sacks of this, bales of that, crates or whatever of the other, and I'd be shifting the cargo into the transit sheds and out again onto the lorries.'

'And the tally clerk's count is the only record the owners of the cargo have? They accept whatever he says?'

'Yes. What are you getting at?'

'Oh, nothing. I'm just making sure I understand what Mr Lambert's job was.'

'Well, that's what it was, and he was very good at it. Got it all written down neat and tidy, and no mistakes.'

'So, Mr Potter, how long have you been a docker?'

'Pretty much all my life, I suppose – I started working in the docks just before the last war. My dad was in the

West India Docks and he got me in there. That's where the navy had its stores depot, and that's where I worked, so I came under the Admiralty. It turned out once the war got going that meant I was a starred man – I was in a reserved occupation, so I didn't have to go into the forces. But looking at you, you're probably old enough to remember all that, aren't you?'

Jago nodded slowly.

'Anyway,' Potter continued, 'this time round I think they've made all kinds of dock workers reserved occupations, with no age limit.'

'And you now work in the Royal Albert Dock?' said Jago. 'The same as Mr Lambert did?'

'Yes, that's right.'

'Are you in the Home Guard too?'

'No, not me – after a day's work in the docks I haven't got the energy.'

'I see. Now, it's been suggested to me that a certain amount of pilfering can occur in the docks, and that someone in Mr Lambert's position as a tally clerk and a man in yours might find themselves on opposite sides of the fence, as it were. Is that true?'

'No,' Potter replied, 'there was never any trouble between me and Ray. Always mates, that was us.'

'Quite. So forgive me for being personal, but as a close friend of Mr Lambert, how would you describe his marriage?'

Potter looked surprised.

'Well, that's not an easy question to answer, is it? Not

the sort of thing men talk about. I don't think he had any complaints – she was the kind of woman he wanted for his wife. I know she'd had a hard time before she met Ray. He told me once her first old man got badly wounded at Amiens in 1918 after two years in the trenches and went a bit funny in the head, but of course I never knew him, and I only got to know Brenda after she married Ray.'

'Did Mr Lambert serve in the war?'

'Yes, he did. Ray's mistake was leaving the docks – he got another job that paid a bit more, but it meant he wasn't starred any more, so he could be conscripted. It still didn't turn out too bad, though – the war was nearly over by the time he got called up, and his battalion was shipped out to India, so he missed the worst of it, lucky so-and-so. That's how he knew that bloke in charge of his Home Guard platoon – the major. Served with him out there, I believe.'

'I see. I didn't know that. So they met up again in the Home Guard?'

'I think that's it, yes. You'd have to ask that major, whatever his name is. I'm not sure Brenda knows a lot about what Ray got up to before she became his missus – but that's probably just as well in any marriage, isn't it? If you want to know more about their married life, though, I don't think I'm your man – you'd do better talking to my wife. She and Brenda probably talked about it – you know what women are.'

'When might we catch her?'

'What, Doris? She'll be here in the morning – she

might be able to give you the inside story. As far as I'm concerned, what goes on behind closed doors is none of my business, and in any case, people round here are generally a bit cagey about things like that. Ray was my mate, so I'm not going to start telling tales about him now he's not here to defend himself, and as for Brenda, all I can say is I reckon she's had a very hard life and she's had to fight for herself. She can marry a man without necessarily being all soft about him. Besides, who can tell what a woman sees in a man – or what a man sees in a woman? It's a mystery, isn't it? Leastways, it is to me.'

CHAPTER SEVENTEEN

It was late afternoon when they stepped out of Len Potter's house back onto the street, and Jago was troubled. It was something Potter had said. Brenda Lambert had spoken of her first husband suffering a wound to his mind in the Great War, but Potter had dismissed him as being 'funny in the head'. Jago was only too painfully aware of what that conflict had done to men. Every day he passed them on the street: this one on crutches, the next with an eye patch, another marked by the empty sleeve pinned to his jacket. And these were the men with respectable, manageable wounds – wounds that the public could cope with and, when necessary, ignore. But for every such man in open view there were the others, hideously broken by bullet, bomb or artillery shell, hidden away in the back wards of hospitals for the rest of their lives. And it was no different for those with wounded minds: some who struggled through the day and kept their weeping for the solitude of the night, others who were forcibly kept out of sight for ever.

There but for the grace of God go I, he thought: that's what people said. It wasn't an expression he used himself, but he knew he bore the scars of the shrapnel that had pierced his leg at Cambrai in 1917, and that that single shard of metal could just as easily have cost him his leg, his face or his life. And what of the wounds in his own mind? It was all just a matter of degree.

To belittle a man's mental anguish as Potter had done was callous: it was the response of the hard-hearted. And if Potter was quoting Ray Lambert's words, where had Lambert got them from? His wife Brenda? Where did the absence of compassion begin and end? Jago felt the need to find some open space to clear his mind.

He glanced down Barge House Road to its southern end, where the Thames was flowing by as ever, indifferent to the woes of those who lived on its shores.

'Let's go down to the river, Peter,' he said. 'It's a shame to be this close and not see it.'

They walked slowly down towards the end of the road. It seemed to Jago it was years since he'd last been here and seen the old causeway where the watermen of the previous century used to ferry people across to the other side of the river. The opening of the free Woolwich ferry just a few hundred yards upriver had put paid to their trade, but the remains of the causeway were still a reminder of a quieter, slower age. Those watermen and their passengers could never have imagined the waves of mechanised destruction that had broken on this place in the last two months.

'There's a pub down here,' he said to Cradock. 'Just by the entrance to Sankey's Wharf. I had a drink there once with an old retired sergeant who'd been a copper at the siege of Sidney Street in 1911, armed with a shotgun, when the police had to call the troops in. Winston Churchill was the Home Secretary then, so he came down to take charge. This old copper said the people of Stepney gave him quite an earful, and he thought he might have to use the shotgun to keep them at bay. The pub's called the Old Barge House. Been here for donkey's years – because of the old ferry, I suppose.'

He stopped: the Old Barge House had come into view.

'Well, just look at that,' he said.

The pub was still there, but now it was a ruin. The windows and doors had been blown out and the roof had gone, leaving a gaping, burnt-out shell, with only the chimneys still sprouting incongruously above the wreckage. Another casualty of the air raids, but to Jago another link to a more tranquil past now lost.

They continued down to where the causeway ran out across the muddy foreshore to the river. On the far side of the water a russet-sailed Thames sailing barge was gliding past – still, to Jago, the most beautiful and majestic vessel to be seen on the river. To their right lay the Royal Victoria Gardens, a rare oasis of greenery in this wilderness of factories and chimneys, and beyond them the London and North Eastern Railway's North Woolwich steam boat pier, where the Thames pleasure steamers had once called on their way down to Southend and Margate, until the outbreak of war put a stop to all such pleasure.

In front of them, the river churned by in all its customary filth. Jago had watched it as a child, when the water was black and choked with rubbish. People used to say it took eighty days for untreated sewage to make its way down the Thames from London Bridge to the sea, making the river little more than a giant open sewer itself, where the eels were the only creatures tough enough to survive. He wondered whether things were any better today.

'It's funny, isn't it?' said Cradock. 'When you're standing here, and it's all quiet, just the river rolling by, you wouldn't think we were at war, would you? It's hard to imagine German troops landing here and fighting for the docks.'

'Yes,' Jago replied. 'And if they do, it'll be retired old soldiers like Danbury and Lambert and the rest of the Home Guard going into action to defend us, heaven help them. They're brave men.'

Cradock stifled a laugh.

'Those old geezers? If the Germans do land and start running into the docks, our blokes won't even be able to catch up with them. I don't mean to be unkind, but what about that Lambert? I mean, he was there to defend the docks against their paratroopers and he had a rifle, but he couldn't even defend himself.'

'Don't be too harsh, Peter. We don't know the

circumstances – we've found a rifle and we assume it's his, but we don't know whether he put it down and left himself vulnerable or whether the killer overpowered him and took it. Lambert was stabbed in the back, so he could've still been carrying the rifle when he died and had no chance to use it. He was patrolling, and when you're on sentry duty or patrolling a site perimeter you're very vulnerable, especially in the dark. It's no fun, I can tell you. Your enemy knows how to creep up on you and kill you, and you don't know where he might come from. That's why they patrol in pairs.'

'Sorry, sir, I didn't mean to be rude. So do you think whoever did it saw Bell go onto the ship and reckoned that was his chance, while Lambert was alone?'

'You mean a spontaneous attack, unplanned?'

'Well, it could've been. You couldn't make a plan that Bell would get invited on board for a toddy at that moment, could you?'

'No, I suppose not.'

The two men were silent for a while, then Jago spoke. 'It wasn't always so quiet and peaceful here, you know. Have you ever heard about the *Princess Alice*?'

'No, sir.'

'Just over there it happened, about sixty years ago.'

Jago gestured to his left, where the riverfront curled round and out of sight.

'It was just round there, past Harland & Wolff's and the gasworks – that stretch of water's called Gallions Reach. The *Princess Alice* was a pleasure boat, a paddle steamer, that collided with a collier and sank – 1878 it was. Nine hundred people on board, and more than seven hundred of them died. It wasn't long after the Northern Outfall Sewer was built, and the boat went down just by the place where all the sewage gets discharged into the Thames.'

'Blimey,' said Cradock. 'And I don't suppose many people could swim in those days.'

'No, I don't suppose they could,' said Jago quietly. He stared out at the river, and his eyes tracked back to the swirling eddies before them, picturing the horror of men, women and children struggling to survive, the nightmare of impending death, the impossibility of escape, the senseless waste of life. Drowning.

He thought he glimpsed a face again, the face of a drowning man, just as he had in the dark waters of the Royal Albert Dock. But no: it was different. This time it was a face he recognised, the face of a real man he'd seen in flesh and in blood. He wanted to turn away, but its hypnotic shimmering just beneath the surface held him. In a blink he was back on the Western Front, his ears deafened by shell blasts, his body soaked in foul water and caked with mud, his mind no longer even sure which way was forward. He heard the rattle of machine-gun fire and hurled himself into a shell hole. He scrambled round and saw, not ten feet away, a German soldier staring wide-eyed at him, not dead but terrifyingly alive, bayonet poised.

A tugboat's horn sounded. Jago took half a step back

from the river and clenched his eyes shut, straining to expel the picture from his mind, not opening them again until it had faded.

'You all right, guv'nor?' said Cradock.

The unvarnished concern in Cradock's voice touched him. He heard in it a gentle innocence and simplicity, the voice of a young man uncorrupted by the devil's choice of kill or be killed, not yet burdened by guilt or regret. He couldn't pray, but his desire that somehow life might spare Peter what had crossed his own path was intense.

'I'm fine, thanks, Peter,' he replied, and gave what he hoped was a reassuring smile. 'I think it's time we knocked off for the day.'

CHAPTER EIGHTEEN

Thursday morning came all too quickly, and Jago felt as though he was still waking up as he made his way to work. He slowed the car to a halt at a pedestrian crossing so that a woman with two children could cross, and saw a man in a flat cap and a threadbare suit selling newspapers outside the smoke-blackened remains of what until a recent air raid had been a chemist's shop. The old printed placards that newsvendors used to display had vanished from the streets months ago because of the paper shortage, and now this man, like many others, improvised his own with chalk on a blackboard. Jago could see just two words written on it: 'Roosevelt landslide'. He stopped the car beyond the crossing, ran back to give the newspaper-seller a penny, then returned and dropped the paper onto the car's back seat.

So if the paper had got the story right, he thought, President Roosevelt had just won a third term. He wondered whether Dorothy would be pleased. She hadn't given much away about her own political persuasion as the election approached; in fact, he couldn't remember her stating any preference for either Roosevelt or his Republican rival Willkie. Perhaps she was concerned to maintain a journalistic impartiality, or maybe she didn't want to embarrass him by trying to draw out his own political convictions if he felt that was inappropriate for a police officer. He liked to think the second explanation was true, because he thought of her as a sensitive person.

The newspaper would have to wait until later, however. Jago drove on to West Ham police station, where he picked up Cradock so that they could go in search of Doris Potter together. All being well, Len Potter would have been at work in the dock since eight o'clock, and Jago had often found that women spoke more freely when their husband was out of the house.

'I trust you slept well, Peter,' he said.

'Not too bad, sir, considering the anti-aircraft guns were at it half the night. No nightmares about being trapped on that *Princess Alice*, though, I'm glad to say.'

'Good.' Jago's night had not been quite so peaceful, but that was not something he had to discuss with Cradock. He released the car's handbrake and set off down West Ham Lane. 'Anything to report on the knife? Have any of those pawnbrokers or bric-a-brac shops seen it before?'

'Yes, sir, and no, sir. I heard this morning – the men have checked all the shops, and no one's had anyone bringing anything like that in. And there's no prints on it either, so I suppose it must've been wiped, or the killer wore gloves.'

'That wouldn't be surprising, given that it was a cold night when it was used. Either way it doesn't help us. Have you got it with you?'

'Yes, here it is.' Cradock handed the knife to Jago, who slipped it into his pocket.

'Any news on the rifle?' said Jago.

'Yes. There were prints, so it wasn't wiped, but they were all Lambert's, so that suggests he put it down before he was killed – if he'd dropped it when he was attacked, I think it probably would've bounced off that mooring rope. So assuming he put it down carefully like that himself before he was attacked, do you think it means the murderer was someone he knew?'

'Possibly, I suppose, if Lambert was stopping to have a chat with his killer. But equally he might've put it down so he could tie his bootlace, and the murderer might've sneaked up behind him while he wasn't looking. Don't forget he was stabbed in the back.'

'I see, sir, yes. So we're no further forward, then.'

'I wouldn't say that. All this information's useful, but I suspect the presence of someone else's prints on that rifle would've been more significant than their absence.'

They drove on. The closer they got to the Potters' home in North Woolwich, the more shocking was the evidence of the previous night's bombing. As they went down East Ham Manor Way past the area of dock workers' housing known as Cyprus they could see a number of homes reduced to pitiful heaps of rubble and others still standing but left as burnt-out shells. Jago slowed to avoid an obstruction in the road: the remains of a bus were parked by the kerb. With windows smashed and bodywork panels torn off, it looked as though a gang of crazed vandals had descended upon it from all sides with the sole intention of destroying every part of it. Jago guessed it must be the 101, because this was its route, but there was no other way of knowing, as the entire upper storey had been ripped away and dashed in pieces to the ground. Only one corner, complete with an intact tyre and a mudguard neatly painted with a white edge for the blackout, remained in its original condition.

He stopped the car: if the bus had been full when hit, there might be many dead or injured. An ambulance was parked close by, and a police constable and rescue workers were examining the wreckage.

'Anything we can do to help?' he asked the constable, identifying himself.

'No, sir, I'm afraid not,' said the policeman. 'Them that could get out have got out, and them that couldn't – well, we're clearing them up now. I think you can leave it to us.'

Jago and Cradock returned to the car, the inspector glad it had not fallen to him to gather up the fragments of the dead so they could be transported to the morgue and reassembled into a semblance of humanity. They drove on in silence. When they reached the Potters' house, they found Doris at home on her own.

'Come in,' she said breezily, welcoming them into their

little house. 'Len said you might be calling this morning, so I've held off going to the shop to get something for his tea – that's if it's still there. He went off to the call-on at the Albert this morning and hasn't come back, so either he's got some work today or he's stopped off at the pub with his mates.'

'Ah, yes,' said Jago. 'I was told some of the pubs by the docks are allowed to open early.'

'That's right – and if you want to know which ones, ask Len. He knows a sight too much about the local pubs, if you ask me. A bit too fond of his pint, is our Len. The dock workers all got a pay rise in July – a shilling a day, which he's probably drinking as we speak, but they only get that if they're working. If it wasn't for what I earn I doubt we'd be able to pay the rent, not unless he suddenly took the pledge, which is about as likely as a squadron of pigs looping the loop over the Royal Docks. Mind you, Maureen's working too now, so that helps.'

'Maureen?'

'Yes, my daughter. She works at Tate & Lyle, down by the river – you know, the Thames Refinery. She's got a cousin who works there who said he could get her a job there or in his dad's shop, up Plaistow way, but she reckoned there'd be better prospects at Tate's. She doesn't get paid much yet – she's a junior clerk in the accounts department – so I just take a few bob for her keep and leave her the rest. I mean, you're only young once, aren't you? She's nineteen, and a girl should be able to get out a bit and have some fun, even if there's a war on. I worry about her down there, though, especially if there's a daytime raid.'

'The refinery produces about half the country's sugar, doesn't it?'

'I wouldn't be surprised, dear – it's a very big place. It must be a target for those bombers, mustn't it, although some people are saying the Germans are actually making sure they don't bomb it, because that dirty great chimney it's got is too good a landmark for them when they're flying in to bomb the docks. Mind you, you'd think if they can see one chimney they ought to be able to see a whole dock right behind it, wouldn't you?'

'Quite possibly, yes. And may I ask what work you do?'

'Of course you can,' she said with a broad smile that looked almost affectionate. 'For the first time in my life I've got what I call a real job, so I'm feeling very pleased with myself. When I left school I worked in a cafe just outside the docks for ten bob a week – more like slavery, really. Then I worked in a greengrocer's shop. You had to be good at adding up for that, remembering how much all the different vegetables cost and adding it up in your head as you went along, then making sure you gave the right change. That's useful in my new job too.'

'And what's that?'

'I'm a clippie, on the buses. One of the first women conductors, I reckon. I'm on the 101 – we go up the Manor Way from here to the Royal Albert, then East Ham, Manor Park and all the way up to Wanstead. The pay's good – three pounds and fourpence a week, rising to three pounds eleven.'

Jago thought of the scene he'd just witnessed on the 101 bus route and wondered how the pay weighed up against the risks. But then that applied to just about any job these days, and it was perhaps better not to mention it.

'We take a lot of the dockers home and bring them back the next morning,' Doris continued, 'so it can be quite entertaining.'

'I can imagine,' he replied. 'How do the men take to having a conductress on the bus instead of a conductor?'

'Do I get any cheek from the dockers, do you mean?' She gave a rasping laugh. 'Nothing that I can't handle. Listen – I'm the queen of that bus. I ring the bell and it stops, I ring again and it goes. I'm in charge, and I don't take any lip from anyone. Besides, I know a lot of those men – Len's mates, they are. There's plenty of rogues working there, but they've got good hearts. They'd do anything for you. And I treat them right, not like some of those old conductors did when they were all men. Treated those dockers like dirt, they did. You just imagine – you've spent all day down the hold shifting old meat that's gone rotten, or wet cowhides that've come all the way from somewhere in South America and are all covered in disgusting slime. You stink to high heaven, and the PLA doesn't give you anywhere to wash except under a cold tap outside the back of the shed, so all you want to do is get home and get cleaned up, then this old conductor won't let you on his bus because he says his other passengers don't like the smell. So people like my husband get chucked off and have to walk home. That's not fair, but now on my bus I'm the one who decides who gets on and who doesn't, and I let those men on. And if anyone doesn't like it, well . . . I don't stand for nonsense from anyone, not even the London Passenger Transport Board.'

The confidence with which she made these claims left Jago thinking that they probably weren't exaggerated. He could picture her holding sway on the platform of the number 101 bus and taking no cheek, as she said, from anyone.

'Will you have a cup of tea?' she said. 'I may be a dragon on the bus, but not in my own home.'

'That's very kind of you, but no, thank you. We won't be long – I just wanted to ask you a few questions. I expect your husband's told you that we're investigating the death of Ray Lambert.'

'Oh, yes. Terrible thing that, isn't it? I can't say I knew Ray very well – not as well as I know Brenda, anyway. You know he was a tally clerk, don't you?'

'Yes.'

'Well, that means he was no fool. He used to say he got the job because he was so good with numbers, and he had to be for things like converting American tons into British ones. I reckon I could do that job too – I'm good at adding up, like I said. But of course there's no tally clerk jobs for women in the docks. I don't know about Ray, but you do hear that some of those tally clerks make a fair bit on the side too – you know, the quay foreman might offer to slip something your way if you let a few crates of this or that through to sell on the black market. Of course, if you say no he might try a bit of strongarm stuff, but I wouldn't put up with anything like that. But anyway, what else can I tell you about Ray? I'd say basically he liked women and football, and I always had the impression he scored more goals away than at home, if you know what I mean. Not that I've got any evidence, mind – it's just the feeling I had.'

'I see. You said you know Brenda Lambert better. Would you say you're close to her?'

'As close as anyone, I should think. Why?'

'Because I'd like to know whether you can shed any light on the nature of their marriage. I was asking your husband if he could, but he said I should ask you.'

'Yes, well, he would say that. Always happy to pass the buck for a quiet life, my Len. What exactly did you want to know?'

'Well, were they happily married, for example?'

Doris Potter greeted this question with a snort of a laugh that was both dismissive and derisive.

'You should be asking her about that, not me.'

'I did ask her, but all she said was that they were "happy enough". What do you think she meant by that?'

'A bit of an academic question, as they say, I reckon.'

'Why's that?'

'I don't think happy came into it. I think as far as Brenda's concerned, they were married, and that was that. And what does happy mean, anyway? You ask a woman if she's happy in her marriage, and what'll she say? It'll depend on what her idea of happiness is, won't it? I don't think Brenda was necessarily looking for what some other women do. She just needed someone, and Ray came along. Her old man – her first husband, I mean, although he wasn't her husband strictly speaking – he wasn't any use to her after the war.'

'I understand he ended up in West Ham Mental Hospital.'

'That's right, the lunatic asylum.'

'I believe they changed the name to "mental hospital" some years ago.'

'Yes, but it's still the loony bin, isn't it? Not that I'm saying anything against him, mark you. I mean, it was the war that finished him, wasn't it? Not his fault.'

'I'd like to get back to her marriage to Mr Lambert.'

'Oh, yes, well, as I was saying, she needed someone. Sometimes any husband's better than no husband, and when the war finished that's the choice a lot of us women faced. We'd lost our men to the war, and there weren't so many around after it to choose from, so you took whatever came your way. It sounds hard, but it was a matter of survival. That's what we are, you know, women like Brenda and me – survivors. Life round here doesn't do us any favours, so you have to make the best of any chances that come along. It's one big fight, and we have to do anything we can just to survive.'

'Are you saying Mrs Lambert had to fight to survive her marriage?'

'That's the problem. I'm not sure she fought enough. You know he used to knock her about, I suppose?'

'Who did?'

'Ray. He was careful to hit her where it wouldn't

172

show, mind – most of the time, anyway.'

'Mrs Lambert didn't mention this to me.'

'Well, what's the point, eh? She's probably told a copper before and learnt her lesson. Any woman who complains to the police gets the same old answer. A man round here can beat his wife black and blue, and all your lot say is it's a domestic – you know, a marital dispute, within the home, and they can't interfere. They say it's a civil matter, not a criminal one. Some of them even say maybe you should take out a summons against your husband. Who's going to do that round here? No, it's a waste of time – you're all the same.'

'Not all of us, I hope.'

'Well, you may be different, but I've never met a copper on the beat who was. No – I told Brenda she'd have to stand up for herself. That's what I do. I wouldn't let any man hit me. My old dad was a boxer over in Bethnal Green and he taught me how to look after myself when I was a girl. I don't care whether it's my husband or anyone else – I'd like to see them try. Like I said, you've got to fight to survive. I just don't think poor Brenda's got enough left in her to see it through – if I'd been in her shoes I'd have left him long ago.'

'I see,' said Jago, nodding his head slowly.

'Do you? Well, maybe you do, but it won't help her. When a woman's had a life like Brenda's, people say well, she'll get her reward in heaven. That's as may be, but I'd like to think just once in a while she might get a bit of reward here on earth too.'

CHAPTER NINETEEN

As the front door of the Potters' house swung shut behind them, Jago and Cradock narrowly escaped colliding with a young woman. Dressed in a red coat and knitted beret, with dark brown shoes and white ankle socks, she was running at full tilt towards the house. Cradock put his arms out to protect himself as the girl clattered into him.

'I'm so sorry,' she spluttered, out of breath. 'I was halfway to work and realised I'd left my purse behind. I had to come back for it, and now I'll be late.'

Jago noticed that his young colleague was blushing and seemed unable to speak as she extricated herself from his inadvertent grasp. He raised his hat to her.

'That's all right, miss,' he said, stepping to one side. 'You live here?'

'Yes. Who are you?'

'We're the police – I'm Detective Inspector Jago and this is Detective Constable Cradock. Would you be Miss Maureen Potter?'

'That's right. How did you know?'

'Just a guess. We've been talking to your mother – she's been helping us with our enquiries.'

'Ah,' said Maureen with a bright laugh. 'Well, whatever it is, I'm sure she didn't do it.' She looked as though she was about to laugh again, but her expression turned suddenly serious. 'She's not in any trouble, is she?'

'No, miss, nothing to worry about. Just a friendly chat.'

'Good. That's a relief. Well, look, I can't stop – I need to get my purse and run back to work, otherwise they'll be docking the time from my wages. Excuse me, please.'

She squeezed past Cradock and put her key in the lock, opened the door and let herself in.

As the door closed behind her, Jago noticed that Cradock still looked a little unsettled by the experience.

'So, Peter, is she what you'd call a looker? The sort that makes you lose the power of speech?'

'No, sir,' Cradock protested, looking hard done by. 'It's not like that at all. I was just thinking.'

'Yes?'

'Well, I was wondering, you see. She works at Tate & Lyle, and that's where they make sugar.'

'They don't make it – it grows out of the ground in places like Barbados. What they do is refine it.'

'OK, they refine it, but the thing is, could she be mixed up with that sugar thing that Sergeant Tompkins told us about? Her mum did say Maureen's got a cousin who works at the refinery and the cousin's dad has a shop in Plaistow.'

'Yes, she did, but that doesn't exactly place Maureen red-handed at the scene of the crime, does it? There must be hundreds of people working at Tate's, if not thousands, and there's a lot of shops in Plaistow, so there's bound to be plenty of people with connections in both places, but that doesn't mean Maureen's cousin is stealing sugar, or Maureen herself for that matter. In any case, it could've been someone from outside doing it, so I don't think we can jump to any conclusions just because we've met young Maureen.'

He gave Cradock a sly look.

'Or is it perhaps because you'd like to have the opportunity to question her on the matter? I saw the way you looked at her.'

'Certainly not, sir. I don't know what you're talking about.'

'Good. If I thought she was turning your head, I'd advise you to concentrate on young Emily, or you might lose her. But she's not, and you are, so that's all right. I'll say no more.'

'Thank you, sir,' said Cradock. He still looked a little sheepish, and Jago felt a stab of guilt for speaking like a Dutch uncle when he himself might do well to heed his own advice.

When they reached Jago's car they saw a uniformed constable hurrying towards them, looking a little out of breath. Jago didn't recognise him, but in this area the man was probably based at North Woolwich police station, and he didn't know all the officers there.

'Excuse me, sir,' said the constable as he got close enough to speak. 'I had a phone call from the station on the police pillar – West Ham station, that is – with a message for you, to say you're wanted. They said you were down here, so I came to find you.' He drew a deep breath to recover from his exertions. 'They told me to look out for your car, and I spotted it here on the street. Very nice motor, sir, if you don't mind me saying.'

'Did they say what I was wanted for?'

'Oh, yes, sir, they said there's a lady waiting to see you.'

Jago was surprised to find that his first thought was that it might be Dorothy wanting to see him, and he was thankful that Cradock did not possess the power of mind-reading. He was both relieved and disappointed when the constable continued.

'She's a Mrs Parsloe, sir. A food inspector.'

'Right. Thank you, Constable. We'll go back and see what she wants.'

Jago and Cradock drove back to the station, where they found a woman waiting for them. She was tall and thin, in her mid-thirties, with a pinched face and wire-framed spectacles, and was dressed in a shapeless tweed suit. She held her head inclined to one side and her chin slightly raised, as if she were trying to avoid an unpleasant smell somewhere in front of her.

'My name is Mrs Enid Parsloe,' she said. 'I'm the new Ministry of Food inspector.'

'Good morning, Mrs Parsloe,' said Jago. 'How can I help you?'

'I'm sure you're busy, Detective Inspector, as am I. I don't want to waste your time or mine, so I shall be brief. We received a report about suspected illegal trading at Morris's butcher's shop in Plaistow, so I've just been down there – normally I'd send one of the clerical staff from the Food Office, because they wouldn't be recognised, but I haven't been in this area long enough for the local tradesmen to know my face, so I went myself. According to the information received, he'd been seen selling bacon to people without checking their ration books and passing sugar to customers from under the counter without being licensed to sell it. I went in and posed as a customer and asked if he had any bacon I could have to make a bacon stew, as I had three sickly children at home and needed to build up their strength with something nutritious. I wasn't registered with him, of course, but I said I'd been bombed out and had just moved into the area, and I hadn't yet been able to take my ration book to the Food Office to get re-registered with a local butcher.'

'And I suppose he accepted that?'

'Yes. I told him I was willing to pay over the odds, but he said he'd sold out of bacon. I was about to ask if he had some sugar so I could make the children plenty of hot sweet tea when he said he had something else that might help – one of the protective foods the government said we should all be eating. He had a quick look round to make sure no one could see, then pulled out a couple of cans from behind the counter – cans of salmon. Fat fish, he said – full of vitamins and very nutritious for the kiddies. I said that would suit me very well, and I asked what they would cost.'

'A little over the odds, I dare say.'

'Exactly. Now, canned salmon may not be rationed, but it is subject to a controlled price. The Canned Salmon (Provisional Maximum Prices) Order that the government brought in when the war started is still in force, as I expect you know.'

Jago said nothing. He wasn't intimately acquainted with the government order in question, but he had little doubt that Mrs Parsloe would be able to quote it chapter and verse if required.

'The controlled retail price for that type of salmon is eightpence per tin,' she continued, with all the gravity of the Chancellor of the Exchequer standing at the dispatch box in the House of Commons, 'but he wanted half a crown for the two. That's one and threepence each, almost double the maximum price. I bought one – for evidence, of course.'

'Of course. And presumably he's not licensed to sell canned fish either.'

'Of course not. He's a butcher. He's clearly in breach of the regulations, and if he's trading illegally in multiple commodities it's a serious offence, so I'd like you to question him and, if you find you have a case, charge him.'

179

'Do you have the can with you?'

'Yes, I do.'

'May I have a look?'

She bent down to the capacious bag by her feet and pulled out the can of salmon. Jago turned it over and scanned the print on the back.

'Hmm,' he said. 'I see. "Produce of Canada". Yes, I think I'd like to interview this man as soon as possible.'

For the first time since entering the office the food inspector smiled.

'Thank you, Detective Inspector. I'm very pleased to hear that. I look forward to learning the outcome of your interview. Good day to you.'

She picked up her bag and left the office without further ado.

'Right, Peter,' said Jago as soon as she'd gone. 'I think we should get back down to the docks and see if the *Magnolia* still has any of that cargo of salmon on board. If not, we'll have to hope there's still some of it in the transit sheds. I want to have a word with young Tom Lightfoot too, so I'll drop you off at the dock and you can go in search of a can of salmon. When you've done that, come and find me at Brenda Lambert's house.'

CHAPTER TWENTY

Jago dropped Cradock off at the Royal Albert Dock and continued alone to Saville Road. He thought again about Dorothy, conscious of how he'd been irritated by Philip Eliot the previous day and of the sharp words he'd said about the man she'd described not just as a colleague but as a friend. He'd probably hurt her, and he hated himself for doing so. He'd have to make amends before another day passed: he resolved to phone her this evening at the Savoy as soon as he could get away from his work, and try to take her out for a quiet drink somewhere.

His arrival at Saville Road forced him to push all thought of Dorothy from his mind. He parked the car and took a few brisk strides to Brenda Lambert's house. He could hear the energetic dance rhythm of 'In the Mood' coming from a gramophone turned up to full volume inside the house, so he knocked loudly at the door.

'Ah, hello, Inspector,' the murdered man's widow said when she opened it, her voice raised over the scratchy noise of the music. 'You'll be wanting to speak to my Tom, won't you? Do come in – I'm just getting something ready for his dinner. He'll be going back to his ship soon, so I'm giving him as much home cooking as I can.' She turned round to face back into the house and shouted, 'Hey, Tom, turn those records off – you've got a visitor.'

The music stopped suddenly as she led Jago through to the kitchen at the back of the little house, where he found Tom Lightfoot taking a record off the gramophone and slipping it into a brown paper sleeve. A stocky figure of average height, he was dressed in khaki battledress with two stripes on each arm and a blue shoulder flash bearing the words 'Royal Marines' in bold red. With his large hands, broad shoulders and sturdy neck he struck Jago as a man you wouldn't lightly pick a fight with.

'Here, Tom, this is Detective Inspector Jago, from the police,' said Brenda. 'He wants to talk to you.'

Lightfoot glanced at him, a flicker of wariness discernible in his eyes as he put the record down on the table.

'Sorry to disturb you, Mr Lightfoot,' said Jago. 'Just a quick word.'

'By all means,' said Lightfoot. 'Fire away.'

'Why don't you men go into the front room?' Brenda interrupted. 'You won't want me fussing around while you're trying to talk.'

'Very well,' said Jago. 'Thank you.'

He followed Lightfoot down the hall to the front room. It was cold and had the musty smell of disuse and damp. In the middle stood a small square dining table, clear except for an empty fruit bowl, and four chairs.

'Take a seat,' said Lightfoot.

'Thanks. I won't keep you long,' said Jago, sitting down. 'I understand you're on embarkation leave.'

'That's right.'

'Have you been in the Marines for long?'

'Longer than some. I joined in 1937 – couldn't find a decent job and fancied an adventure, so I signed up.'

'And saw the world?'

'Well, a fair bit of it, and of course it was more fun in peacetime, with no one shooting at us. I started out on a cruiser on the East Indies Station, so I saw Aden, Trincomalee and Bombay, then we came home for a refit just in time for the war to start. When they'd finished all the work on her we joined the Home Fleet, but then unfortunately she got knocked about a bit in an air raid on Scapa Flow, so it's only now she's really been ready to fight. I'm due back at the Depot in Deal on Sunday, and then I expect I'll be sailing off to some place I can't say where, to do something I don't know what.'

'I suppose what with all that, you haven't seen much action yet.'

'Don't you believe it. I haven't been sitting around all this time waiting for them to get the ship fixed. It's probably OK to mention it now, even if walls do have ears, because it's all history, but in April I got shipped out to Norway and suddenly there I was, fighting the Germans. And a right mess it was too.'

'In my day it was Gallipoli, although luckily for me I wasn't there.'

'Yes, well, Norway was probably just a sideshow compared to that, but even so, we never had a chance. The Germans were better equipped than us and better supplied. We had no airfields and no air cover, so their bombers could play merry hell with us, and they were free to bring up all the reinforcements they wanted. We were lucky to get out. So now Germany's captured seven hundred miles of coastline with a navy only a quarter the size of ours. No wonder Chamberlain resigned.'

'Well, I hope your next deployment proves more successful.'

'So do I, mate. So do I. But I don't suppose you came here to talk about the war. What's so interesting about me that you come round here to talk to me?'

Before Jago could answer he heard the front door slamming.

'Is that your mother going out?' he asked.

'Yes, she said she had to go round and see a friend in Wythes Road who's had some bad news. A telegram, she said. You know how it is. Anyway, do carry on.'

'We're investigating the death of Ray Lambert, and I understand that you're his stepson. Please accept my condolences.'

Lightfoot nodded his acknowledgement, but said nothing.

'I just wanted to know what you can tell me about him,' Jago continued.

'What sort of thing do you want to know?'

'Well, for one thing, can you think of why anyone would want to kill him?'

'I don't think I can, no. I don't imagine he was the most popular person around, but that doesn't mean anyone'd want to do him in. To be honest, though, I can't say I knew him that well. I mean, he wasn't my real dad, and when he and my mum got married I don't think he made much of an effort to get to know me or be a dad to me. Then when I grew up I was overseas with the Marines a lot of the time. He wasn't the sort of bloke I'd go out for a drink with if I got some leave. As far as I was concerned he was just my mum's old man. You know what I mean? A stranger, really. He didn't seem bothered about getting to know me, and I was quite happy with my life without getting to know him.'

'What about your real father? Do you see him?'

'No. He got locked up in the asylum when I was a kid, and I haven't seen him since. I think when my mum got married to Ray she didn't want to see him any more, and I couldn't very well go and visit him on my own at that age.'

'And more recently?'

'No. I tried once, just before I went into the Marines. I had some idea about seeing him before I went away, so I went over to Goodmayes, but they said he'd been released. They gave me an address, but when I checked it the people there said he'd moved on and they didn't know where to. After that I didn't try again. I didn't have the time, and I didn't really have the inclination either. He's not part of my life any more, and if I did go and see him I doubt we'd have anything to talk about. Besides, I'd probably have got an earful from Ray.'

'Had Mr Lambert ever met your father?'

'I don't think so – why would he? He didn't like my dad, and I expect the feeling was mutual. But look, I thought it was Ray you wanted to talk to me about, not my dad.'

'That's correct. I'm trying to build up a picture of the kind of man he was, what he did in his work, in his spare time and so on. For example, I understand he worked as a tally clerk in the docks.'

'Yes, well, what I know about that I could write on the back of a penny stamp. All I can say is it was something to do with checking how much stuff went onto the ships and how much came off them. If you want to know more than that you've got the wrong bloke. And as for what he did in his spare time, that's easy – he was down the pub. I don't know how much effort he put into his work, but he certainly put enough into his drinking. Nasty piece of work he was, too, when he'd had a skinful.'

'So he was a heavy drinker?'

'You bet he was. Drank like a fish. Someone once told me it went back to the old days when he was a docker. That was before he was a tally clerk. He was working in the West India Docks in those days, and that's where all the rum comes in. Need I say more? It was like a drunk's paradise for those blokes – from what I've heard, they could help themselves to as much as they liked. So what did my mum tell you?'

'She didn't say a lot. I think she was still shocked from learning that he'd been killed. She said he was good with numbers, and that he was a bit of a restless soul.'

Lightfoot gave a bitter laugh.

'I wouldn't be surprised if his soul had a few things to be restless about.'

'What do you mean?'

'Nothing in particular. I just didn't trust him. When you talked to him he didn't give much away – as if he had things to hide. What you might call shifty. You know?'

'Was there anything specific you think he might've wanted to hide?'

'There was, yes. Did she tell you he hit her?'

'No, your mother hasn't said that to us. But it has been alleged by someone else.'

'There you are, then. That's one thing. Funny she didn't mention that, isn't it?'

'What do you mean?'

'Nothing. It tells you something about Ray Lambert, though, doesn't it? Even when he's dead she's still scared of him.'

Lightfoot glanced towards the door as if Lambert might yet enter and join them.

'Thank you, Mr Lightfoot,' said Jago. 'That'll be all for now. Are you leaving for Deal on Sunday, or will it be earlier?'

'Saturday afternoon, I think.'

'So if I need to speak to you again, you'll be here until then?'

'That's right. If I'm not in, my mum'll probably be able to tell you where you can find me.'

'Good. Well, thank you for your help, and goodbye.'

After leaving Brenda's house, Jago returned to the car to wait for Cradock's return. He reflected on the new picture of Lambert's home life that the dead man's young stepson had revealed – if what he'd said was true. It might explain why Brenda had seemed curiously unmoved by her husband's death, but there could be other reasons for that. His musing was interrupted by the sight of Cradock hurrying along the street towards him. He leant over to open the passenger door, and Cradock slid into the front seat.

'Well,' said Jago, 'what did you find out?'

'I found that Carlisle, the mate, on the ship,' Cradock replied, 'and he said the boxes of salmon had all been unloaded, but he got a bloke to take me down to the transit shed, and some of it was still there, waiting for the customer to collect it. They opened a box for me and gave me a can.'

'And it matches?'

'See for yourself.'

Cradock reached into his coat pocket and pulled out a can. To Jago's eye it was identical to the one the food inspector had given him.

'Interesting,' he said. 'So Mr Morris the butcher may have a little explaining to do. I want you to go and see him before the day's out, Peter, and tell him there's been a report that he may've been involved in a breach of trading regulations. Ask him if he'll be kind enough to come along to the station at two o'clock tomorrow afternoon to assist us with our enquiries. If he's not keen, offer him the alternative of being arrested. Oh, and if he's got a daughter, keep your eyes off her and on his cleaver.'

Cradock smirked. 'Yes, sir.'

Jago weighed the can of salmon in his hand.

'Very tasty, I'm sure,' he said. 'They let you keep it, then?'

'Yes,' said Cradock. 'They said it was the property of the Co-operative Wholesale Society, so it wasn't their place to start handing out free samples, but I told them we needed it for evidence, and they said in that case I could take it away. They made me sign for it, though.'

'Of course – otherwise someone might think they'd pinched it, and they'd be in hot water. Nothing gets past the PLA Police, does it?'

Cradock replied with a knowing smile.

'It's a well-known fact, sir.'

CHAPTER TWENTY-ONE

'You know, Peter,' said Jago as he turned the Riley's ignition key and pressed the starter button, 'the longer I spend around these docks, the more I hear about people working rackets with the cargo. You get the impression that whichever way you turn you'll find someone nicking something. Low-level stuff, I'll grant you, but it's making me wonder what else might be going on.'

'You mean like that business with the whisky that DDI Soper mentioned? If that involves the docks in London and Scotland, it could be a bit more serious.'

'Exactly. He wanted us to have a word with DI Burton about it next time we saw him, so I think it's about time we did just that. We'll see if he's in his office.'

'Do you think we could stop on the way, sir?'

Jago knew what was coming: a quick glance at his watch was enough to tell.

'Oh? Why's that?'

'I think it was just having that can of salmon in my

hand, sir. Made me come over all hungry. Any chance of us getting something to eat on the way?'

'I'll see what we can do,' said Jago.

It was a short drive up the Connaught Road to the Albert Dock's No. 9 Gate, but before they went into the dock Jago made sure he'd stopped to buy a sandwich for himself and Cradock.

'There,' he said, handing Cradock a brown paper bag containing a cheese and pickle sandwich. 'Will that be enough to keep you from death's door?'

'Yes, thank you, sir. That should do nicely.'

They both ate quickly in the car before Jago drove on and into the dock, where they found Burton at his desk in the police office again. Jago had not seen enough of his PLA Police opposite number to form a fair judgement, but he had the impression that Burton spent more time at his desk than he did. Perhaps Jago was old-fashioned, but he believed you didn't catch criminals by sitting at your desk.

'Good afternoon, Jim,' said Jago, and Burton returned the greeting, inviting them to take a seat. Jago and Cradock pulled up a chair each on the other side of the desk.

'How can I help you today?' asked Burton.

'I'd like to pick your brains, if you don't mind,' Jago replied. 'You see, we've got this old station sergeant up at West Ham nick – Frank Tompkins, he's called – who's been dragged out of retirement to reinforce our numbers at the station, and he's been telling us stories about what used to go on in the old days in these docks that'd make your hair stand on end. Like Ali Baba and the Forty

Thieves, he said it was – people pinching stuff left, right and centre. Now, I'm sure things aren't like that now, and you did say you come down on anything like that like a ton of bricks, but I wonder whether you could tell me how much pilfering and suchlike really goes on.'

Burton seemed to spend a little time thinking about the question before responding.

'It's not like it used to be,' he said. 'Nowadays the dock management tends to tolerate a certain amount of pilfering, as long as it doesn't get out of hand. I think they're prepared to accept that if dockers are handling alcohol they'll help themselves to a drink – what they call "having a waxer" – and as far as we're concerned, as long as the man can get himself home we don't mind. So they can get away with that sort of thing, but nothing large-scale gets past us. Mind you, you have to understand the pressures on the dock police too. The PLA are saying they've got to make savings, and they're talking about cutting the number of jobs. From what I've heard, that'll mean we lose about two dozen uniformed constables, but there's one other cut that could be very serious. We've currently got just four CID inspectors across the whole of the London docks, and they're talking about cutting that to three.'

'I see – and one of those four is you.'

'That's right. So I could be out of a job myself any time.'

'It seems strange to cut police numbers in a strategic facility like this when we're at war.'

'I couldn't agree more, but I think it's because there's not so many ships coming in here now, so the Port of London's losing money, and we're the Port of London's police. So anyway, if they do that, there'll be fewer coppers in the docks to keep things under control and legal.'

'Right. Now, talking of keeping things under control and legal, I've heard there's some kind of racket going on in Scotland with whisky. Do you know anything about it?'

'Why do you ask?' said Burton, his voice sounding a little wary. Jago thought that was odd, given that it was the PLA Police's own divisional inspector for the Royal Docks, Burton's immediate boss, who'd told Soper about it. He was about to invoke the name of Divisional Inspector Grayson but suspected he might learn more about this wariness if he didn't.

'Because my DDI seems to think there could be a connection with the London docks,' he replied. 'So do you know anything?'

'I've got one or two suspicions,' said Burton cautiously.

'Why didn't you mention them?'

'You didn't ask. We don't just sit around here twiddling our thumbs all day until there's a murder and then call you big boys in. We have plenty of things to deal with ourselves, and we can get on and do it without your help. Besides, I don't see that it's relevant to your investigation.'

'Well, perhaps you could tell me what it's about, just so I don't look a fool in my boss's eyes – he expects me to know everything, and he'll no doubt expect me to know about this, even if it is irrelevant.'

'All right. It's to do with that business of shipping being diverted to other ports.'

'What Carlisle told us about?'

'That's right. As I understand it, in September, when the big air raids started, the government set up what they called the Clyde Emergency Anchorages, to beef up the Scottish ports so they could handle the extra cargo. The PLA sent three hundred Thames dumb barges and scores of dockers up there to help. Heroes to a man, I'm sure, but the thing is, I've heard from a police colleague in Scotland that they suspect some of the ex-London dockers up there in Clydebank are working a racket, stealing cases of whisky that are supposed to be exported to the USA – although I haven't heard anything to suggest any of their old mates down here are mixed up in it too.'

'Clydebank, eh? That's where one of our Home Guards comes from – the one who was patrolling with Lambert the night he was killed. He's called Charlie Bell. Do you know him?'

'I haven't had the pleasure personally, but I've heard his name mentioned. Bit of a troublemaker, they say. Some kind of communist, I expect – there's a few of them in the docks. Very keen on the class struggle and robbing the rich to pay the poor. There's no shortage of grievances for a man like him to play on, either. The bosses don't trust the dockers, the dockers don't trust the management, and even the workers in here aren't just one big happy family. You may remember there was a big strike in the docks in 1912. It went on for months, and the management brought in strike-breakers to do the work when the men walked out. These dockers have long memories, and there's still a lot of resentment on both sides. The men who went on strike remember who worked, and their sons remember too. A lot of old grudges.'

'I see. But this whisky – do you know how it's going astray?'

'No, I don't. But what I do know is that we've got tight security here – as I told you before, there's a PC on every gate, so it won't get out that way.'

'Are you sure?'

'Yes. The PLA has a system. If anyone from outside's trying to get into the dock to pick up some goods, they have to show us a release note. We don't let them in without it.'

'And for getting out?'

'Then they have to show us a dock pass, otherwise we don't let them or what they're carrying out. You wouldn't believe how much paperwork there is in the docks. Hundreds of clerks, all scribbling away all day on different bits of paper, to make sure everything's fair and square. Seems to me every time the bosses in here think there's a security problem they try to solve it by adding some new paperwork and employing more clerks to deal with it.'

'But surely a determined crook can get round any system.'

'In theory, I suppose, yes.'

'So if someone was determined enough, he could get a case of whisky out of the dock?'

'Well, yes – I mean you can never say something

like that's impossible, can you? But I'd be surprised if it happened here. It's just too risky for the men – if they're caught nicking anything, they're finished.'

'So to cut a long story short, you're aware of the suspicions, but you don't have any evidence or leads that might connect anything dubious going on up there with the men working down here.'

'That's right. You're welcome to look into it, of course, if Grayson thinks I can't handle it, but I don't think you'll find much. Now, I've got a lot on my plate today, so is there anything else I can do for you?'

'No. Thanks for giving us your time.'

'You're welcome. And by the way, before you go you might like to know the master's returned – the master of the *Magnolia*, that is. He's called Munroe, a Scotsman. I dare say he has a Christian name too, but I only know of him as Captain Munroe. The old-fashioned type, if you know what I mean. You might want to call on him. Oh, and you remember that lascar you were talking to on the *Magnolia*? Jamal, wasn't it? I've just heard something about him. Seems he's gone missing – absent without official leave since last night.'

'Have you made any enquiries as to where he might've gone?'

'No. It's your case and he's your witness, so I thought I'd leave it to you.'

CHAPTER TWENTY-TWO

To walk along the quayside on the southern side of the Royal Albert Dock was like taking a stroll through an ants' nest. Scores of men, all seemingly clad in the same battered old black jacket, trousers and boots, with a waistcoat, tie and cap, moved rapidly and purposefully this way and that, pushing barrows and trolleys, spearing sacks with the vicious-looking docker's hook that each of them carried, stacking crates, coiling ropes, all in apparently random patterns and yet equally all with a sense of hidden order. Above their heads, crane jibs swung swaying pallets of goods out of ships' holds and towards the waiting dockers, each load a perilous threat to the unwary. As Jago picked his way carefully through this organised human chaos, he could not help but note the contrast with the atmosphere in DI Burton's office. Detectives all had their own way of getting the job done, of course – Jago's own experience of working with DDI Soper was evidence enough of that – but what he found strange about Burton was his apparent indifference. Perhaps, just this once, Soper was right: somehow Jago had managed to put Burton's nose out of joint. If that was the case, he thought, the offence was unintended, so he'd just have to put up with it – and so would Burton.

'Excuse me, guv'nor,' said Cradock, hopping over a trailing rope to come alongside him.

'Yes, Peter?'

'I wasn't sure whether you were thinking, sir.'

'I'm always thinking, Peter. What do you do when you're walking through a dock?'

'I think too, sir. In fact, that's what I was just about to say – I've been thinking.'

'I'm glad to hear it. About what?'

'About these burglaries. Well, about the one at Major Danbury's house, actually. It's what you were saying back there about men working in the docks nicking stuff, and what DI Burton said about that Charlie Bell character – that he's a bit of a hothead, no time for rich people or bosses.'

'I'm with you so far. So what's your theory?'

'Well, Bell works in the docks, and he knows Danbury through the Home Guard, so he probably knows where he lives and might even have been there. He'd also know when Danbury was on duty, and if he managed somehow to find out when Mrs Danbury and her daughter were working on the mobile canteen, he'd know when the house was empty. And it was what Bell said when you mentioned Robin Hood – he said we could do with a few more like him, didn't he? Do you think he could've done it, maybe to get even with Danbury for something, or just to get a bit of cash?'

'So he sees himself as a latter-day Robin Hood, eh? Well, he doesn't dress in Lincoln green, but he does have a rather natty Errol Flynn moustache. Let's keep an eye out for him on our way down to the *Magnolia* – he might be working somewhere down this side. It could be interesting to have a word with him, and I'd like to see his reaction if we show him this.'

He pulled the knife out of his coat pocket and turned it over in his hand.

'Do you think he could've killed Lambert too?' said Cradock.

'One step at a time, Peter,' Jago replied, putting the knife away. 'We don't know whether he's the burglar yet, let alone a murderer.'

After making brief enquiries on their way, they located Bell working on a barge halfway down the quay. When they caught his eye he climbed up to meet them, slapped a cloud of black dust out of his clothes and removed a pair of old gloves.

'Excuse the mess,' he said, gesturing back towards the barge. 'Carbon black. One of the worst things to handle. Half a hundredweight in each sack, and it gets everywhere – it takes days to wash it out of your skin. The only good thing about it is it doesn't make your clothes stink. Anyway, what can I do for you?'

'A brief word with you, if we may,' said Jago. 'I don't want to stop you working for too long.'

'That's very considerate of you. This is piecework, you know – we don't get paid for standing around watching the world go by, like some I could mention. This is real work, and you can thank your lucky stars this isn't how you have to earn your living.'

'I can see what you mean.'

'I'm not sure which is worse, this stuff or the sugar. If you're working on sugar it's back-breaking – you're carrying three-hundredweight sacks of it, and when it gets on your skin it's like sticky sandpaper rubbing away at you. It can make you bleed. The sugar men have to wrap sacking round their legs and boots to keep it off them, and by the time they get to about forty-five they're finished – they can't physically do it any more.'

'So is it all right to talk?'

'Aye, that's fine by me. But if I'm going to stop for a while, I'd sooner sit down. Let's go over there.'

He pointed to some wooden chests positioned outside the nearby transit shed. The three men moved across and sat on them.

'Do you sometimes wish you'd stayed a riveter?' asked Jago.

'Maybe I should've done, but in the end it wasn't my choice. I think I told you I used to build warships – that was at William Beardmore & Co's Dalmuir yard, at Clydebank. There were thirteen thousand of us working there – when I was fifteen years old we were building

200

the Dreadnoughts, and then when I was nineteen the Great War started, and I spent the whole war in the yard. But then it ended and nobody needed ships built – tens of thousands of men were thrown out of work in the industry, and on top of that all the soldiers came home, so there were no other jobs to be had.'

Jago nodded sympathetically.

'The last ship I built was the SS *Duchess of Atholl*,' Bell continued. 'That was real work – six thousand men a day working for more than two years, riveters like me in pairs, hammering in two million white-hot rivets by hand. There was even a film about us building her – it was on the newsreels, in all the cinemas. You can't imagine what it's like, seeing twenty thousand tons of ship edging down the slipway into the River Clyde and knowing that we built her, with our own hands, our sweat, our muscles and our skills. I tell you, I loved that ship. Still do. It's the most beautiful thing I ever made.'

'I'm surprised, though,' said Jago. 'From what I've heard about your political views I wouldn't have thought you'd have too much affection for anything to do with a duchess.'

'I see you've been doing your homework, Inspector. But come on, man – it's not a woman, it's a ship. Besides, the real Duchess of Atholl is the one member of the ruling class I'd make an exception for. The rest of them you could put up against a wall for all I care. But she's different – she's the one they call the Red Duchess, isn't she? The one who went to Spain and had the guts to stand up and protest about the fascists' bombing raids on open towns. She may be a Tory and a toff, but at least she's made herself useful. She spoke up for shipbuilding, too, when she made her first speech in Parliament, and for families on the Clyde whose lives depended on jobs in the shipyards. Mind you, it wasn't enough for our place – by 1930 the whole yard had closed.'

'So was that when you moved down here?'

'Aye, I had to, to find work. I was fit and strong, and I got a job in the docks – that's all there is to it.'

'And you're in the Home Guard?'

'That's right. If any Nazis turn up here I'll happily kill the lot of them.'

'For king and country?'

'Let's just say for justice.'

'I hear you're a bit short of weaponry, though.'

'Aye, well, it's the same old story – good men willing and able to work, with incompetent management all the way up the line. I mean, we're supposed to be saving the country but we haven't even got enough tin helmets to go round.'

'So your platoon commander was telling me. Do you have one?'

'No. I did, but that was only because I bought it myself – fifteen bob post-free from some place in Manor Park. How is it a member of the Home Guard can buy a helmet by mail order but can't get one issued by the government?'

'So you did have one, but not now?' Jago asked, not wishing to get into a discussion of the government's military supply problems.

'Yes, I gave it to one of the other men – he's got a wife and kids to provide for. So now I'm back to taking on the world's most powerful army in my field service cap. It's a joke, isn't it? And the training's no better – we go to parades, but that just means standing around doing nothing for twenty minutes at a time, then doing a bit of basic drill that we already know, with a rifle if you've got one and a broomstick if you haven't, and no one seems to know what kind of training we should be having.'

'Teething troubles, perhaps?'

Bell looked askance at him as if not sure whether he was joking, then gave a half-hearted laugh.

'Maybe, but we started in May and now it's November, so while we're still marching up and down and doing precious little else, the Germans could be parachuting right into these docks. Where will we be then? I'm telling you, these men need to be toughened up, taught how to fight, not left pussyfooting around in drill halls with broomsticks. I decided if I was going to be ready I'd have to take matters into my own hands.'

'What do you mean?'

'Well, it was very interesting. About three months ago someone showed me a letter in one of the papers about a place over in Middlesex where you could do a course on guerrilla warfare – two days' intensive training, free of charge. It was called the Osterley Park LDV Training

School, so I thought it was something official, but it turned out it was private, run by a man called Tom Wintringham. He's a real fighter – he was in the civil war in Spain. I signed up, and it was exactly what I needed. He trained us in street fighting, harassing the enemy, how to make a petrol bomb, how to kill a sentry.'

'Ah, yes, I've seen stories about that in the press. The government's taken it over now, hasn't it?'

'Yes. I think it probably frightened them. I don't imagine they were keen on the idea of men running round on the streets with tricks like that up their sleeves – could be a threat to what they like to think is the established social order. Anyway, now they've got it where they want it, under their control – you can only attend if you're a commander or a section leader, and you have to be nominated by regional headquarters.'

Jago took the knife from his pocket again and held it towards Bell, handle first.

'When you were doing your training at Osterley Park, were you taught to use a weapon like this?' he asked.

Bell took the knife from Jago and examined it, then placed it on the edge of his finger to test its balance.

'No,' he said. 'We used a straight dagger. Besides, this looks very foreign. Why do you ask?'

'Have you seen this knife before?'

'No. What's so interesting about it?'

'It's the weapon used to kill Mr Lambert.'

Bell's face was suddenly flushed with anger.

'What? Are you suggesting I'm a murderer? You want

to be careful, throwing accusations like that around.'

'No one's accusing you of anything, Mr Bell. I simply wanted to know whether you've seen it before.'

'Well, I haven't, and I hope that satisfies you.'

'Thank you, Mr Bell. I'll have it back now, if you don't mind.'

Bell turned the handle towards Jago and thrust it into his waiting hand, his face set in a scowl.

'You think I'm some kind of fiery Scot, don't you, Inspector? The kind of man your sort always see as trouble. You and your masters. You don't like men who think for themselves, who ask questions they shouldn't. Well, listen to me. I may be just a filthy stevedore who works with his hands and his muscle, but without people like me this country would starve. And if the Nazis march in today it won't be the bosses who fight them – they'll all be cosy and safe in their country mansions, looking to please their new customers. It'll be people like me, the people nobody's heard of, doing their dirty work for them as usual, risking our necks so they can be free.'

Jago thought of suggesting that Bell should consult DDI Soper about men who think for themselves before rushing to judge him, but he was keen to get down to the *Magnolia*. He waited for a moment to give Bell's head of steam time to dissipate.

'Just one question before we go, Mr Bell,' he said quietly.

'Yes? What's that?'

'Can you tell me what you were doing on the night of

the twenty-seventh of October?'

'I don't know. What day was that?'

'It was the Sunday before last.'

'I thought you were trying to find out who killed Ray Lambert – that was the day before yesterday.'

'We are, but this is something different. Where were you?'

Bell thought.

'I wasn't on duty – my Home Guard duty nights are Friday and Monday. If it was that Sunday, I was at home in the Anderson shelter all night, trying to get some sleep.'

'Can anyone confirm that?'

Bell hesitated before replying.

'Well, yes. Mrs Higgs was there too – my landlady. But before you start imagining things, she's a respectable woman, and she lets me share her shelter because she's got a kind and tender heart. Understand?'

'Of course I understand, Mr Bell. And thank you for your help.'

CHAPTER TWENTY-THREE

'That Major Danbury was right about Bell, wasn't he, sir?' said Cradock as he and Jago left the stevedore to resume his work and continued their walk down the quay to the SS *Magnolia*.

'In what respect?'

'When he said he was a bit of a hothead. I mean, that's not the half of it, is it? Bell seemed very touchy to me.'

'Perhaps you'd be touchy if you'd spent all day shifting sacks of carbon black in a barge.'

'Maybe, sir, but he struck me as like the sort of bloke you see in the pub, always spoiling for a fight.'

'Well, as long as he didn't get one, we've preserved the King's Peace. He's denied seeing the knife and he's come up with an alibi for the night of the Danburys' burglary, which we shall have to check, of course.'

'Yes, sir. It's got me thinking again, though.'

'Well done, Peter. About what?'

'That thing DI Burton said about "old grudges". Do

you think there could've been some trouble between Ray Lambert and Charlie Bell to do with the past?'

'Are you thinking about that dock strike in 1912?'

'Yes. I mean, if Lambert was thirty-seven when he got married in 1931, he would've been about eighteen then. If he'd been a strike-breaker he certainly wouldn't see eye to eye with Bell.'

'But was Lambert working in the docks at that time?'

'I'm not sure. Len Potter said Ray left the docks and wasn't starred any more, so he must've been working there at some point after the war began, but we don't know when he started.'

'Potter said he started working in the docks himself just before the war, so it's possible he was there by 1912.'

'Not in the Royals, though – he said he was in the West India Docks, didn't he?'

'Yes, but I think that strike in 1912 involved all the London docks, not just the Royals. Either way, though, Charlie Bell can't have been mixed up in it – in 1912 he'd still have been an apprentice on the Clyde. So I don't think there'd be any enmity between him and Lambert that went back to the strike.'

'Still, it'd be interesting to know what Lambert did before he was called up, wouldn't it?'

'Indeed it would – we'll have to find out. But first we must see if Captain Munroe's on his ship.'

* * *

A member of the SS *Magnolia*'s crew met them at the top of the ladder and confirmed that the captain was on board, then took them up to the bridge to meet him. They found a man of about sixty with blue eyes, a creased brow and a full head of grey hair, and wearing a uniform that looked as though it had seen a good many years at this post. He was standing with legs apart, as if expecting the ship to roll, and gazing out over the dock with a pipe clenched between his teeth. He swung round when he heard them arrive and extended his hand in greeting.

'Welcome aboard the *Magnolia*,' he said when they had introduced themselves. 'Not the noblest vessel I've served on, but a reliable old girl. Built in 1919 in Ayrshire, she was, where I was born myself. We've been through a good few scrapes together, especially in the last year or so.'

'Yes, Mr Carlisle told us a little about your trips up and down the east coast.'

'Aye, a little alarming from time to time, but I take it all as it comes – I've been at sea for forty-six years now. It's the only life I know, and I don't know what I'll do when I have to stop. Mind you, this war might decide that before me – the way things are going, I'm quite likely to end up like Edward Kennedy.'

Jago did not recognise the name, and he realised that his face must have betrayed his ignorance.

'Captain Kennedy,' Munroe explained, 'of the *Rawalpindi*. Did you know her?'

'No, I'm afraid not.'

'Then you haven't spent enough time here in these docks. She was beautiful – a P&O liner on the India route. She was built on the Clyde in the twenties, but her home berth was here in the King George V Dock, and I believe a lot of her crew came from round here – West Ham men. When the war started she was converted into an armed merchant cruiser in the Royal Albert, which basically means they bolted a few old guns onto her and painted her grey, and last November she ran into two of the biggest German battleships up near Iceland. She didn't stand a chance, but Captain Kennedy chose to fight rather than surrender. He was sixty, same as I am now, and he went down with his ship. A terrible end for the *Rawalpindi*, but an honourable way for an old sea dog to go, don't you think?'

'I'm sure,' said Jago, 'but I hope that won't be the case for you.'

'We all have to go sometime – speaking of which, I assume you're here because of that poor fellow who was killed the other night. Stabbed in the back, I gather.'

'That's right. Is there anything you can tell us about the incident?'

'No, there isn't. I was ashore at the time, and Carlisle was in charge here. Whatever he's told you, that's all there is – I can't add anything, because I wasn't here.'

'There's something else I'd like to ask – was the ship carrying any whisky on your last run down here? As cargo, I mean.'

'No, not as far as I know.'

'As far as you know? Forgive me, but don't you know what you're carrying?'

'Yes and no. I mean, we know what the customer tells us we're carrying, but we don't open everything up to check. What I need to know is how much the cargo's worth, and is it safely stored. We're not really very interested in what we're carrying, as long as we're getting paid to carry it.'

'So would it be possible for you to be carrying a certain amount of cargo without knowing you had it?'

'How do you mean?'

'Well, supposing the dockers loaded a bit of extra cargo of their own, as you might say, and then discharged it at the other end of their voyage. Would you know about it?'

'The cargo's the mate's responsibility. It's his job to make sure everything's stowed properly and that we discharge it at the right port. So it's Carlisle again. I hope he's been helpful to you.'

'Oh, yes, he has.'

'Good – he's been in this game nearly as long as me. He can be a bit of a curmudgeonly old salt if the mood takes him, but there's nothing he doesn't know about seafaring. I've been working with him for seven years now, since I was appointed master of the *Magnolia* – I inherited him with the ship, you might say. He'd already been the mate for a couple of years. Knows the ship inside out – every nook and cranny.'

'He doesn't want to be master of his own ship, then?'

'Perhaps when he was younger he might have, but not now. I don't think he'd want the extra responsibility, especially in wartime. He could probably retire tomorrow if he chose to. He's no wife or children to support, as far as I know. He's got a very nice house in Erskine, on the Clyde, and another little place in a fishing village down in Fife. Better off than I am, I should think. I reckon he's just waiting until he's got enough tucked away in the bank and then he'll be off for a life of leisure. Not like me – I'd like to die in harness, as they say, keep working till I drop. All I want to know from you is how soon I can get my ship on its way – time is money, and my owners won't be pleased if I sit around in London for too long on an empty ship.'

'I'm sorry, Captain Munroe – at this stage I can't tell you. We need to complete our enquiries, but I can assure you we're working on it as fast as we can. We're well aware of how vital your work is, so we won't detain you any longer than is absolutely necessary.'

'Aye, well, that's all right then, isn't it?'

212

CHAPTER TWENTY-FOUR

Jago and Cradock navigated their way carefully along the bustling quayside back to where they had left the car.

'Where next, guv'nor?' said Cradock as Jago unlocked the door.

'I'd like to see if Major Danbury's at home,' said Jago. 'I want to find out a bit more about his past – there's something a touch mysterious about it, I think.'

'Righto. And talking of mysterious, sir, that thing that DI Burton said about the lascar, Jamal – do you think it's significant that he's gone missing?'

'I think it could be. If he's gone without permission, maybe he's running away from something. As Burton said, he's our witness, so it's possible someone's decided they don't want him around.'

'So where would a man like that go? He told us he doesn't know anyone here and said he always stays on the ship, so if that's true he won't have any friends who can take him in.'

'If he's frightened, though, he'll probably just run and then worry about where to spend the night later. There's plenty of places round here now that've been bombed but might still offer a bit of shelter to a man in his position. I'm inclined to check the West Ham Seamen's Mission first, though. It's only round the corner in Victoria Dock Road, and they'd give him a roof over his head if he went there – I expect all the seafarers know where it is. We'll call there on our way.'

They got into the car and drove to the dock gate, where they found PC Wilkinson standing outside the small police box, his hands clasped behind his back.

'We meet again,' said Jago. 'You've finished your nights, I see.'

'That's right, sir,' Wilkinson replied. 'I had a day off and now I'm starting a month on early turn.'

Jago glanced at his wristwatch. It showed the time as nearly half past four.

'On early turn, you say? Finishing a bit late then, aren't you?'

'Yes, sir, I should've been off two and a half hours ago, but a couple of the blokes on gate duty got bombed out of their homes last night and one of them's injured, so I've been told to stay on here until I can be relieved. Don't know when that'll be yet.'

'And I suppose that new war duty allowance the government's brought in applies to the PLA Police as much as to the Mets, does it?'

'That's right, sir, same for every constable in the

country – now they can make us work up to twelve hours a day without getting overtime or time off, and no right to a rest day once a week either. Seems a lot to give up for an extra three shillings a week, but it's not my place to complain.'

'So you've been here since six this morning, yes?'

'That's right, sir.'

'On the gate.'

'Yes, sir. I think I told you before we only have two types of duty in the dock police – gate duty or beat duty. I was on beat duty when I found that dead bloke, and now I'm on gate duty.'

'So as you said before, your job today is to stop people walking off with things they're not entitled to.'

'And walking in with things they shouldn't be walking in with too – we've had blokes coming through the gate with chisels and the like, so they can steal from the cargo. But mainly it's stopping them taking stuff out. We keep an eye on all the men as they leave. You get a bit of a nose for it – and my dad was a docker, so I knew some of the old tricks even before I started here. You learn what to look out for. For instance, if any of them's walking a bit funny or looks a bit bulkier than they should, we stop them and search them – to see if they're trying to sneak anything out.'

'And some of them do, I imagine?'

'Oh, yes. I've seen all sorts over the years – the bloke who seems to have put a few pounds on, but it turns out he's got a length of silk wound round himself, underneath his clothes, or the one with a bottle of

215

whisky slipped into his pocket. And then there's the dolly bags.'

'Dolly bags?'

'Yes, sir, that's what the dockers call 'em. To me and you it'd be a stocking they've borrowed off their missus. They fill it with anything useful – tea's a favourite – then slip it down inside their trouser leg and walk out bold as brass. We've had a few of them. Of course, since the war started we haven't had the time or the men to check everything as much as we used to, so there's probably a bit more slipping through, but we do our best.'

'But what about bigger items, or bigger quantities? The kind of thing you can't hide in your clothes.'

'Well, that's what we do the vehicle checks for. Before we let lorries or vans or what have you out through the gate we have a look at what they've got on them and we check their passes. Basically, if they're taking anything out that they didn't bring in, they've got to have a pass – and if they haven't, we detain them for enquiries and hand them over to the sergeant or the inspector.'

'How do you know what they brought in?'

'Well, we're not talking about the clothes they stand up in, but if a man brings in some cigarettes or tobacco, say, he has to book it in on his way in through the gate. It gets written down in the book, and we cross it off when he goes out again.'

'So what you're saying is you catch some of them, but some still get through.'

Wilkinson hesitated.

'The trouble is, sir, when it comes to nicking stuff, I reckon once a man's been working in the docks for a bit he's going to know every trick in the book – and a few more that aren't. Like I said, though, we do our best under the circumstances.'

'And you're here on the gate for the whole shift?'

'Yes, sir. I get my half-hour meal break, of course, and I'm supposed to be relieved for that, but it doesn't always happen. If I'm lucky I can slip into the box for a bite to eat. Some of them have a gas ring you can cook something up on, but otherwise it's a sandwich.'

'What about toilet breaks?'

'There's no toilet in this box – I'm supposed to wait till I'm off duty. If you can't manage that you have to nip round the back of one of the sheds.'

'Do all the gates have a police box?'

'Most of them do, sir, but there are some gates that are hardly ever opened, so there's no box on them.'

'Are any of the gates open at night?'

'Yes, sir. No. 11 Gate, down the far eastern end, on Manor Way, that's open round the clock, but most of them close about ten or ten-thirty at night. The ships generally stop working about six-thirty or seven in the evening. In peacetime the docks used to keep working all night if necessary, and officially that's still the case, although the blackout's made it a bit tricky.'

'Has anyone ever tried to bribe you to turn a blind eye on the gate and let them come into the docks?'

'Yes, sir, they have.'

'Tell me more.'

Again Wilkinson hesitated, as if wary of saying the wrong thing.

'Well, you know the way it is, sir. Some of the crew on the ships that come in here, they've been at sea for days, for weeks sometimes, and then they're stuck in the docks here, so some nights they try to get a certain type of lady to come back onto their ship with them. It's been known for men like that to offer an inducement to an officer on the gate.'

'And you've experienced this?'

'Yes, sir.'

'And did you let them in?'

'Of course not, sir. More than my job's worth, isn't it?'

'Yes, it is. And speaking of crew members, can you tell me whether a lascar's come through here while you've been on duty?'

'In or out, sir?'

'On his way out. Apparently he's gone missing. He's Indian and his name's Abdul Jamal.'

'No, not today, sir. Not through here, at least. But there's a lot of gates to these docks, and we can only do our best with the manpower available, can't we?'

Jago didn't answer him. He left, followed by Cradock, wondering what else might have got past PC Wilkinson.

CHAPTER TWENTY-FIVE

The Missions to Seamen hostel looked like a young new arrival from another world, a soaring art deco edifice that had landed among the elderly shops and commercial properties on the northern side of Victoria Dock Road. Completed only three years before the war started, it commanded a view over Custom House station on the opposite side of the road and the Royal Victoria Dock beyond. It also, Jago thought, probably presented another conspicuous landmark to approaching Luftwaffe bombers, like the Thames Refinery chimney. For whatever reason, it too seemed to have escaped damage so far.

Cradock opened the front entrance door for Jago and followed him into the lobby, where an ornate wall-mounted clock was showing just after five. Beneath it a tousle-headed man in his twenties was seated at a wooden desk. He got up and strode over to meet them, his face creasing into a broad smile.

'Can I help you?' he said.

'I hope so,' said Jago. 'There's a small matter you may be able to assist me with. My colleague and I are from West Ham police and we're looking for a man who's gone missing from a ship – he's not been seen since last night.'

'Is he in trouble?'

'No, but he's a witness in a case we're investigating, and I'm concerned for his safety. He's Indian, about forty, and his name's Abdul Jamal.'

'Abdul Jamal? Yes, there was a man here this morning who I think gave that name.'

'What did he want?'

'He was a lascar and he was trying to find the Coloured Men's Institute. He'd heard it wasn't in Tidal Basin Road any more, but didn't know where it had moved to.'

'It was demolished, wasn't it?'

'Yes, when Silvertown Way was built.'

'So where is it now?'

'I understand the Institute didn't have enough money to buy a new place, so now they're based at the Presbyterian Church Hall in Hack Road.'

'Did he say why he wanted to go to the Institute?'

'No, and I didn't ask him. I gave him directions and he left. I can only suggest you go down there and see if they can help you.'

'Thank you,' said Jago. 'We'll do that. Come along, Peter.'

With a nod of thanks he left the mission building, followed by Cradock, and they returned to the car.

'So what is this Institute?' asked Cradock as Jago started the engine.

'It supports the black and Asian population in West Ham,' Jago replied. 'It was set up sometime in the twenties I think, by a Mr Chunchie, a Muslim fellow from Ceylon who served in the army during the war and then became a Methodist minister. A good man, by all accounts, although I've never met him.'

'So a place where Jamal would get a sympathetic response?'

'Exactly. Now let's go.'

Jago put the car into gear and set off down Victoria Dock Road. Hack Road was little more than half a mile to the west, and within minutes they were outside the church hall.

The front door was open, and they went in. The hall was full of busy-looking people with no one obviously in charge, so Jago enquired of a passing woman, who offered to fetch the duty supervisor. Moments later she returned with a middle-aged, wiry-haired man, whom Jago would have described as of athletic build had it not been for his limp, which was clearly discernible as he crossed the room. He was dressed in old flannels and a knitted roll-top pullover and carrying a mop and bucket, which he deposited on the floor when he reached them.

'Good afternoon, gentlemen,' he said.

'Good afternoon,' said Jago. 'I'm Detective Inspector Jago, West Ham CID, and this is Detective Constable Cradock.'

The man nodded silently.

'Hibbert,' he replied. 'Ronald Hibbert. I work here. What can I do for you?'

'I wonder if you might be able to help us, Mr Hibbert. We're looking for a man called Abdul Jamal, a seaman. Is he here by any chance? We'd like to talk to him.'

'Talk to him about what?'

'About a case we're investigating. We think Mr Jamal may be able to assist us in our enquiries.'

Hibbert looked Jago and Cradock up and down slowly, as if sizing them up.

'We did have a man by that name earlier today,' he said, 'but he's not here now. And forgive me for asking, but is he likely to want to talk to you? You'll appreciate some of the men who come here have learnt to avoid people like you.'

'People like us?'

'Yes, white people. Policemen. I've been here a long time now, and I know what it's like. I came over from Jamaica in 1915 – volunteered for the British West Indies Regiment when the war started. When it finished I stayed on, but then there was all that unemployment, and a lot of people didn't want us here any more. Have you been a policeman long enough to remember the riots in Canning Town in 1919?'

'That was the year I joined the police, so I heard about them but wasn't actually involved.'

'Just as well, perhaps, if you were new to the job – it was a serious business. We don't want to see that sort of thing again round here. You may not know it, but there's more than a thousand Indians living in West Ham, and Canning Town's got the biggest population of black people in the London area – maybe in the whole country. Most people get along fine, but it only takes a few bigots to stir up trouble. I don't want trouble for Mr Jamal or for any other man who comes to this mission.'

'Quite right – I understand that.'

'Good. Now, you said he might be able to help you. How?'

'He's a witness to a crime committed in the docks. That's why we'd like to talk to him. But now he's gone missing from his ship, and I'm keen to know why he felt he must get away from it.'

'Isn't it always the same reason – the colour of his skin? Do you know what it's like for those lascars on British ships? They spend their days down in the boiler room, choking on coal dust, and as soon as they're not needed for shovelling they're put to work on the filthiest jobs in the engine room. And that's just in peacetime. In wartime, if the ship's torpedoed they'll be the first ones to drown.'

A picture of this scene began to crowd into Jago's mind; he shuddered as he tried to stop it.

'When they're in port,' Hibbert continued, 'the rest of the crew can go ashore, but the lascars have to stay on board and keep working. They're the lowest of the low.'

'I understand that. I'm concerned about him, because if he's jumped ship, he's put himself in a risky position –

and that means there must've been some very important reason for him to run away.'

'You think he could be in danger?'

'It's possible. That why I want to find him – I don't want him to come to any harm.'

'OK,' said Hibbert with a nod. 'So what do you want me to do if he comes back?'

'I'd be grateful if you could just ask him to get in touch with me as soon as possible – he can phone me at West Ham police station or leave me a message if I'm not there. The number's Maryland 1113.'

'I shall do that.'

'Thank you very much, Mr Hibbert, and goodbye.'

'Goodbye.'

Jago and Cradock left the church hall and returned to the car.

'I didn't know there'd been riots in Canning Town in 1919,' said Cradock.

'Well, a bit before your time, I suppose,' Jago replied. 'You'd have been just a kid.'

'What was it about?'

'I think it was like that man Hibbert said. People welcomed the Jamaicans when they came here to fight for us, but after the war there weren't enough jobs to go round and some of the locals resented them being here. A white man – a stevedore from the docks, I think – insulted a West Indian man on the street, and the result was a riot.'

'Who started it?'

'I don't know, but the thing that surprised a lot of people was that it was the white man who ended up before the police court. The magistrate tore him off a strip – he told him the Jamaicans were British subjects who'd served the Empire while men like him were just loafing around, and sentenced him to two months' hard labour.'

'Interesting,' said Cradock thoughtfully. 'Shame we didn't manage to find Jamal, though.'

'Yes,' Jago replied, taking a discreet glance at his watch. They had spent enough time chasing halfway round dockland for their elusive witness. 'But on the other hand if we get a move on we might just be able to get up to Danbury's house before the blackout. I didn't want to be delayed too long down here.'

Jago chose not to mention why he was reluctant to be delayed. If Cradock knew that he was hoping to meet Dorothy in London, there might be schoolboy humour to contend with. He started up the engine and pulled away.

When they arrived at The Cedars, it was Mrs Danbury who came to the door. Jago's assumption that the major and his wife had had no success in finding a replacement maid was confirmed when she asked him and Cradock to help her by drawing the blackout curtains downstairs while she did the upstairs rooms. Once that job was done, she sat down with them in the drawing room.

'I must apologise for my husband's absence, Inspector,' she said. 'He went out about half an hour ago to get the accumulator charged. We find we're listening to the wireless more these days than we used to – one really can't afford to miss the news – so the accumulator needs recharging more frequently. He was glad of the opportunity to take a little exercise too, but I'm sure he'll be back shortly. He likes to keep fit, you know – he always says he can't expect his men to take on any physical challenge that he can't do himself. I find keeping the garden under control is enough exercise for me. We had a little man who came to do it for us twice a week, but he's an air-raid warden now, so he's cut back, and as with so many things these days one now has to do it oneself. The garden's a little smaller than it was, of course – we had to get part of the lawn dug up to put in an Anderson shelter, which made me feel very sad, but we've hidden it away right at the far end and tried to make the best of it by planting flowers on top. Gardening's my one pleasure in life, really. If I had my way I'd live out in the countryside, but there are worse places than Forest Gate to live, I suppose.'

'Have you always lived here?' said Jago.

'No, I spent my childhood in Hampshire. Such a happy time. My father was an army officer and my mother had been a nurse. Not an ordinary nurse, of course – they tended to come from the lower classes. She was what they called a lady probationer. As you may know, they were the educated women who were expected to rise to positions of responsibility within the profession, and I'm sure she would have, had she not married my father. He was one of her patients. I was educated at home, and then when I grew up I decided to follow in her footsteps and trained as a nurse myself.'

'A noble calling.'

'Yes, but looking back now I think I was just a naive and idealistic girl. I see the same thing in my daughter. I thought it would be romantic to be a nurse and save people's lives, just as I fear she thinks it would be romantic to defend the innocent and send the guilty to the gallows. But after three years of making beds and changing dressings I came to my senses. I realised I didn't want to be a spinster in a starched apron for the rest of my life – I wanted to get married. So in 1908 I sailed out with the fishing fleet. My, what a long time ago that seems now, and how the world has—'

She broke off, glimpsing Cradock's puzzled expression and giving a short laugh which seemed to Jago to strike a slightly false note.

'Oh dear, Inspector,' she said. 'Your colleague looks a little confused.' She gave Cradock a maternal but patronising smile. 'When I say I sailed with the fishing fleet, I don't mean I set off in a Grimsby trawler to catch haddock for the nation's breakfast tables. It was just an expression people used in those days. It was the way they talked about young Englishwomen who went out to India to get married – a rather pejorative term, I might add, and flippant. For me and many others it was a very serious matter – it was our duty to the Empire. There was a shortage out there, you see – a shortage of European women for the British men to marry. Some of the men had married native women – can you imagine what that was doing to the future of the British race?'

Jago declined to respond to this question, sensing that the subject might be something of a hobby horse for Mrs Danbury.

'Whether in India or here,' she continued earnestly, 'I believe intelligent women have a duty to bear children for the future benefit of the nation, but also an even greater responsibility to marry well – to join their lives to men of quality and breeding, so that we'll produce the sort of stock that this country needs if it's to avoid sliding into degeneracy.'

It sounded to Jago as though she was repeating lines she'd heard in a speech.

'Are you interested in eugenics, Inspector?' she asked in the same tone.

'It's a little outside my remit,' he replied.

'Really?' She looked genuinely surprised. 'But your job is to suppress crime. I'd have thought it was very relevant to your work. The problem is obvious – working-class people seem incapable of bringing up children, so their sons grow up not as honest, hard-working men but as lawless thugs. Most criminals come from the lower classes, and those classes already outnumber us. They're breeding too fast, and if we don't do something, we'll be overwhelmed. It's as simple as that.'

Jago wasn't sure whether to be flattered to be included in Mrs Danbury's use of the term 'us'.

'You should come to one of our meetings, you know,'

she said. 'The West Ham Eugenics Society – we take an active interest in the creation of a healthy and hygienic society and we meet monthly. I've been telling people for the last ten years what this country needs – we must clear away all those dreadful slums, ensure pure and fresh food for everyone, and introduce voluntary sterilisation to prevent feeble-minded women becoming mothers. But what's actually happened? Nothing. The politicians have been too weak to do anything. The 1930s were a wasted decade – and now look where we are.'

Jago felt he was being drawn into deep water.

'So when you went to India in 1908,' he interjected in an attempt to rein the conversation back, 'was that how you met Major Danbury? The fishing fleet, I mean.'

'Yes, that's right. Of course, he wasn't a major then, just a subaltern, but clearly a man the commanding officer had his eye on for promotion. When I sailed out to India I was young and fearless – the only thing I was afraid of was not finding a husband and having to come back as what we used to call a "returned empty". But I needn't have worried. Not long after I'd arrived I went to a dance, and that's where I first met Royston. By the way, some people try to call him Roy, but he's most insistent on being called Royston – it's an old family name, you see. His great-grandfather, Sir Royston Blake-Danbury, was a Member of Parliament and made a fortune out of the railways, although sadly he lost it in the financial panic of 1847 and the family was never able to recover its former position. Nevertheless, I could see that Royston was a man of breeding. He was handsome and brave, and an outstanding sportsman. He was awarded the Military Cross during the last war, you know – so brave.'

'Yes, I noticed the medal ribbon when I met him in the docks.'

'And did you know he's the president of Wanstead Cricket Club? He's well known locally, and very respected. What I believe people call a pillar of society. As far as I was concerned, I could think of no better man to be my husband. It was love at first sight, you know. We married in 1909, and I can tell you it was a very different world in those days.' She gave a sigh of resignation. 'Back then it really was the British Empire. Everything seems to have gone to pot since then.'

She was interrupted by the sound of the front door slamming shut and a loud male voice in the hall. Shortly afterwards her husband entered the room.

'Ah, Jago,' he said, ignoring Cradock. 'Good evening.'

'I was just telling Inspector Jago how we met, dear, in India,' said his wife.

'Were you indeed?' Danbury replied, looking annoyed. 'Well, I'm sure these gentlemen haven't come here to find out about our courtship, my dear. They must be very busy.'

He turned back to Jago.

'So, Inspector, how can I help you?'

'Actually, Major Danbury,' said Jago, 'what your wife was telling us is relevant to our visit. You didn't mention that you'd lived in India.'

'You didn't ask.'

'Quite, but I'd be interested to know a little more about it. I gather you were serving as an officer in the Indian Army.'

Danbury looked anxiously at his watch.

'Do sit down, dear,' said Mrs Danbury. 'I'm sure the inspector wouldn't have come to talk to you if it wasn't very important.'

'Oh, very well,' he replied, and sat down opposite Jago and Cradock.

'Yes, Inspector,' he continued. 'I was in the Indian Army. I joined the Scinde Rifles in 1907, a fine regiment, and by the time I left after sixteen years' service I was a major. And speaking of rifles, I must ask – are you finished with Lambert's rifle yet? We're short, you know, and I could do with having it back.'

'I'm sorry, I can't let you have it yet. But tell me more about your regiment. I know that some of those Indian Army regiments did very distinguished service in France in the last war.'

'Indeed they did. In my own case we were in France for the first two years, then in Mesopotamia and finally in Palestine, before we got back to India at the end of the war. By that time we'd seen a lot of fighting, some of it very unpleasant.'

'And you say you left India after sixteen years, so that would be in 1923?'

'Yes, that's right. By then, of course, things were in turmoil. When the war ended, the government of India was in a terrible state financially, and the Indian Army had to make huge cuts in its costs. A lot of regiments were amalgamated to save money, including my own – we were merged with four others in 1922. Then the following year the government decided to begin the Indianisation programme.'

'Indianisation?'

'Yes, that's what they called it. The idea was to start giving proper king's commissions in some of the Indian regiments to Indians – before that, they could be officers, but only with viceroy's commissions, and no matter how senior their rank they were automatically inferior to the lowest-ranking British soldier. Actually, that's very similar to the position Home Guard commanders like me are in now – I may be in command of a platoon, but officially in relation to a regular army officer or even a regular NCO I only rank as a private. But anyway, to get back to this Indianisation idea, it meant now they'd be ranked equally with British officers and could even command them. All part of keeping the Indians happy and preparing them for self-government, I suppose, or some such nonsense, but I wasn't happy about it myself. Some of them were splendid chaps, but they weren't British, were they? In the first instance the government decided eight units of the Indian Army would be completely Indianised, and mine was one of them. I could see which way the wind was blowing, so I managed to pull a few strings and get a transfer to a British Army regiment, and came home. That's how my association with the Royal Docks began – in 1926 I found myself commanding armed military escorts for food convoys so they could get out of the docks.'

'That was during the General Strike, I assume?'

'Exactly. Those were difficult days. Did you ever hear about West Ham council and the submarines?'

'I'm not sure.'

'Well, the borough council was Labour-controlled, of course, as always, and during the General Strike it took the side of the striking dockers and threatened to cut off the electricity supply to the Royal Docks. That would have meant all the frozen meat in store there would be ruined, so the Admiralty sent in two submarines to sit by the entrance to the King George V Dock and use their generators to power the cold stores. Jolly resourceful, I thought.'

'I don't suppose the dockers saw it like that.'

'I don't suppose they did, but in those days the docks were a den of thieves. The strike was all got up by the Bolsheviks, I don't doubt, but the politics of it were of no interest to me. A soldier just follows his orders, doesn't he? Anyway, as time went by there were more cuts to the British defence budget, and a few years later I had to retire from the army. That was in 1929 – and then I started my job with the Port of London Authority.'

'Ah, yes, you mentioned that you'd worked in management for the PLA. What exactly was your job?'

'I was a traffic officer.'

'And what did that entail?'

'It's quite simple. Each transit shed in the dock has a shed foreman, who's the PLA member of staff in charge of that shed and its contents, and above him is the traffic officer, who's in charge of a number of sheds. In my case I was responsible for all the transit sheds on the south side of the Royal Albert Dock – ensuring security, seeing to it that everything ran smoothly and generally managing their operations. Not senior management, of course, but still an important role.'

'I'm sure. So I imagine you know the dock inside out.'

'Er, yes, I suppose you could say that.'

'I see. Now, I'd like to ask you one more question about the deceased man, Mr Lambert. I've been told that he served with you in India. Can you confirm that?'

'Served with me? Surely not – the man was a docker, wasn't he? He can't have been an officer.'

'No. I believe he was a private.'

'Then I definitely wouldn't have known him.'

'You sound very certain.'

'Of course I do. If he'd been in my regiment he wouldn't have been a private, he'd have been called a sepoy – and more to the point, he'd have been an Indian. In Indian Army regiments like mine the officers were all British, and the other ranks were all Indians.'

'I see. Perhaps he'd simply heard of you.'

'That's possible. He'd never said anything to that effect to me since I'd been his commanding officer in the Home Guard, though. Now, is that enough of my history, Inspector? I have things to do, you know.'

'There is just one more thing you might be able to help us with, if you don't mind.'

'Very well.'

Jago took out the knife and showed it to Danbury and his wife.

'Have you ever seen a knife like this before?'

Danbury took the knife by the handle and pulled it from its sheath to examine it.

'Yes, I've seen hundreds of the things. It's a *kirpan*, a ceremonial dagger that Sikhs carry.'

'And have you seen this one in particular?'

'I'm not sure, but it looks very like one I used to have myself.'

'Used to have?'

'Yes, mine was one of the things I lost when we were burgled.'

'And you, Mrs Danbury, do you recognise it?'

'Me? I'm not sure I could say. I've seen one like it lying around gathering dust for years, but I've never taken it out of that sheath thing. I don't like weapons – I think they're horrid.'

Jago took the knife back and replaced it in its sheath.

'Thank you,' he said. 'That will do for now.'

'You're welcome,' said Danbury, getting to his feet. 'My wife will show you out.'

With that, he strode out of the room. His wife smiled apologetically at them and showed them to the front door. Jago and Cradock returned to the car.

'Bit of a character, isn't he, sir?' said Cradock as they got in. 'Proper officer and gentleman.'

'Yes – I've met a lot like him in my time. A real old-fashioned military type, right down to his army moustache. Reminded me of Billy Bennett.'

'Is he that old comedian? I've heard of him.'

'That's the one. He's getting on a bit now, but he was very big on the music halls and famous for his moustache. Had a distinguished record in the army in the last war too, although he wasn't an officer. They used to be compulsory, you know.'

'What, moustaches?'

'Yes, it was in King's Regulations – all men in the army had to have their chin shaved but not their upper lip, so it was the bane of a young soldier's life – not old enough to grow convincing facial hair but forced to prove it to the whole world. Luckily for me they abolished that bit of the regulations in 1916, the year I was conscripted, so I never had to try. Anyway, when I saw Danbury, with his build and his magnificent tash, all I could think of was old Billy doing his act on the stage. They always used to bill him as Billy Bennett, "almost a gentleman".'

'You mean you think Danbury's just putting on an act?'

'Not at all. I'm sure Danbury's what he appears to be, every inch of him. It's just that in my experience there are gentlemen and gentlemen. I've met some who know they're real gentlemen – they're the sort who have a serviced apartment in the Albany and a place in the country. Danbury's an officer and a gentleman, as you say, and he has a maid – or at least had one – but the thing is, he lives in Forest Gate. In the Albany I think he'd be regarded as a lesser degree of gentleman.'

CHAPTER TWENTY-SIX

Jago dropped Cradock off on their way back to the station with the briefest of instructions for the following day and continued his journey alone. He was keen to get on the phone to the Savoy as soon as possible without being overheard, so went straight to the CID office and closed the door behind him. On his third time of trying to get through to the hotel he was successful and discovered that Dorothy was in and could see him. He left immediately.

It was dark when he arrived at the Savoy. He pushed through the revolving doors and into the front hall, where he asked a smartly dressed man at the reception desk to call her. Within minutes she came down to meet him.

'I thought you might like a quiet drink somewhere,' Jago began. He was nervous about how she might be feeling towards him and was relieved when she responded with a warm smile.

'You mean you know someplace in London where it's quiet after dark? What with your guns and their bombs, this must be the noisiest city on earth.'

'Sorry – figure of speech,' he replied. He could hear his own voice lightening.

'How about right here in the hotel?' she asked.

'That would be nice, but . . .' He didn't like the prospect of running into her American colleagues, especially if one of them was Philip Eliot. 'I know a little bar down the Strand that might be more private.'

'That sounds intriguing.'

Now he felt embarrassed. She could sense it, and laughed.

'Don't worry – only joking. A little bar down the Strand sounds perfect.'

The place in question was only about three minutes' walk away. They set off down the Strand to Southampton Street, then turned into Maiden Lane. The bar was about halfway down on the left. Inside, it was small and, as Jago had hoped, quiet.

He bought them drinks and they found a table in a secluded corner. Taking his seat, Jago pulled the newspaper he'd bought that morning from his coat pocket.

'Landslide victory for Roosevelt,' he said, pointing to the front-page headline. 'Is that good news?'

'It is for those who voted for him.'

'Are you being evasive?'

'Just discreet.'

He smiled.

'I would've voted for him.'

'But that's because you want America to come into the war. There's plenty of people in the States who don't.'

'So you voted for Willkie?'

She laughed.

'Let's just put it this way. You know there's a lot of American journalists living at the Savoy?'

'Yes.'

'Well, that includes the entire London bureau of the *New York Times*. They all moved into the hotel when their offices were destroyed in that terrible air raid on September seventh – you'll remember that one.'

'We all remember that one.'

'The night before last they organised a special presidential election party at the hotel and invited all the American correspondents. The place was packed.'

'And you were there?'

'Of course. The *Boston Post* people were all there. *The Times* boys rigged up a couple of voting booths, one marked Roosevelt and the other Willkie, so we could have our own little election. Then as the real voting figures started coming in from New York on the wire someone chalked them up on a blackboard.'

'How appropriate – the first news I saw of the result was on a blackboard too.'

'What?'

'Never mind – carry on.'

'A total of one hundred and ten reporters voted.'

'And the result?'

'Interestingly, in view of your newspaper headline, it was a landslide.'

'For Roosevelt?'

'When the votes were counted, the result of our little poll was Roosevelt one hundred and six votes, Willkie four votes.'

'So the journalists certainly know who they want.'

'Yes – but then they're living here and being bombed just like you are, so maybe they see things differently to, say, a farmer in the Midwest, where enemy bombers can't reach.'

'And I suspect you were one of those hundred and six Roosevelt supporters.'

Dorothy laughed again.

'The voting was secret, of course, but I guess statistically speaking, the odds are in favour of your assumption being correct.'

Jago found himself smiling: she seemed to be teasing him, and he loved it. There was an easy charm in her playful coyness, but he wondered whether this was a game only those without deep, dark secrets could play. He found this thought disturbing and tried to get back onto safer ground.

'So, what have you been doing today?' he asked airily.

'Writing a piece about the election result, of course – probably what every American journalist is doing today. Even Philip Eliot.'

She looked at him, waiting to see his response to the name.

'Ah, yes,' he said. 'I was going to mention that. Look, I'm sorry for the way I spoke to him. I was a bit harsh, I know, and I probably embarrassed you, so I apologise.'

'That's OK, John. I'm sure he didn't mind, and I wasn't embarrassed. I guess you were very tired.'

He was conscious that he had spoken only of his desire to apologise to her, not to Eliot, but he felt little inclination to apologise to her colleague. He didn't know whether she'd noticed that, but either way he was grateful to her for providing him with an excuse for his rudeness.

'Yes, I suppose I was,' he replied. 'But thank you.'

He paused briefly, still feeling awkward.

'And your article,' he resumed. 'What are you saying about the result?'

'Raising the obvious question, I guess. I'm reporting from London, so it's about what it'll mean for your country – "Britain stands alone: will America now stand with her?" That kind of thing.'

'Very interesting. When we were having lunch with your friend Eliot he said if Britain goes down, we all go down with you. What did he mean by that?'

'I think he meant this war isn't just about you – if Britain's defeated it'll leave America very vulnerable. Supposing Hitler wins and your navy falls into his hands, not to mention maybe Bermuda, or even Canada and Newfoundland too? Then there's the Pacific. Since Holland fell, Washington's concerned that Japan may have its eyes on the Dutch East Indies, with all that rubber and oil – that's why the president moved the Pacific Fleet out of California and based it in Pearl Harbour, Hawaii, to deter Japanese aggression. So what if Germany defeated you, and Japan decided to grab Singapore? If it ever comes to a fight, our air force would be no match for the Luftwaffe, and if we found ourselves up against the combined power of the German, Italian and Japanese navies – let alone your own fleet if Hitler had that too – the US Navy wouldn't stand a chance. The thing is, Roosevelt knows that if he can keep Britain afloat and fighting there's a chance America can stay out of the war.'

'And that's why people voted for him?'

'Willkie agreed with him that only Britain was holding back the German threat and so the USA should do everything it could to support you, short of going to war itself. But Roosevelt won because he was the one who'd seen all this coming and actually started rearming and giving help to Britain.'

'So what's in it for us now that Roosevelt's won?'

'Well, the important thing, I think, is it's not just a win for him but a defeat for the isolationists and the new America First Committee. They don't want a war and they don't want the USA to help Britain, so were backing Willkie. In practical terms it means there'll be more American warplanes for Britain and maybe more ships, possibly loans, and more cooperation with Britain against Japanese threats in the Far East. I think it means the mood's changing in America. Only the other day I read something that said the average American believes the USA will be in this war in a year's time. That wouldn't have been the case a year ago.'

'Something to look forward to, then.'

'A lot of people would say so, yes. But not everyone, so it remains to be seen.'

Dorothy looked around the bar.

'Still quiet in here, isn't it? I guess most people don't want to be sitting round in a bar in the blackout.'

'Yes, but I happen to know this place has a cellar, and if the sirens go, the landlord's happy for his customers to take shelter in it.'

'That's reassuring.'

She adjusted her position on the chair to get more comfortable and flashed him a smile.

'So, now it's your turn. What have you been doing today?'

'I've been here, there and everywhere, including talking to a man in the Home Guard this afternoon who's going to be very pleased, as will your friend Eliot – today's paper says the government's going to give men in the Home Guard proper army ranks. Apparently at least half the volunteers are veterans from the last war, and they can't get used to not having normal ranks. The government's promising to give them proper uniforms and weapons, too.'

'Not before time, judging by what Philip's told me.'

'There's been a lot of complaints about it, I gather, which is not surprising considering we're depending on the Home Guard to keep the German army at bay if they try to invade. I was talking to another volunteer today, and he said he'd been to some special training camp to learn guerrilla warfare techniques. Said he'd been trained by a fellow called Tom Wintringham, who'd been in the fighting in Spain, and I wondered whether you'd come across him when you were there.'

'Tom Wintringham? Oh, yes, everyone knew him. He was a communist – a member of the Communist Party here in Britain, although they expelled him a couple of years back for not toeing the line. When the civil war started he went out to Spain as a reporter for the *Daily Worker*, but then he joined in the fighting and ended up as commander of the British Battalion, part of the International Brigades fighting for the Republicans.'

'Sounds like an interesting man. Did you meet him?'

'Oh, yes. I met him when I was in Spain and I've seen him once or twice here in London – he's the *Daily Mirror*'s military correspondent now. I can't say I knew him, though – not as well as my friend Kitty did. She's an American war correspondent, a Massachusetts girl like me, and she was out in Spain. They became very close – so close that they eventually set up home together in London, and last I heard, he and his wife were getting divorced. I'm not surprised he ended up training your Home Guard in guerrilla warfare techniques – he had some very strong views on how you should fight a modern war if you want to win it.'

'Yes. But the man I was talking to said the powers that be probably weren't too keen on the idea of men being let loose on the streets with skills like that. In the wrong hands, that sort of knowledge could be very dangerous. I prefer my villains to rely on their fists – it helps to keep things on an even footing if we get into a bit of trouble with them.'

'You said the murder you're investigating was of a Home Guard man, didn't you? How's it going?'

'That's right. I'm not sure we've got very far with it yet. Somebody obviously had it in for him, but we don't know who. And I sometimes think even when we do get to the bottom of a business like this, have we really made anything better?'

'What do you mean?'

'It's to do with the last murder case I had. It seemed to me my pursuit of justice meant I destroyed a man's life – I didn't kill him, but I might as well have done. I separated him from his wife and ruined everything that was precious to him, and all because of the law. I'm supposed to be helping people, but it feels like I'm just bringing revenge and pain and death. That man's going to hate me now. You told me once you thought I was on the side of the angels, but I sometimes wonder whether I'm just the angel of vengeance. Maybe I'm as guilty as they are.'

'Don't be too hard on yourself, John. Isn't it supposed to be a good thing to temper justice with mercy? Maybe you should show yourself a bit of mercy.'

'Mercy? Mercy's a dangerous thing. Did you ever hear about Private Tandey?'

'I don't think so.'

'He was in the army in the Great War and won the Victoria Cross, but apparently one day he came across a wounded German soldier. Tandey could've killed him, but he decided to show him mercy instead and spared him. Later it turned out this soldier was the man we all know and love today as Adolf Hitler. So if Tandey had shot him instead, we'd have been spared all the trouble we've got now.'

'Is that a true story?'

'I don't know. It was in the newspaper.'

She laughed.

'In that case I'd better make no comment, but it's certainly a good story. Now let me try one on you – do you know that speech by Portia in *The Merchant of Venice*, where she talks about the quality of mercy?'

'I've seen the play – years ago at the Borough Theatre in Stratford High Street, before it was turned into a cinema. I can't remember much about it, though.'

'Well, I can go one better – I've played the part, although only when I was at school. I like it where she says mercy is an attribute of God himself – she says, "earthly power doth then show likest God's when mercy seasons justice". How about that? You could try seasoning your justice with mercy.'

Jago sat back in his chair. He wasn't sure whether he'd been reproved or encouraged. But when he saw the kindness in Dorothy's eyes, he decided he must take it as the challenge of a friend who cared about him – perhaps someone to whom he mattered.

CHAPTER TWENTY-SEVEN

When Jago walked through the door of West Ham police station on Friday morning he found Station Sergeant Tompkins at the front desk, leafing through a newspaper.

'Catching up with today's news, Frank?' he enquired.

Tompkins gave what sounded like a derisive snort.

'Wish I were. It's been so busy in here I'm having a job catching up with yesterday's. It says they still reckon Hitler could invade us. I thought that was all over and done with, but it says here the RAF's been bombing invasion bases and barges on the French coast again. What do you make of that?'

'I don't know. I've seen enough barges down in the Royal Docks to last me a lifetime, without having a load of German ones chugging across the Channel full of stormtroopers.'

'You've seen a fair bit of the Home Guard of late too, haven't you? How do you rate their chances?'

'No comment.'

Tompkins folded the newspaper and stowed it away, then pulled out a small cardboard box and rattled it at him.

'What's that, Frank?' said Jago. 'Collecting for the Police Benevolent Fund?'

'No, this is my shrapnel box. The Ministry of Supply says any old bits of anti-aircraft shell are useful scrap metal, and we're all supposed to have a box at work to collect it in. So next time you see some street urchin picking up bits for his shrapnel collection, confiscate it and bring it in here for me.'

'You must be joking.'

'Course I am. It's true, though – hot off the press, as you might've said in your journalistic youth. Personally, I think the average police officer's got enough on his plate already without scouring the streets for scrap metal. Mind you, when I tried it on Mr Soper he said he'd certainly do his best. Very devoted to his duty is Mr Soper.'

'Now, now, Frank.'

'Sorry, sir. But you know what I mean.'

'Mr Soper has many and varied duties of which we know nothing, and he must fulfil them as he sees fit.'

'Yes, sir, and I'm sure whatever duties he spends all his time on in that office must be very important.'

'But we won't discuss them here, will we, Frank?'

'Oh, no, sir. Mum's the word.' He raised a theatrical finger to his lips. 'Walls have ears.'

Jago laughed.

'You're the second person this week to say that to me – the propaganda campaign must be working.'

'Oh, yes, and who was the other person? Mr Soper?'

'Actually it was a young corporal in the Royal Marines I was talking to only yesterday – he's the stepson of the murdered man. Lightfoot, he was called. Sounds more like a name for a ballroom dancer, not a marine, but he looked tough enough to be one.'

'A ballroom dancer?'

'No, a marine. You want to be careful, Frank. If anyone hears you talking like that, they'll think you're losing your marbles and force you back into retirement.'

'Fine by me, sir, fine by me.'

Tompkins paused, then chuckled to himself.

'Remember that Lightfoot we had in here a few years ago? I remember nicking him. Light fingers would've been a better name for him, I remember thinking – he was a regular little tea leaf.'

Jago tried to recall a thief called Lightfoot passing through their hands, but nothing came to mind.

'Not sure I remember that one, Frank. When was it?'

'Oh, it must've been three or four years ago, 1936 or '37, I should think. Tommy Lightfoot. Just a lad, he was. Of course, that might've been when you were away seconded to the Special Branch in sunnier climes, mightn't it. When was that?'

'That was in thirty-six.'

'That must be it, then. You were enjoying yourself out in France or Spain or wherever it was with those arms smugglers in the Civil War and missing all the real action back here.'

'Yes. So what was he nicked for?'

'Oh, just general thieving – he'd been pinching bits and pieces off the stalls in Rathbone Market, and one of the stallholders caught him. He'd given young Tommy a bit of correction before we got to the scene too, as I recall. A lovely shiner the poor lad had – a proper black eye.'

'Do you remember how old he was?'

'Yes, he was seventeen – I remember because he was just too old for the juvenile court. He'd been at it since he was a kid, by all accounts, but this was the first time anyone had actually caught him red-handed.'

'What happened to him, then?'

'Little blighter got away with it, didn't he? First offence, see. He was bound over to be of good behaviour and put on probation – for two years, if memory serves me right.'

'Hmm . . . no record, then,' said Jago, wondering whether the young thief had changed his ways and decided on a career in the Royal Marines instead.

'By the way, sir, talking of marines has just reminded me – I took a call first thing this morning from another seafarer, a Mr Carlisle. He said you knew who he was, and he had a message for you. Said he'd been talking to you about someone he had a drink with on a ship down in the Albert Dock. Ring a bell, does it?'

'Yes. What did he say?'

'He said he wanted to withdraw it. Said it wasn't true.'

250

'So he didn't have a drink with that man after all?'

'That's what he said.'

'He was lying, then.'

'Funnily enough, that's what I said to him. Not as blunt as that, of course, but I asked him did he mean he'd been mistaken, or did he mean he'd not told you the truth. He said it wasn't the truth. "I lied to him," he said. Now what do you make of that?'

'I'm not sure, Frank. Not sure at all.'

CHAPTER TWENTY-EIGHT

Jago stepped into the CID office and noticed two things. One was that the clock showed the time was ten to nine, and the other was that Cradock was seated at his desk, but not in the usual manner. To his surprise the usually energetic constable had his head slumped on his folded arms, and the sound coming from him was on the point of effecting a glissando from heavy breathing to a full-blown snore. Jago shut the office door a little more noisily than usual, and the slumbering head rose from the desk. Cradock peered at him through bleary eyes and then straightened up in a flash.

'Sorry, sir. Good morning, sir.'

'Good morning, Peter. A little early for an afternoon nap, isn't it?'

'Yes, sir. Very sorry, but it was a bad night. Those ack-ack guns were at it like hammer and tongs. Thought I'd try to get a spot of shut-eye before you arrived.'

'In that case I'm sorry to disturb your beauty sleep,

but I'm afraid we have things to do. I want to go and see Mrs Lambert.'

Cradock tried to stifle a protracted yawn.

'Mrs Lambert? Right . . . To see whether she'll spill the beans about her hubby hitting her?'

'Exactly. And one or two other matters as well. Let's go.'

Jago strode out to the car in the chilly November sunlight, with Cradock trailing behind him. As they set off, the motion of the Riley seemed to make his passenger drowsy again, so Jago left him in peace to wake up in his own time. Eventually Cradock sat up in the seat, rubbed his eyes and looked round with what Jago thought of as the eagerness of the young.

'Firing on all cylinders now, guv'nor,' he said cheerily. 'That little nap must've done the trick.'

'Good,' said Jago. 'So perhaps we can turn our thoughts to the day's work. First I need to tell you what I've just heard from Frank Tompkins. He says Carlisle's called in to withdraw what he said about having a drink with Charlie Bell on the *Magnolia* on Monday night. It seems Carlisle says he lied to us.'

'Blimey, that's a turn-up for the book, isn't it, sir? I mean, when he confirmed Bell's story about being invited onto the ship for a drink, that more or less put Bell in the clear, didn't it?'

'More or less, although Anderson reckons the murder occurred between half past two and half past four in the morning, so if Bell did need an alibi, saying that he was with Carlisle for half an hour or so at about four o'clock isn't exactly cast iron, is it? And anyway, why would Bell want to kill Lambert?'

'I don't know. Maybe they were both mixed up with those whisky thefts in Scotland. Bell comes from up that way, doesn't he? Or maybe they just fell out over something, or Bell wanted to get rid of Lambert for some reason we don't know. He certainly had the opportunity. They were patrolling together, just the two of them in the blackout, and Bell was the last person with Lambert before he was murdered. Either way, if Carlisle's gone back on what he told us, that makes Bell more of a suspect than he was.'

'Do you think Carlisle gave that alibi under duress?'

'You mean Bell forced him to cover up for him?' He paused to give the idea consideration. 'Well, he's not the kind of bloke you'd want to pick a fight with, is he? But that makes it all the more surprising for Carlisle to change his mind now – it's not going to go down well with our Charlie, is it?'

Ahead of them, a police constable on point duty at the junction with Barking Road raised his right hand to stop them. Jago slowed the car to a halt and drummed his fingers on the steering wheel while they waited.

'Supposing Carlisle withdrew the alibi because he wanted to incriminate Bell?' he said as the traffic passed in front of them.

'Why would he want to do that?' said Cradock.

'What do you think?'

'Well, I suppose in theory it could be to divert suspicion from himself, but there's no more reason to think Carlisle might've wanted to kill Lambert than to think Bell did.'

'So what if it was Carlisle rather than Bell who was involved in the whisky thefts with Lambert?'

'Then Carlisle might've had some kind of motive for murdering Lambert. Maybe he could've slipped off the ship somehow without Bell noticing, killed Lambert, then got back on board in time for Bell not to suspect anything. Would that be possible?'

The policeman had now stopped the Barking Road traffic in turn and waved them on across the junction.

'To quote you, Peter – in theory,' said Jago as the car moved off. 'But then it'd be Carlisle who needed the alibi, so why destroy it? It's also possible – in theory – that Bell and Carlisle were in cahoots and concocted the alibi between them, but now for some reason they've fallen out. It's still not clear, though. As things stand I can't see a strong reason why either of them should've killed Lambert, let alone both of them.'

'I think I'm getting a headache, sir,' said Cradock.

'All right, Peter, we'd better leave it at that until we have more evidence. We need to ask Carlisle why he changed his mind and whether Bell put pressure on him to provide an alibi. But that may have to wait till tomorrow – first we need to see Brenda Lambert.'

When they reached Saville Road they found Brenda Lambert at home. She welcomed them in with a smile and led them through to the kitchen.

'Cup of tea?' she said, gesturing towards the range. 'Kettle's on.'

'No, thank you,' said Jago. 'We won't be long.'

'Well, at least take the weight off your feet. Here you are.'

She moved a pile of ironing off one of the chairs and motioned them to sit down. Compared to the last time they'd seen her, she seemed quite chatty, perhaps already adjusting to her husband's death. Jago wondered whether that was due to her temperament or just to the fact that for everyone who lived in this area death had become a more frequent visitor in the last two months.

'Thank you,' he said, taking a seat. 'I'm glad we've managed to catch you in, Mrs Lambert – I wasn't sure whether this was one of your cleaning days.'

'No, I do it Tuesdays and Thursdays, and sometimes a bit extra on Saturdays if Mrs Danbury asks me.'

'Mrs Danbury? Would that be Mrs Louise Danbury by any chance?'

'Yes, that's right, the major's wife. He's in charge of the Home Guard mob that Ray was part of. She sometimes wants me to do a bit of clearing up if they've got guests coming for the weekend or something special like that. Mostly it's just sweeping and dusting, though, that sort of thing. Mind you, there's plenty of dusting to do in their place – it's a big house, and full of old junk.'

'How did you come to be cleaning for Mrs Danbury?'

'Well, I think the major asked his men if they knew

anyone looking for a few hours a week cleaning. Ray told me he'd said I could do it, and that pal of his, Charlie, he said his landlady might be interested, but then it turned out she couldn't do the time Mrs D wanted.'

'Would that be Charlie Bell?'

'That's right. His landlady's called Mavis Higgs. Have you met her?'

'Yes, I have.'

She grinned at some unspoken thought.

'I say landlady, and I suppose that's right, but I reckon she's a bit more than just his landlady. Very fond of Charlie, she is. I ran into her yesterday down the shops, and she was full of it. Charlie this, Charlie that, all about how he gives her money to help with her bills, helps round the house, even gives her little presents. Anything she wants, he says you just name it and I'll get it for you. Nick it from the docks, more like – that's what I reckon. Ray always said Charlie was a light-fingered – well, I won't tell you exactly what he called him, but he reckoned Charlie didn't mind helping himself to stuff he took a fancy to. And if he's taken a fancy to that Mavis, I wouldn't be surprised if he kept her supplied with a bit of this and that without necessarily going to all the inconvenience of paying for it, if you know what I mean.'

'Did your husband ever talk about Major Danbury?'

'A bit, yes, but only the usual kind of stuff. You know, moaning about him from time to time.'

'Why was that?'

'I don't know. I think he reckoned the major was

a – what do you call it? A stuffed shirt, that's it – pulling the men up if their collars weren't straight or their boots weren't shiny enough. Bit of a cheek, I think, considering they're all volunteers. I don't think Ray thought much of him, but then some of those old military gents can be a bit funny, can't they? Probably a bit too posh for Ray's liking. His wife's the same. Full of airs and graces, you know, talks like Lady Muck, walks around with her nose in the air, but watches me like a hawk and won't pay a penny more than four bob a week. Likes to live like a toff, but I reckon she hasn't got two ha'pennies to rub together. They're all show, her sort. Him too, I wouldn't be surprised. Mind you, I think some married couples deserve each other. Don't you? Are you married, Inspector?'

'No, I'm not. Now, there's a small point I'd like to check with you about your husband, if you don't mind. I recall you saying Mr Lambert had been an ordinary docker before he became a tally clerk, but do you happen to know whether he worked in the docks before the last war?'

'Now you come to ask, I'm not sure we ever discussed it. Apart from saying he'd been in the army for a bit in the war, he only ever talked about being a docker, so I've always assumed he'd been a docker all his life.'

'So might he have been working in the docks by 1912?'

'Well, he'd have been, what, eighteen then, so he could well've been. But I couldn't tell you for certain. Len might know, though – they were pals when they were kids.'

'Thank you,' said Jago, pausing for a moment. 'Mrs Lambert, there's something else I'd like to ask you about your husband, on a slightly more delicate matter.'

She looked at him, a new wariness clouding her expression.

'Oh, yes? What's that?'

'I'm sorry to intrude on private matters, but it's about his relationship with you.'

'Somebody's been telling tales, have they? Now look, Inspector – I mean, we had our ups and downs, and I'm not saying my Ray was perfect. Far from it, in fact, but . . .'

Her voice petered out into silence.

'It's been suggested to me that your husband was quite a heavy drinker,' said Jago.

'Oh, so you know that, then,' she replied. 'All right. Yes, it's true. To be honest, I think it was just a habit he'd got into. He liked a few pints, but the spirits were worse. He always seemed to have a couple of bottles on the go – rum, brandy, whisky. Never seemed to run out. It was the spirits that really got him going.'

'Got him going? What exactly do you mean by that, Mrs Lambert?'

'Well, I mean he used to get a bit cross. Not like his real self at all. It wasn't him – it was just the drink.'

'Was he ever violent towards you?'

Jago looked into her eyes and saw only a dull and unresponsive sadness.

'I suppose you know about that too,' she said, hope draining from her voice. 'Yes, he used to hit me sometimes. Marriage doesn't always work out the way we think it will, does it? I thought it was all going to be so much better than before. I thought he'd love me, but now I sometimes wonder whether what he wanted was just a skivvy to clear up after him, not a wife. We never learn, do we? We ought to take a look at other people's marriages before we get too keen on tying the knot ourselves. There's so many youngsters rushing into getting wed these days, what with the war and everything. I only hope my Tom doesn't make that mistake.'

'Does he have any plans?'

'None that he's told me of. He's sweet on that girl of Doris's, though, that Maureen. Have you met her?'

'Yes, but only briefly.'

'She's always seemed a very nice girl to me, but she's just a kid. I hope it's not the uniform that's taken her fancy. You know what these girls are like. But that's all by the by, isn't it? And anyway, who am I to talk? I'm not exactly a great example when it comes to choosing husbands, am I? Who told you about Ray hitting me?'

'Someone suggested it. That's all I can say.'

'All right. Anyway, it was my own fault, I suppose. It seemed like all I had to do was say the wrong thing to Ray or do something not quite the way he liked it, and it'd set him off. It's just the way men are. There's nothing you can do about it, is there?'

Jago left her question unanswered.

'I'm sorry, Mrs Lambert. There's just one last thing I'd like to ask you. We've also been told that after the Great War Mr Lambert's army service took him to India. Can you confirm that?'

'India? No, I didn't know that. All I know is that he was in the army and didn't want to talk about it. I assumed he must've come out when the war finished, but he never said, and I never asked him. That was long before I knew him, of course.'

'Yes. Did he ever tell you where he served, or what regiment or corps he was in?'

'No. He never said anything about it – but then I get the impression most men who were in it have never really spoken about it. At least, maybe they talk to their old pals, but not their wives or families.'

'Do you know who any of those old friends of your husband are?'

'No, I don't think I know any of his mates from those days. But that's the way it is with a lot of marriages, isn't it? The man lives in his man's world, and his wife in her women's world, and they don't cross over much. Sad, really, isn't it?'

CHAPTER TWENTY-NINE

When the front door of Brenda Lambert's house clicked shut behind the two detectives, Jago stood on the pavement for a moment, contemplating the superstructure of the freighter that towered what seemed like only feet away on the other side of the dock fence.

'I wouldn't like to live here,' he said, 'not with that on my doorstep. I should think any bomber pilot would be thrilled to hit a monster like that. It must be like having Winston Churchill camping in your back yard – you'd be a magnet for every enemy plane in the sky.'

'Too true,' Cradock agreed. 'And I don't suppose they're going to be too careful which side of the fence their bombs drop.'

'Of course not – it's impossible. The best bomb aimer in the world couldn't guarantee that sort of accuracy.'

'Someone told me the Americans have made a bomb sight that means you can aim a bomb into a barrel from ten thousand feet up. It'd be good if we could get some of those for our planes.'

'Yes, I've read about that, but apparently the Americans are worried about it falling into enemy hands, so even if such a miracle machine exists, which I doubt, we're not going to see it over here for a while.'

'It'll be a sight for sore eyes when we do, though, sir, won't it?' said Cradock, beaming at his own cleverness.

'I dare say,' Jago replied with such forbearance as he could muster. 'But if you can just bring yourself back down to earth, there are one or two matters a little closer to home that we must deal with.'

'Yes, sir. What's next then?'

Jago glanced at his watch.

'We've got Mr Morris the butcher coming to the station at two o'clock, so we need to be back by then, but we've got time to fit in one or two other things before that. I'm curious about this business of whether Ray Lambert and Major Danbury served together in India – Len Potter maintains that they did, but Danbury's positive they didn't.'

'Mrs Lambert doesn't know anything about it either, so does that make Potter the odd man out?'

'I think we need to dig a bit deeper with both of those gentlemen, and since Potter's the closer of the two, I think we'll start with him.'

They drove to Barge House Road and knocked on the door. Len Potter opened it.

'Oh, it's you two again, is it?' he said. 'If it's the missus you want, she's out playing on her bus.'

'Actually, it's you we'd like a quick word with, Mr

Potter. Can we come in?'

'Help yourselves,' said Potter, letting them into the house. 'It looks like you're in luck and I'm not.'

'What do you mean?'

'Work's still thin on the ground – I didn't get taken on this morning, so it's hard cheese for me, but luckily for you it means I'm in and you haven't wasted your journey.'

'Ah, I see. I'm sorry to hear about the work.'

'Don't worry – you get used to it. So how can I help you now?'

'It's about Major Danbury. I'm wondering whether you can help us clear up an apparent contradiction between what you told us and what he's said. We've spoken to him since we last saw you, and he has no recollection of serving with Mr Lambert or knowing him in India.'

'Well, that's as may be, but Ray certainly mentioned him. He didn't speak too kindly of him, either. Made him sound like a nasty piece of work – said he'd pay for it one day.'

'Who'd pay for what?'

'Danbury would, but for what, I don't know.'

'This still doesn't help us to establish whether Mr Lambert and Major Danbury actually knew each other.'

'I know. I'm sorry, but there's not much I can do about that. All I can say is that's the impression I got from the way Ray used to talk about him.'

'What else did Mr Lambert tell you about Major Danbury?'

'Not a lot, really. I got the feeling he thought Danbury

was a bit of a Colonel Blimp – you know, he huffed and puffed, and he talked a lot about the old days, but at least he was doing his bit. It can't be fun for any of them at their age creeping round the docks in the middle of the night while the Germans are trying to bomb us to kingdom come, can it? Even the major could probably be sitting tight at home all night with a bottle of gin for company – or even his wife. But no, he's out there with the rest of them, doing his bit for king and country. You can't say fairer than that, can you?'

'And what can you tell me about Mr Lambert's time in the army, when he was in India?'

'Well, just one or two stories he told me, really. I remember him saying people thought he must've had a cushy time of it, being out in India, but it wasn't all polo and cocktail parties for the likes of him out there – in fact, it got worse after the war ended than it was when the war was on. He was in the Punjab, and he said they had some very sticky moments. The thing is, everything was in a bit of a pickle in India by then. The Indian Army troops who'd been fighting for us all over the place came home and were getting demobbed, and something like half of them were from the Punjab, and that's where there was all sorts of trouble brewing. The nationalists – Gandhi and all that mob – didn't want to be ruled by us any more.'

'And still don't, from what I understand of it.'

'That's right. Anyway, he said eventually there was some kind of riot by the natives in 1919, and it got a bit out of hand. A scandal, apparently. It was in a place called Amritsar, I think, in a sort of public square – a big open space with buildings on three sides. Some brigadier-general marched in with a load of troops and opened fire on the crowd without warning – they say hundreds of people were killed, and it wasn't just political agitators, it was women and children and passers-by too.'

'Did he see this for himself?'

'Not exactly, but he was there. He was stationed at the garrison in Lahore, which I think he said is the capital of Punjab. He was an armoured car driver, and this brigadier-general trying to quieten the mob down ordered a couple of armoured cars up to the square too. One was our Ray's. Only trouble was, to get there they had to go down these alleys, but they were too narrow, so the cars couldn't get through. Mind you, Ray reckoned that was a blessing, because later on he heard that the brigadier-general was planning to get those armoured cars to fire on the crowd with their machine guns, and Ray said he could never have slept again if he'd known he'd shot innocent civilians.'

'So Mr Lambert wasn't involved in the shooting himself?'

'No. But he said he saw some of it. There was one bloke, he told me, a soldier, who came up the alley away from the square, pushing some Indian civilian in front of him and shouting at him. When he got clear of the square he stopped, threw the man up against a wall, then pulled out a pistol and shot him in the head, just like that. Then he marched straight off back to the square.'

'And Mr Lambert saw all this with his own eyes?'

'Yes, he swore to me what he told me was exactly what he'd seen.'

'Did he know who the men were?'

'No. He just said it was a soldier and an Indian.'

'Did he report the incident?'

'Report it? No. He was in the army, wasn't he? You don't go round stirring up trouble in the army, do you? You don't get very far doing that. No, you keep your head down. He said he didn't let on to anyone – I was the only person he'd ever told about it.'

'And have you told anyone else?'

'No. He made me swear not to, and I didn't. But now he's been murdered, well, I think you ought to know, that's all. I mean, somebody obviously wanted to do him in, didn't they?'

'Thank you, Mr Potter, you've been most helpful. By the way, does Mrs Lambert know all this?'

'I don't think she does. What I've just told you, that's about the only thing he ever said to me about the war. Apart from that, I don't think he ever talked about it, not even to her.'

'I see. And just one last question. You said you and Mr Lambert had been friends when you were boys and went to school together. You mentioned that Mr Lambert was called up towards the end of the war because he'd left a starred job in the docks, but you didn't say when he started working there, so I'm just wondering – did Mr Lambert work in the docks before the last war?'

'Yes, he did.'

'Was that in the Royal Docks?'

'No. It was in the West India Docks, same as me. Why?'

'Just trying to complete the picture, Mr Potter, that's all. Thank you for your assistance.'

CHAPTER THIRTY

'That was interesting,' said Jago once they'd taken their leave of Potter and started motoring back towards the north of the borough.

'That stuff about India, you mean?' said Cradock.

'Yes. It was all hearsay, of course, so it's not proper evidence, but still interesting. Unfortunately it doesn't get us any further forward regarding whether Danbury and Lambert knew each other, but what Potter said about the rioting in India got me thinking about that bit of paper again.'

'The paper with the name written on it?'

'Exactly. Dayabir Singh. Whoever he is, I'm wondering if there's some sort of connection. That lascar Abdul Jamal said men called Singh are Sikhs, so Dayabir Singh's a Sikh, and Sikhs are a religious majority in the Punjab, and that's where the rioting was. Potter said a lot of Indian Army soldiers who fought for us in the Great War came from the Punjab, so most of them would've likely been Sikhs, if not all.'

'You mean Dayabir Singh might've been a soldier?'

'It's possible. I remember when I was in the army they used to call the Sikhs one of India's martial races, which meant they made good soldiers. And there's something else – Potter's just told us the Punjab is where Ray Lambert was stationed when he was a soldier.'

'And he was mixed up in that riot, where all those Indian people were killed. Do you think this Dayabir Singh might've known Lambert was there and thought he was involved in shooting the Indians, and killed him because of that? I mean, Potter did say somebody wanted to do him in.'

'Or maybe Lambert was carrying that name because Dayabir Singh had threatened him. But even if that were the case, it wouldn't necessarily mean Singh killed Lambert himself.'

'He got someone else to do it, you mean?'

'It's a possibility. But if what Lambert told Potter was true, he was shut up in his armoured car at the time, so he wasn't actually harming any of the people who were rioting.'

'Maybe he just said that to cover himself. And anyway, it sounds as though he would've done it if he'd been ordered to by the commanding officer.'

'That can only be a matter of speculation, I think.'

'I suppose so, yes. But talking of officers, sir, if Lambert served with Major Danbury in India, suppose Danbury was there too – in that place where the riots were, I mean.'

'Amritsar.'

'Yes, that's it. What if Danbury was the officer who gave the order to fire?'

'No. Potter said that was a brigadier-general, but Danbury said he came out of the army as a major. It's possible he could've held a much higher temporary rank during the war – lots of men did – and brigadier-general was always a temporary rank in those days, but my recollection is that when the War Office abolished it after the war they said men who'd held the rank in wartime were entitled to use it when they retired. So given how keen he is to be addressed as Major, I can't imagine him declining to be known as Brigadier-General.'

'All right, then, what if he was Lambert's commanding officer? That would've been more like a captain or major, wouldn't it?'

'Yes, but Danbury's already said he couldn't have been, because he was in the Indian Army, where all the privates were Indian. Lambert must've been serving in a British Army regiment stationed in India, which is totally different to the Indian Army.'

'All right, so supposing it was Dayabir Singh who was serving under Danbury, not Lambert?'

'Now that's an interesting thought. Danbury said the name meant nothing to him, but perhaps we should ask the gallant major again next time we see him.'

Cradock nodded his head in agreement and lapsed into a silence which Jago hoped meant he was reflecting on what they had just discussed rather than simply recovering from the mental exertion.

Half an hour later they pulled up outside the Danburys' house and got out of the car. Jago stretched his legs before approaching the front door of The Cedars, which this time was opened by Evelyn Danbury.

'Good morning, Miss Danbury,' he said. 'Not at the university this morning?'

'No,' she said as she let them in. 'It was hit in the air raid last night, so when I got there this morning I discovered my lectures had been cancelled. I've only just got back.'

'Actually, it's your father I was hoping to speak to.'

'I see. I'm afraid he's out – he's at the Home Guard HQ. He seems to be busier now he's retired than he ever was before. What did you want to know about?'

'About his time in India. He mentioned it last time we saw him, and I was interested in knowing a little more about it.'

'I doubt whether I can help you with that, although I was born there, you know. I believe my father returned from Palestine or somewhere like that in the Middle East when the Great War ended, and I was born, er, about a year later.'

For a moment Jago expected her to blush, but she merely gave him an easy smile.

'So I was only four when we left,' she continued, 'and I remember hardly anything about it, which is a shame, as it must have been a very romantic place to live.'

'Quite. And a welcome respite for your father,

272

after four years of war.'

'I dare say. My father's not a very communicative man, you know. He's never spoken about the war, so I know virtually nothing of his experiences.'

'That's not uncommon. And now he's lost a man from his Home Guard platoon. Has that been difficult for him?'

'I don't think so. I suppose he got used to losing men during the war.'

'Has he said anything about the man who's been killed?'

'He said his name was Lambert, that's all.'

'Your mother said she hadn't come across Mr Lambert at the mobile canteen and didn't know him, but I wonder whether you had. Did you know him?'

'Know him? No, I can't say I knew him, but I knew who he was.'

'What do you mean?'

'I mean I'd probably seen him around at the mobile canteen, but it was only on Monday evening that I found out who he was, and it wasn't a pleasant experience.'

'Can you tell me more?'

'Certainly. Until that evening he was just one of the usual Home Guard men I serve cups of tea to, and to be quite honest they all look the same to me. It's dark, of course, and quite a few of them are wearing the same type of coat and tin helmet. Trying to look like soldiers, I suppose, but a lot of them are probably twice as old as me. I don't know their names, but I find it interesting to chat with them. They're all dock workers, of course, and the sort of people I would never come across socially in the normal course of life, but if I end up specialising in criminal law they're probably the class of person I'll find myself dealing with in court. So it's quite useful to talk to them and listen to their conversation – it gives me an insight into how that sort of person thinks.'

'And Mr Lambert? Did you chat with him?'

'Not exactly. To tell you the truth, he seemed to be one of the least pleasant of the lot. A rather odious fellow, from what I could see of him. He had a kind of swagger, strutting around as if he were General Gort himself. A man with ideas above his station, I thought. Do you know the sort? I expect you meet them in your line of work – people with an overinflated sense of self-confidence.'

Jago suppressed the smile he felt coming to his lips. Pots and kettles, he thought.

'How could you tell?' he asked.

'It wasn't just the way he walked, Inspector,' she continued. 'He waited until I'd served everyone else, then came over and – well, all I can say is he was very forward with me. He introduced himself with what I can only call a leer and said, "My name's Lambert, but my friends call me Ray. What's yours?" "None of your business," I said, and gave him his tea. He said some other things that I can't remember precisely, but they were quite improper. Nor the sort of things he'd say if my father had been there, I can tell you.'

'Where was your father?'

'Oh, I don't know. Attending to something, I expect. Men in his position always have things to attend to, always have to keep working while their men lounge about drinking tea, don't they?'

'Did you tell him about Lambert's behaviour?'

'No. My father has far too much to worry about already, and I didn't want to add to his concerns. Besides, I'm old enough to look after myself. I don't take any nonsense from old men with wandering hands.'

'Do you mean Lambert's hands wandered?'

'No. He could hardly do that while he was standing on the quay and I was in the canteen van handing down drinks. I just mean he was that type. They may think they can get their way with some foolish girls, but they don't with me.'

'And what time was this?'

'It would have been sometime between eleven and half past eleven on Monday night.'

'Did you see him again that night?'

'No.'

'Would you have expected to see him again in the normal run of things?'

'I can't really say. I mean, we move around the docks during the night, but the men don't necessarily all come to the van every time we stop. I couldn't tell you who comes when, or how many times any particular man comes.'

'Right. Now, when we spoke to you before, you told

us you'd seen two people having an argument further down the quay.'

Evelyn nodded.

'Was one of those people Mr Lambert?'

'I'm sorry, Inspector, I really couldn't tell in the dark, and I hadn't seen where either of them had come from.'

'And their voices – male, female? Any accent or anything else to distinguish them?'

'From what I could hear, male, but they were too far away for me to pick out an accent.'

'And you told us before that they were both wearing overcoats, but I don't think you mentioned what they had on their heads. Were they wearing hats?'

Evelyn thought for a moment, her eyes screwed shut.

'Not hats as such, no, but . . . Yes, I think one of them was wearing a steel helmet. The one nearest the water. But not the other one, no.'

'Thank you, Miss Danbury, that's most helpful. I think now we'll see if we can find your father at the Home Guard HQ. It's just down at the end of the road, isn't it?'

'Yes, that's right. It's number 22 to 26 Woodgrange Road – above Burton's the tailor. The Home Guard's got the first floor, which used to be the snooker hall, and the second floor's being used by the Ministry of Food. You can't miss it.'

CHAPTER THIRTY-ONE

Jago and Cradock took the car to the end of Claremont Road and turned left into Woodgrange Road. Evelyn Danbury had been right, thought Jago: you couldn't miss the premises where the Home Guard had set up its headquarters. He wasn't keen on the art deco style of architecture, but he couldn't deny that the new Burton's building on their left, just across the road from the Forest Gate roller-skating rink, was striking and, perhaps appropriately for a tailoring establishment, cut a distinctive figure that some would no doubt find elegant.

It didn't take them long to find Danbury: he was engaged in a loud conversation with a mild-looking man in steel-rimmed spectacles who appeared to be on the receiving end of the major's advice on how to do his duty. Jago and Cradock waited until he'd finished and approached him.

'I'm sorry to interrupt you, Major Danbury, but there's something I need to know and I thought you might be a good person to help me. Your daughter told us we'd find you here.'

Danbury was looking flustered, but at the mention of his daughter he appeared to calm down in the way, it seemed to Jago, a man of his type and background might moderate his behaviour upon hearing the words 'ladies present'.

'To be frank with you,' said Danbury, 'right now I'm extremely busy, as you can probably see, but I'm sure I can spare a few minutes to assist you. Come into my office – it's little more than a cupboard over there, but it affords a modicum of privacy.'

They followed Danbury into a small area in the corner that had been partitioned off for his use and sat down round a battered wooden table bearing a telephone and piles of official-looking papers. A map of the area hung on the wall opposite a taped window that overlooked the street below. The major folded his arms on the table and leant forward slightly, as if about to interview them.

'So, what is it you want to know?' he said.

'It's a couple of things to do with India,' Jago began. 'Firstly, you told me before that all the men in your regiment apart from the officers were Indian.'

'That's correct.'

'I asked you the other day whether the name Dayabir Singh meant anything to you, and you said no. But it's an Indian name, and since then you've told us that you served in the Indian Army and that in your regiment only the officers were British – all the other ranks were Indian.

I've been wondering whether this Dayabir Singh might have been a soldier, and whether you might perhaps have had an Indian man of that name under your command.'

Danbury looked blank and shook his head.

'It doesn't sound familiar,' he said, 'but of course one didn't know all the native troops by name – there were too many of them. There were plenty of Singhs, but I don't remember any by the name of Dayabir. What's the second thing?'

'That's to do with Ray Lambert. You may remember me saying we'd been told he'd served with you in India.'

'Yes, and I told you then that I didn't know the man – I'd never clapped eyes on him until he joined my Home Guard platoon.'

A hint of exasperation had crept into Danbury's voice, so Jago used his calmest tone.

'Indeed. Since then we've been told that Mr Lambert served in the Punjab, and was at a place called Amritsar, where there were riots in 1919, and since you'll know vastly more than I do about India, I'd be grateful if you could tell me a little about what happened there.'

This seemed to have the desired effect. Danbury looked somewhat mollified, although he still had a suspicious look in his eye, as though wondering what Jago was up to.

'I'm not necessarily an expert,' he began, 'but I'll help you if I can.'

'Thank you. Perhaps first you could help me ensure my understanding is correct. In 1919, I was only just out of the army myself and about to join the police, so I wasn't too aware of what was happening in India.'

'You were in the army, were you? Where was that?'

'In France – the Western Front.'

'Officer, or other ranks?'

'I was a second lieutenant, but I started out in the ranks.'

Danbury looked unimpressed.

'I see. Well, what can I tell you about Amritsar?'

'First of all, what was the disturbance about?'

'That's simple. There was a lot of unrest at the time, and we – the British authorities, that is – had arrested three subversives. One of them was that Hindu fellow Gandhi, who everyone seems to have heard of these days.'

'Ah, yes, I've seen him in the newspapers – he appears to have quite a following. And he's even been over here and visited the East End, hasn't he?'

'Yes,' said Danbury with an almost imperceptible sniff, as if an unsavoury odour had drifted into the room. 'He came to London in 1931 for the big conference on home rule for India, and instead of accepting the government's hospitality he spent six weeks in some kind of centre for the poor in Bromley-by-Bow, of all places. An odd chap, but in 1919 he was still useful to us. He was a nationalist, you see, which made him our enemy, but he also did everything he could to prevent violence, so from our point of view that meant he was effectively protecting us from violent action. It's all turned rather sour since then, but I say it's our own fault – if we hadn't allowed a free press and freedom of assembly in India, no one would ever have heard of him.'

'You said three people were arrested. Who were the other two?'

'A man called Satya Pal, and another called Saifuddin Kitchlew. Natives, obviously.'

'Were they Hindus too?'

'Satya Pal was, but Saifuddin Kitchlew was a Muslim.'

'And what happened?'

'Well, some undesirables and ruffians in Amritsar began protesting about the arrests. The trouble started in a public area called the Jallianwala Bagh, a sort of garden, enclosed on all sides. Pretty soon it turned into a riot, so the troops were called in to stop it.'

'And these troops opened fire on the crowd?'

'Yes, as a matter of fact they did. But there was no alternative – we'd already had three days of rioting in various parts of northern India, and our commanding officer had to use force to restore order and show that rebellion of that kind would not be tolerated.'

'Am I right in understanding there were civilian casualties?'

'Yes, there were. But look, you have to understand the circumstances – those people were politically organised. They weren't going to go home quietly just because we asked them nicely.'

'You've said two of the men arrested were Hindus and one was a Muslim, so I assume no Sikhs had been arrested. But am I right in thinking a lot of Sikhs were killed in the riot?'

'Yes, I believe so, but there were a lot of Sikhs living in that area – it was in the Punjab, after all. The crowd was just whoever had turned up to protest, so there were all sorts – Hindus, Sikhs, Muslims, the lot. They were simply a rabble.'

'A rabble who found themselves up against armed troops.'

Danbury's voice and expression suggested that he'd had this conversation with other people many times.

'I know what you're thinking,' he said. 'The fact is, a lot of nonsense has been spoken and written about it since then. People call it a massacre, but I say it was a necessary action to subdue revolutionaries and maintain the peace, and that's all there is to it. If drastic action hadn't been taken, the trouble would have spread right across the country, and where would that have left us?'

'Were you there yourself?'

'Yes, I was, as it happens.'

Danbury looked away from Jago and out of the window. His voice dropped, and for the first time the note of confidence in it seemed to fade.

'I'm afraid the Indians never forgave us,' he continued, 'but we were only doing our duty. We were upholding the law and maintaining the King's Peace, just as you and your colleagues in the police force do here, on the streets of West Ham.'

Yes, thought Jago, *except that we don't open fire on protesters*. But he left the thought unspoken.

CHAPTER THIRTY-TWO

Morris the butcher was waiting for them when they got back to the police station. He was a short, tubby man of about fifty with a fleshy face and a snub nose, whose frame suggested that whatever privations his customers might be suffering, he himself had reliable access to a more than adequate supply of food. He hauled himself awkwardly to his feet when Jago introduced himself and Cradock, and then followed them to the interview room.

'Thank you for agreeing to come along and see us, Mr Morris,' Jago began. 'Do take a seat.'

'Well, I hope it won't take long,' said Morris, puffing slightly as he eased himself onto the wooden chair Jago had offered. 'I've had to leave the shop in my young assistant's hands.'

He rolled his eyes as if to signify that this represented a serious risk to his business.

'We shan't keep you for any longer than necessary,' said Jago, 'but we have a few questions we'd like to ask.

How long that takes will depend on how well you can explain your trading activities to us. Now, you have a butcher's shop, yes?'

'That's right.'

'So you'll be familiar with the current regulations about what you're allowed to sell – and what you're not allowed to sell.'

'Yes.'

'For example, canned fish.'

'Fish? What's that got to do with anything?'

'I believe DC Cradock here told you there's been a report that you've been involved in illegal trading. That's a serious matter, and I'm going to ask you a few questions about it. I should add that you're not obliged to say anything, but anything you say may be given in evidence.'

'What?' cried Morris. 'This is a damned impertinence. I don't know what you're talking about.'

'In that case I'll explain. A Ministry of Food inspector visited your shop yesterday.'

'A Ministry of Food inspector? I don't remember anyone like that coming in.'

'She asked you for some bacon, because she said she had three sickly children at home, but you said you didn't have any bacon. You did, however, sell her a tin of salmon for sevenpence above the controlled price, and that's against the law.'

'One measly tin of salmon? Haven't you people got anything better to do than harass reputable tradesmen?

284

We're supposed to be fighting a war, people are dying out there, and all you're interested in is a tin of salmon? Give me strength.'

'The inspector was only doing her job.'

The butcher snorted in disgust.

'Doing her job? What about my job? I'm providing a public service, keeping people fed. The government's spending fifty million pounds a week on this war, and they send you round here because I might've accidentally charged sevenpence extra on a tin of salmon? They must want their heads examining.'

'Accidentally?'

'I don't know – but in any case, what difference does it make? Look, she came into my shop and gave me some sob story about her children – three kids, she says, all evacuated to a farm somewhere at the other end of the country, and she finds out the farmer who's meant to be looking after them for her's got them out milking his perishing cows at four o'clock every morning, so she's brought them back home, and now she's been bombed out. The kids are starving and ill, and she's trying to get them back up to strength, but she hasn't got her ration book sorted out or something, and she needs a bit extra to get them well. The way she told it, she was in real trouble, so of course I tried to help her. Now you're telling me she was just some government snooper trying to catch me out. She deliberately played on my sympathy by telling me a pack of lies. She deceived me. I'm just trying to do the best I can for a customer, and next thing I know I'm being treated as a criminal.'

He slumped back angrily into his chair.

'A criminal is someone who breaks the law,' said Jago, 'and the law says you can't sell salmon for more than eightpence a tin and you can't sell stolen goods to the public.'

Morris sat up again abruptly.

'Who said anything about stolen?' he demanded.

'You're saying it wasn't?' said Jago.

'Of course not. I bought it fair and square.'

'Who did you buy it from?'

'From some bloke.'

'You'll have to do better than that, Mr Morris.'

'Well, I don't know who he was. He said it was all above board. He came into the shop and said he had a load of salvaged goods he'd been told to sell off – by the Ministry of Food, he said, as it happens. He said a warehouse had caught on fire and had its roof blown off in an air raid, and all the water from the fire hoses had damaged the goods inside, so it had to be sold off. So as not to go to waste, see. You must've seen the adverts – the government's always telling us we mustn't waste food, isn't it?'

'Yes. And you're telling me this was flood-damaged food? Salmon are fish – or didn't you know? They live in water, and when they've finished living in water they live in cans, and cans are waterproof. Don't make me laugh.'

'I'm sorry, Officer, I was only telling you what the bloke said. I just thought I was helping out by preventing wastage, doing my civic duty, like.'

Jago felt a surge of annoyance at the man's impudence

but resisted the urge to shout in his face. The thought of a tradesman using even as trivial an item as a tin of salmon to deceive others for profit made him angry.

'This salmon's imported, from Canada,' he said. 'Was that warehouse you mentioned in the Royal Docks, by any chance?'

'I don't know, do I?'

'What was the man's name?'

Morris gave him a blank look.

'I'm sorry, I don't quite recall.'

'What did he look like, then?'

'Just an ordinary sort of bloke – about your height and build, about your age too.'

'What did you pay him for the salmon?'

'I can't remember that, I'm afraid.'

'You didn't get a receipt?'

'No, he said he was in a hurry.'

'You're under arrest, Mr Morris.'

'But I haven't done anything wrong!' Morris shouted.

'You can save your explanations for the magistrate,' said Jago. He turned to Cradock. 'Detective Constable, would you please take Mr Morris to a cell?'

Having deposited Morris in the cells, Cradock returned to the CID office, where he found Jago at his desk, sifting through some paperwork.

'He's not happy, guv'nor,' said Cradock. 'Says he's got a shop to run and we've no right to lock him up.'

'He's probably worried what that assistant of his

might get up to while he's away. We'll give Mr Morris a few hours of enforced leisure, so he's got time to reflect on his business practices, and then I think we'll release him on bail and get him back in front of the magistrate next week.'

'Very good, sir. You didn't ask him about the sugar, though.'

'No. He didn't actually sell any to the food inspector, and the only solid evidence we've got from her is about the fish. We'll see whether he decides he wants the business with the sugar and any other relevant offences taken into consideration when we charge him.'

Cradock looked thoughtful.

'Talking of fish, sir, that salmon he's selling,' he said. 'It's from Canada, same as the stuff the *Magnolia* was carrying, and it's the same make too. So do you reckon it was nicked off that ship?'

'It's possible, but of course the fact that it's the same make isn't proof. It could just be a popular brand, and it could be coming over from Canada on all sorts of ships. But at the very least it's a coincidence, and our Mr Morris is a slippery customer for sure.'

'He must know it was nicked, mustn't he?'

'I'd say he's wily enough to work that out if he wants to. But a man like him might prefer not to know where his goods come from – and not to ask.'

'If this particular lot came in on the *Magnolia* and it's been stolen, there's still the question of how whoever pinched it got it out of the docks though, isn't there?'

'Yes, but from what we've heard I imagine a tally clerk might well overlook a few cases of tinned salmon, or a docker or stevedore might temporarily misplace them somewhere in the docks, or a member of the crew might stow them away privately somewhere on the ship. Then all they'd need would be someone to get them over the fence and into a van at a suitable moment.'

'In the dark, you mean?'

'Exactly. Unless they found some way of walking past a policeman on the gate with their trousers full of tinned salmon. But then I'd say almost anything's possible in these docks.'

CHAPTER THIRTY-THREE

Cradock had noticed that Jago was sitting with his back to the clock. Sensing a lull in their conversation, he leant over to one side in an exaggerated pose to stare at it. Jago followed his gaze.

'Look at that, guv'nor,' said Cradock, feigning surprise. 'Nearly three o'clock. Amazing how time flies, isn't it? Especially when you're working hard.'

'I assume this message is coming from your stomach, Peter, and that it has something to do with eating?' said Jago.

'Well, now you come to mention it, sir, we haven't had any lunch yet, have we? Might be a good idea to get a quick bite of something while we can.'

'Very well. We'll slip down to the canteen and see if they've got anything left. I'm talking about a sandwich or a piece of cake, mind – we haven't got time for a three-course meal.'

Cradock was disappointed but didn't want to risk losing this small concession by trying for more. He followed Jago out of the office and they headed for the canteen. His disappointment was compounded, however, when Jago took him by way of the front desk, where they were intercepted by Frank Tompkins.

'Afternoon, sir,' he said to Jago. 'I see you've been having a word with my local butcher, Mr Morris. Was that in connection with certain shady dealings observed by my missus in his shop?'

'It was indeed, Frank. He seemed to think he was providing a public service, which in a way he was, I suppose. It's just unfortunate it was an illegal service. He'll be explaining that to the magistrate next week.'

'Good. I don't like cheating – it's not British, is it?'

'It is in his case, I'm afraid. It's a pity, but you can understand why some of these shopkeepers do it. It can't be easy to resist the temptation, especially when breaking the rules means you can keep your customers happy and make an extra bob or two on the side too.'

'You're not going soft on crime, are you, sir?'

Jago laughed.

'Not me, Frank. I must be going a bit soft on young Peter here, though – I'm on my way to the canteen to buy him something to eat. Just enough to keep him alive, of course. Can we bring anything back for you?'

'That's very kind of you, sir,' said Tompkins. 'A nice cup of tea would be very welcome, thank you.'

'Cup of tea it is, then. All quiet down here?'

'Quiet enough, thanks, although it doesn't take much to keep me busy. And how about you? Any nearer to finding out who murdered that Home Guard?'

Jago pursed his lips in thought as he considered the question, and Cradock resigned himself to a delay in their progress to the canteen. He reluctantly accepted also that Sergeant Tompkins sometimes made a more useful contribution to Jago's deliberations than he did himself.

'Ray Lambert?' said Jago. 'No, I don't think we are. There were only two unusual things at the scene of the crime, and we've been trying to work out what either of them might mean.'

'Oh, yes? What were they?'

'One was the murder weapon and the other was a piece of paper we found on the body. The bit of paper had a name written on it – Dayabir Singh, an Indian name. We don't know who this Dayabir Singh is, or whether Lambert even knew him, so it could mean nothing at all, but the interesting thing is that with a name like Singh he's most likely a Sikh, and another Indian who saw what may've been Lambert shortly before he was killed identified the murder weapon as a Sikh knife. We've also found out that Lambert was in the army in India after the Great War, and so was Major Danbury, who's the Home Guard platoon commander. One of Lambert's pals said the two of them served together, although Danbury says he doesn't remember that.'

'And why's that significant?'

'I don't know – it may not be significant at all. It's just that they were both in a place where there were some nasty riots – in the Punjab, where lots of Sikhs live.'

'Whereabouts in the Punjab?'

'A place called Amritsar.'

'In 1919?'

'Yes, that's right.'

'Ah, well, I remember that.'

'You weren't there too, were you?'

'No, of course not. But I remember it was in the papers at the time, and there was quite a fuss about it. A government enquiry and everything. Our troops opened fire on some kind of protest, and lots of Indians got killed.'

'That's it. And there was something Danbury mentioned when we saw him today – he said that after that, the Indians never forgave us. It just got me thinking again about whether there's a connection of some kind – I mean, Lambert was there in the army in 1919 when all those Indians were killed, including lots of Sikhs no doubt, and then twenty-one years later he ends up stabbed to death with a Sikh dagger.'

'Might be no connection at all.'

'Absolutely, but it's what I've been wondering.'

'I suppose it's possible, of course. There was that bloke who got shot in London a few months ago, wasn't there? O'Dwyer, his name was – he'd been some sort of official out that way, in India. I think he'd been mixed up in those riots in some way too, and then years later an Indian pops up at Caxton Hall in Westminster and kills him. A revenge killing, apparently. Maybe your man Danbury's right – they've never forgiven us. But what did this Ray Lambert do?'

'That's what we've been trying to find out, but we haven't got very far.'

'This other Indian you mentioned, the one who identified the knife – who's he?'

'He's a lascar on the ship that was moored next to where Lambert's body was found.'

'Is he a Sikh?'

'No, he says he's a Muslim.'

'How old is he?'

'About forty, I should say.'

'Old enough to have been around in 1919, then. Perhaps you should ask him what he was doing when those riots were happening.'

'Good idea, but he's gone missing – hasn't been seen since Wednesday night.'

'A disappearing witness? That's interesting. And what about that bloke I told you about this morning? Carlisle, was it? The one who says he's changed his mind – he told you he'd had a drink with someone on a ship and now he says he didn't. What's that all about?'

'Another disappearance, it seems – a disappearing alibi. It's what you might call the case of Bell's whisky.'

Jago smiled at his own little joke, but Tompkins' face was blank.

'There's another Home Guard, you see, called Charlie Bell,' Jago explained, regretting his wisecrack. 'He was on patrol with Lambert, and Carlisle said he'd invited Bell on board for a hot toddy, and now he's told you he didn't. It was about the time Lambert was murdered, so it could mean someone's alibi's just gone up in smoke.'

'I see. I expect you'll be deploying all the skills and experience of the West Ham Criminal Investigation Department to get to the bottom of that little mystery, then.'

'Oh, yes. I've got one of my best men working on it.'

Tompkins glanced in Cradock's direction but made no comment: he didn't want to discourage the poor boy.

'First, though,' said Jago, 'I need to make sure he doesn't pass out from hunger before the canteen runs out of food.'

'Righto,' said Tompkins. He paused in thought for a moment as Jago and his assistant moved away. 'But seriously, sir, thinking of that O'Dwyer business – do you reckon this Lambert case could be some kind of revenge killing too?'

Jago stopped and turned back to face him.

'It could be, Frank, but revenge for what, precisely? That's the question. Any suggestions?'

Tompkins looked surprised.

'Me? Oh, no, sir – you're the clever detective lads. I'm just the old station sergeant hauled out of retirement for the duration. I'll leave all that sort of thing to you.'

CHAPTER THIRTY-FOUR

Twenty minutes later the detectives emerged from the canteen, Cradock newly fortified by a large slab of fruit cake and Jago bearing the promised cup of tea for Tompkins. When they got to the front desk to deliver it, a man in a smart grey suit who had evidently been waiting for them rose from his chair to greet them.

'Detective Inspector Jago,' he said. 'I was hoping you'd be here.'

'Mr Whitton,' Jago replied. 'How can we help?'

Alfred Whitton raised a hand to signal politely that he had not come in search of assistance.

'Actually, I'm here partly because I feel a word of apology is in order. I may have appeared a little aggressive when you came to my house on Wednesday, and I regret that. I'd had a bad night, I'm under a lot of pressure at work, and I think the fact that we'd been burgled was just the last straw. What I said may have sounded somewhat extreme. I hope I didn't offend you – I'm sure you must be working in very trying circumstances too – but if I did, please accept my apologies.'

'That's quite all right, Mr Whitton, I understand. These are difficult days for all of us.'

'Thank you. I appreciate your understanding. The other reason why I've come is because I've found that bicycle frame number you wanted, or rather my wife found it. It's 457296. Here.'

He handed Jago a scrap of paper with the number written on it.

'Thank you, Mr Whitton, that'll be very helpful.'

'I suppose it's too much to hope that you've made any progress with your investigation yet.'

'I'm afraid we haven't, sir. With the best will in the world it'd be unusual for us to have a crime reported on a Wednesday and solve it by Friday. These offences that happen in the blackout are particularly tricky, because there's less chance of us finding any witnesses. It'd be nice to think that at a time like this we'd all be pulling together and crime would be decreasing, but the sad fact is that some people just can't keep their hands off other people's property, and they'll take any chance that comes their way to steal.'

'You don't need to tell me that, Inspector. I see plenty of it in my job.'

'Ah, yes, you mentioned that you're a company director. What line of business are you in?'

'Lighterage. You know what lighters are?'

'Oh, yes,' said Cradock, interrupting. 'We know all about them. Barges, aren't they?'

Whitton gave Cradock the sort of look he might

give to an overkeen puppy.

'Yes, that's right – well done.'

'What's your company called?' asked Jago.

'It's the Thames Lighterage Company. We run a fleet of lighters, working in the docks and on the river too. So if you're talking about people who can't keep their hands off other people's property, there's not much you can tell me that I don't already know. Some of those dockers . . . Well, if you ask me, I think anything that's not screwed down or locked up when they're about is likely to go wandering – and even when it is, it might.'

'Are you suggesting it could be a dock worker who burgled your house?'

'No, not at all. If a man pinches something at work, it doesn't necessarily mean he'll break into someone's house and steal things. I'm just saying I'm probably as sceptical about human nature as you are. When you've seen the things I've seen in my time in the docks, you can't help it.'

'By the way, sir, which docks does your company work in?'

'Most of the London docks, but mainly the Royals. The current circumstances are making things very hard for us – the air raids are causing constant damage and disruption in the ports, not to mention the ships and cargoes being lost at sea on their way before they even get to us. We've got fewer ships coming in, so there's less work for us, and the bomb damage to our lighters is putting our costs up. This war may be good for some businesses, but I swear it'll be the ruin of mine.'

'I'm sorry to hear that, sir. I'm sure our lives depend on the docks.'

'That's no exaggeration, Inspector. So now, if you'll excuse me, I must get back to my office and do my little bit to keep them working. If I can be of any other assistance, just call me.'

Alfred Whitton strode briskly out of the door and was gone. Jago handed the piece of paper on which the stolen bicycle's frame number was written to Cradock.

'Here you are,' he said. 'Look after this. If a bike turns up with this number on it we'll know it's the one stolen from the Whittons.'

'Yes. I've been thinking about that, actually.'

'Thinking about what?'

'Well, about those two burglaries, really.'

'And?'

'It was what I was saying yesterday – Charlie Bell works in the docks and knows where Major Danbury lives and when he's on duty, so I was thinking it might've been him who burgled the major's house. And now we've got two men who're involved in the docks – Danbury with his Home Guard platoon and Whitton with his barges – and they've both been burgled. So what if there's someone who's a bit light-fingered and also knows where they both live because he works in the docks?'

'Someone light-fingered like Charlie Bell, you mean?'

'Well, it's what Brenda Lambert said.'

'Only hearsay again – and quoting the words of a man who's now dead.'

'Yes, but I'm just wondering whether Charlie Bell happens to know Whitton as well. It might be nothing, but what do you think?'

'I think if a bike with that number on the frame happens to turn up in Mr Charlie Bell's possession he'll have some very interesting questions to answer. It seems to me he might have a finger in several pies, and I'd like to know which ones.'

Jago glanced at his watch.

'I think we might have time to pop down to the docks right now and see if we can dig a little deeper with Messrs Carlisle and Bell about that drink they did or didn't have together.'

'Kill two birds in the bush, you mean?'

'Not in the bush, Peter – with a stone.'

Cradock's face gave no indication that he understood.

'A bird in the hand is worth two in the bush, Peter, but if you want to kill the two birds, you don't do it in the bush, you use a stone.'

Cradock now looked only perplexed, as if baffled by Jago's comment but reluctant to appear impertinent by saying so.

'Yes, sir, whatever you say.'

'Good,' said Jago. 'Let's go.'

They drove to the Royal Albert Dock and followed the now-familiar route past the transit sheds to the SS *Magnolia*.

'We'll see if Carlisle's at home, shall we?' said Jago.

They went up the ladder, and as on their previous visit they found Munroe, the ship's master, on board.

'We were hoping to see Mr Carlisle,' said Jago. 'Is he here?'

'I'm afraid you've missed him,' Munroe replied. 'He came to me this morning saying he needed some time ashore, so I said yes.'

'Did he say why he needed it?'

'Just said he had some personal business to attend to. He's a reliable man, and I've no need to go nosing into his private affairs, so I didn't enquire any further.'

'When do you expect him back?'

'Monday at the latest. I can manage without him until then.'

'Very well. When he comes back, could you tell him we'd like to speak to him?'

'Certainly. I'm sure he'll be only too pleased to help you. Now, do you have time to stop for a drink?'

'I'm sorry, Mr Munroe, but we can't. There's someone else we need to see.'

They took their leave of Munroe and walked back to the car.

'Where to now? Mrs Higgs's place?' asked Cradock.

'Yes,' said Jago. 'If Charlie Bell's at home, we can ask him a few questions about hot toddies and bicycles.'

'I think tonight's supposed to be one of his Home Guard nights – he said he's on duty Monday and Friday nights, didn't he?'

'Yes, you're right, but we might catch him having his tea before he goes out,' Jago replied, starting the engine. 'And anyway, if he's out, maybe we should just ask Mavis whether he's given her any more nice presents recently.'

CHAPTER THIRTY-FIVE

The sun was slipping low in the sky above the King George V Dock as Jago and Cradock approached the house where Mavis Higgs and her lodger lived. Mothers were bringing their children in from their games on the street, and in some homes the blackout curtains were already appearing at the windows, ready for whatever horrors the night might bring.

They knocked on the door, and Mavis opened it almost immediately. She looked anxious.

'Hello, Mrs Higgs,' said Jago. 'May we come in?'

'If it's Charlie you want, he's out,' she replied. 'It's his Home Guard night tonight.'

'Never mind. I was hoping we might catch him before he went out.'

'Usually you would – he's normally on duty from nine o'clock in the evening, so he'd be having his tea about now, but today he said he had to go out early. He didn't say where. I'm very sorry if you've wasted your journey.'

'Not at all. I'd like to have a quick little chat with you too, if you don't mind.'

'Me? Oh, all right, then.' She stood aside to let them in, then took them to the kitchen.

'Is everything OK?' Jago asked. 'You look worried.'

'Oh, don't mind me, Inspector. I always get a bit jittery this time of night – it's the air raids, you know. Especially when Charlie's out – it's funny, but I always feel safer when he's here. I'll be going down the shelter in a minute.'

'In that case I'll be brief.'

'Oh, no, don't worry, Inspector. I'll be all right if you're here. I don't know why – it's just having company, I suppose. Makes me feel safe. Here, take a seat.'

'Very well,' said Jago, sitting down. 'Thank you.'

'What is it you want to chat about, then?'

'It's just a little question – do you happen to have a bicycle on the premises?'

'No, I haven't. Why do you ask?'

'We're just trying to find one that's missing. Do you mind if my colleague here has a quick look round?'

'Well, I think I'd have noticed if there was a bike in the house or the back yard, wouldn't I? But if it'll put your mind at rest, help yourself.'

Jago nodded to Cradock, who left the room in search of the bicycle.

'I've another little question, if you don't mind, Mrs Higgs. I wonder if you could tell me whether you were here on the evening of the Sunday before last, the twenty-seventh of October.'

'Oh dear, it's difficult to remember that far back, but I probably was, yes – I'm usually in Sunday evening.'

'And were you here all night?'

'Oh yes, I'm always here at night. Where else would I be? These days I'd be in the shelter, of course, but that's here too.'

'Was Mr Bell here with you?'

'Well, er . . .' she hesitated. 'It's a bit more difficult with him – he comes and goes a lot more than me, what with his job and the Home Guard and all. Have you asked him?'

'Yes.'

'Well, whatever he says is probably right. If he says he was here I'm sure he was.'

'I see. And tell me, how do you find Mr Bell? As a lodger, I mean.'

'Well, I'll take in pretty much anyone. I mean, when money's short you can't be too choosy about who you have, can you? I've only got the one room I can rent out, but that little bit of extra cash comes in very handy. Having said that, he's probably the best lodger I've ever had. Very considerate, he is. Never comes in late at night waking me up with his row like some of them I've known in the past. Always very thoughtful, and a very interesting man to talk to.'

'Yes, I understand he's had an interesting life. He was telling us about his years in the shipyards – those men must've been so proud to know they'd built great ships like that from nothing with their own hands.'

'Oh, yes. He's a proud man, you know. Proud of being Scottish, proud of building ships, and now he's proud of being a stevedore. They're a bit special, you know, have to know a lot about ships to take care of people's cargoes.'

'And I imagine he takes care of you too?'

'Yes, he's very attentive. He's not just a lodger, really. He says there's nothing he wouldn't do for me. And it's nice to have a man about the house again, especially with all the bombing and stuff.'

'Again?'

'Yes, I mean my son, Roger. He's a man now – well, he's nineteen, but he's old enough to be in the navy. The Royal Navy, that is. He's serving on a destroyer somewhere, but he's not allowed to say where – he's been gone a while now, so I was on my own until Charlie came along. I've got a photo of him here somewhere. I'll show you – he's a handsome lad.'

She reached for her handbag and rummaged in it. Behind her, Jago saw Cradock return to the room and shake his head.

'He's turned out a better man than his father, I'll say that for him,' said Mavis. 'I married young, you see, and you know what they say, "Marry in haste, repent at leisure." I didn't know it at the time, but he was a bad 'un, my husband was, and twelve years ago he left me – ran off with a girl I thought was my friend. Now where is that picture?'

She tipped the contents of her bag onto the table.

'Ah, there it is,' she said, picking up a small photo of a young man in a naval rating's uniform, standing at ease in what looked like a back yard, possibly hers.

'A very smart-looking young man,' said Jago. 'You must be very proud of him.'

'Yes, I am,' said Mavis. She stared lovingly at the photo, but Jago's gaze was distracted.

'Excuse me,' he said, 'but is that a powder compact? May I have a look?'

'Course you can, but why are you interested in that old thing?'

'It's this picture on the front. Can you tell me what it is?'

'It's a ship, of course – and look, there's the name at the bottom. The *Duchess of Atholl*. My Charlie built that ship.'

This was the first time she'd referred to him as her Charlie, thought Jago, and he noticed that when she did so her voice had the same affectionately possessive gentleness as when she spoke of her absent son. Sometimes he hated his job.

'May I ask how you came by this?'

'Came by it? It was a present from Charlie, that's all.'

'And do you know how he came by it?'

'Yes, he said he bought it from a man in a pub. I know it's not brand new, but it's as good as, and no man's ever bought me something as nice as that, not even second hand. My husband certainly never did. All he spent his money on was cigarettes and beer.'

'I see. Well, I'm afraid I shall have to borrow it for a while, Mrs Higgs.'

'Oh,' she said weakly. 'All right – but you will look after it, won't you?'

'I shall, Mrs Higgs. I shall. And before we go, could I ask you just one more question?'

'Of course.'

'I know Charlie works in the docks, but do you happen to know who he works for?'

'Well, he's casual, so as far as I know he works for any stevedoring company that wants him, but he's told me the stevedores work in regular gangs, and the companies get to know the ones they prefer to work with. The company he seems to mention most is Thames Lighterage, I think – and usually he's grumbling about them.'

When they were back in the car, Jago gave Cradock the compact.

'Put this in your pocket, Peter, and look after it. We need to show it to Mrs Whitton and see whether she can confirm it's hers.'

'What, show it to her now, sir? It's past blackout time.'

Jago looked at his watch.

'No, you're right. I think we should get back before the Luftwaffe turn up. We'll go when we get a moment tomorrow.'

Cradock took the compact.

'Very good, sir. Is that it for today, then?'

'Not quite. We'll be going almost past the Potters' door on our way back, so if there's no bombs actually falling I'd like to drop in for a couple of minutes and see if their Maureen's at home. After what Evelyn Danbury said about Ray Lambert and his attitude to young women, I'd be interested to know whether that's something Maureen can confirm.'

They drove the short distance to Barge House Road and found Len Potter at home. He welcomed them in and shut the door behind them. No sooner had he explained that his wife was at work on her bus and his daughter wasn't home from work yet than a key rattled in the door behind them and Maureen came in.

'Hello, Dad,' she said, taking off her hat and coat and hanging them on a hook on the wall. 'Hello, Inspector, I didn't expect to see you.'

Jago was about to reply, but Potter spoke first.

'You're late,' he said. 'What's up?'

'Nothing, Dad. There was a problem at work and we all finished a bit late. There's no need to worry.'

'Oh, yes there is. How can I not worry when there's bombs dropping every day? And that reminds me – what were you doing last night? You didn't say you were going out.'

'Oh, come on, Dad, I'm grown up now. I can go out with a friend of an evening if I want to.'

'I'm still your father, and while you're living under my roof I like to know where you are.'

'Give over, Dad. I was perfectly safe. If you must

know, I was having a drink – just one, mind – with Tom Lightfoot.'

Potter's face relaxed.

'Ah, that's all right, then.'

'See? If I'm not safe with a Royal Marine who's also my mum's friend's son, who can I be safe with?'

'Yes, well, I've said that's all right. You could do a lot worse than young Tom, I'm sure.'

Maureen turned to Jago.

'So, Detective Inspector, been having a chat with my dad, have you?'

'Yes, I have, actually. I wonder if I might have a word with you too. In private, if you don't mind.'

'I'm sure I don't mind, as long as my dad doesn't. Is that all right, Dad? Think I'll be safe with this one?'

Potter said nothing, but the gesture he made with his head suggested she should be the one who left the room.

'Shall we step into the hall?' said Maureen.

Jago and Cradock followed her out and shut the door behind them.

'His bark's worse than his bite, you know,' said Maureen, lowering her voice. 'I suppose he just doesn't want to accept that I'm grown up. Have you got any daughters, Inspector?'

'No.'

'Well, if you had, I'm sure you wouldn't mind them going out for a drink with a Royal Marine, would you?'

'I think that would depend on the marine,' said Jago.

'Tom's very sweet, and he looks lovely in that

uniform, doesn't he?'

'Ah, yes, the uniform. Somebody was saying to me only today how girls can fall for a uniform.'

'Well, that's true of course, but I've seen him out of his uniform too.' She stopped suddenly and blushed. 'No, that's not what I mean – I mean I've seen him in civvies. You must think I'm awful.'

'Don't worry, Miss Potter, we know what you mean.'

'Good. Well anyway, Tom's a real gentleman, if you know what I mean.'

'I'm glad to hear it. Now, I won't keep you for long. I expect you know we're investigating the death of your father's friend, Mr Lambert.'

'Uncle Ray? Yes, my mum told me. He worked in the docks with my dad. I don't really know what he did there, though.'

'As a matter of interest, have you ever been inside the docks?'

'Me? No. Why would I do that? I'm not that sort of girl, you know.'

'What do you mean?'

'Well, there are girls that go in there, aren't there? To meet the sailors – you know. When those men are back from being at sea for weeks on end they've usually got a lot of money to spend and they show the girls a good time.'

'I thought people weren't allowed into the docks without good reason.'

'Well, I don't know about that. Maybe that is a good reason. All I know is some girls do. My dad says it's not 'difficult to get in – he says anyone can get past the gate bobby if they slip him half a crown.'

'That's not what I've been told.'

'I suppose it depends who you were asking, doesn't it?'

I suppose it does, Jago reflected, but he kept his thoughts to himself.

'I see,' he said. 'Now, concerning your uncle Ray – Mr Lambert.'

'Yes?'

'I'd just like to know how well you knew him.'

'How well I knew him? That's difficult to answer, really – I mean, he's just my uncle. Not really my uncle, of course, but that's what I've always called him. I don't know anything about when he was younger, or what he did at work, if that's what you mean. I just knew him as my dad's friend.'

'Did you get on well?'

Maureen hesitated before answering.

'All right, I suppose.'

'Did you like spending time with him?'

'Why do you ask that?'

'I'm interested in how he got on with young women of your age.'

'That sounds a bit funny. What are you getting at?'

'I'm sorry, it's rather a sensitive thing to ask about, but I've been talking to another young woman who indicated she didn't feel very comfortable with him. She referred to "wandering hands". I'd like to know whether that's ever been the case with you.'

Her eyes darted towards the door that separated them from her father and then back to Jago.

'Look,' she said quietly, 'can we slip outside for a moment?'

She opened the front door and stepped back to let Jago and Cradock leave first, then came out herself and gently pulled it shut behind them.

'I don't want to tell you lies,' she said, 'but I don't want to upset my mum and dad. You understand that, don't you?'

'Of course,' said Jago. 'Just tell me the truth.'

'In that case, the truth is I made sure I was never alone with him.'

'Why's that?'

'For the same reason any girl doesn't like to be alone with some men.'

'You mean he'd behaved inappropriately towards you?'

'That's one way of putting it, I suppose. I'd put it differently – the fact is, he tried it on with me a couple of years ago. I was only seventeen. Can you believe it? I didn't know that sort of thing went on with friends of your family, but I do now, and since then I've done my best to avoid him.'

'Did you tell anyone?'

'I couldn't tell my dad – it'd be too embarrassing. But I did tell my mum.'

'And what did she say?'

'She said that's what men are like, and I should avoid getting into that situation again, but if I did, I should give him a good kick where it hurts and get away from him. Give as good as you get, she said – it's the only language some men understand. Please don't tell my mum or dad what I've just told you, though – I don't want to stir anything up. As far as I'm concerned now, he's just a creepy old man, and I keep out of his way. Was a creepy old man, I should say.'

'Have you told anyone else?'

'Er, no. It's not a nice thing to talk about.'

'Are you sure you didn't? Did you perhaps mention it to Tom, for example?'

She hesitated briefly before replying.

'Well, yes, I did, actually.'

'And what did he say?'

'He just said, "If it happens again, you let me know."'

'I see. Thank you, Miss Potter. That will be all.'

CHAPTER THIRTY-SIX

'Morning, sir,' said Frank Tompkins as Jago walked into West Ham police station early on Saturday morning. 'We've had a report in overnight that I think might interest you. It's to do with the docks, but it came from one of our lads, not the PLA Police. He was on his beat just outside the Albert Dock boundary about three o'clock this morning when he found a car parked where he wouldn't normally expect to see one. He thinks he saw two or three men standing near it, although of course it was dark and he only had the moonlight to go by, but when he got closer they ran off. He thought that was a bit suspicious, and in any case, as he pointed out, there's that new order by the Ministry of Home Security.'

'The one about not leaving a vehicle unattended? I suppose that's what it would be if they all ran off.'

'Yes, if there's no one in charge and within sight of it, it's unattended. And if you're driving your car after lighting-up time, even if you're caught out in an air raid now you have to lock it up or immobilise it before you run for shelter.'

'So what did our observant constable do?'

Tompkins gave a throaty laugh.

'He immobilised it for them, of course – let a couple of tyres down.'

'Very resourceful.'

'Just doing his duty. He's required to take any reasonable steps to make it incapable of being driven away – in case the German army get their hands on it, I suppose.'

'Fine, but what's it got to do with me?'

'Well, the thing is, it was quite a posh car and it was unlocked as well as unattended, so he had it towed round to North Woolwich police station for safe keeping in case it belonged to someone important. He thought it might've been nicked, and if that was what the blokes who ran off had been up to, he didn't want them to come back and finish the job when he'd gone.'

'Posh, eh? What make was it?'

'That's it, you see. It's an Armstrong Siddeley. Big heavy thing – I remember you mentioned coming across one the other day. You don't see many of those around these parts, especially not down the docks.'

'You certainly don't, Frank. I think I'd like to take a look at that car – it sounds like an interesting specimen. Phone North Woolwich, will you, and tell them I'm on my way. And is DC Cradock in?'

'Yes, I believe he's in the canteen having some breakfast.'

'Good, I'll go and round him up.'

With Cradock retrieved from the canteen and installed in the car, Jago set off for North Woolwich police station. It was situated in the heart of North Woolwich, on the corner of Albert Road and Pier Road, next to the Royal Victoria Gardens.

'See that?' said Jago, pointing to a green-tiled pub as they turned into Pier Road. 'The Three Crowns. That's where my dad started his singing career, when he was just an amateur lad looking for a lucky break. He used to come down here and do turns at the "free and easy" nights they had in the old days – the Three Crowns was a famous place for them back then.'

Cradock nodded, hoping to convey an impression of interest in this piece of ancient history. To his relief, any obligation he felt to maintain the impression was cut short by their arrival as Jago turned into the yard behind the station.

North Woolwich police station looked like a smaller cousin of its West Ham counterpart: just two storeys instead of three, but built in the same smart style of brick and stone and adorned with a turret at the corner of the ground floor, reminiscent of those on New Scotland Yard. Jago parked the Riley and found a uniformed constable waiting for them.

'Good morning, sir,' said the constable. 'I understand you want to see the car we brought in overnight. It's over here – I think you'll find it interesting.'

He led them to a large vehicle in the corner of the yard.

'Take a look round the back, sir.'

Jago and Cradock walked round to the rear of the car, where a large leather luggage trunk was strapped onto a rack. Jago opened the lid and found inside the trunk twelve identical wooden cases, on each of which was painted information to the effect that it contained twelve bottles of Mortlach whisky.

'We've opened one, sir,' said the constable. 'One case, that is, not one bottle.'

He removed the lid from the nearest box and Jago moved some of the straw with which it was packed to reveal, indeed, bottles of Mortlach pure-malt whisky.

Jago took one of the bottles out of the case and examined it.

'Mortlach,' he said. 'That's a very fine pure malt. A bit rare too. I'm taking this one with me as evidence, Constable. You keep the rest here under lock and key.'

'Yes, sir. There's also something a bit fishy inside, sir – on the floor by the back seat.'

He opened the rear passenger door on the driver's side, and Jago saw on the floor four cardboard boxes, smaller than the wooden whisky crates.

'We've opened the nearest one, sir. Have a look.'

Jago peered into the box and saw it was packed with small cans. He took one out and examined it, then passed it to Cradock, who did the same.

'Fishy indeed,' said Jago, pocketing the can when Cradock had finished looking. 'Cans of salmon. And they've come a long way, too – all the way from Canada.

Boxes of salmon and whisky in the same car – that's an interesting combination. Either those boys at the Ritz who create cocktails for people with more money than sense have come up with a new recipe, or this lot has something else in common with the whisky.'

'It looks the same as those cans the butcher was flogging – and that the *Magnolia* was carrying,' said Cradock. 'Could be a coincidence, I suppose – it might just be a popular make, as you said.'

'Yes – or there could be a simpler explanation. Peter, see if you can get hold of DI Burton. Tell him we may have found some stolen property connected with his docks and ask him to get over here to the station so he can have a look too.'

He turned to the local constable.

'Show DC Cradock to the phone, will you?'

'Yes, sir. Oh, and by the way, sir, we're checking the number plate on that car. It's a local number, AN 257, but we haven't been able to get hold of anyone at the council yet.'

'I don't think we need to worry too much about that,' said Jago. 'I believe I know who this car belongs to.'

CHAPTER THIRTY-SEVEN

By the time Burton arrived, Jago and Cradock had examined the rest of the car but found nothing of significance. The PLA detective inspector found them in the police station.

'You wanted me?' he said.

'Yes,' said Jago. 'I thought you'd like to see what we've discovered this morning. One of our North Woolwich constables came across an unattended car just outside the Royal Albert Dock during the night, and our colleagues here found something of interest in it. Take a look at this.'

He handed Burton the bottle of whisky he had removed from the car. Burton studied the label.

'Mortlach,' he said. 'Very nice.'

He passed it back to Jago.

'As DC Cradock may've mentioned on the phone,' Jago continued, 'I'm wondering whether this is stolen property, and in particular whether it could be something to do with that racket in Scotland we were discussing the other day – bottles of Scotch consigned for export to America but mysteriously going missing on the way. What do you think?'

'I don't think I could say,' Burton replied. 'All I know is what I told you. Mortlach's a fine malt, but I haven't heard of a particular brand being mentioned in relation to that Scottish business. What kind of car was it in?'

'The car was rather fine too – it's an Armstrong Siddeley. And what's more, I know it – I recognised the registration. I've seen it before.'

'Really? Where?'

'Parked outside Major Danbury's house. It's his – and there were twelve cases of Mortlach in it.'

'And salmon,' Cradock added.

'Salmon?' said Burton, looking from Cradock to Jago with a puzzled expression.

'We found a quantity of tinned salmon in the car too,' Jago explained, 'and you may recall Carlisle told us tinned salmon from Canada was part of the cargo the SS *Magnolia* was carrying.'

'I see,' said Burton. 'But surely you're not saying the major's involved in that business?'

'What do you think?' said Jago. 'You've been working in the docks for eighteen years. Have you had any previous dealings with him? He was a traffic officer in the Royal Albert for nine years or so until he retired, and before that there was the 1926 strike, when he was in the army, escorting convoys in and out of the dock.'

'You mean the General Strike?'

'That's right. Did you run into him then?'

'No, that was before my time.'

'But you've been working in the docks for the last eighteen years – you said so.'

'Yes, but not in the Royals – I started out in St Katharine Docks, up by the Tower of London, and then I was in the West India Docks.'

'The West India Docks? I've heard there used to be quite a bit of pilfering there – men helping themselves to rum, they say. Did you ever come across any of that?'

'Oh, just the odd bit here and there. Nothing serious, though.'

'I'm told Ray Lambert and his pal Len Potter both used to work there at one time. Are you sure you never met either of them there?'

'No, never.'

'When were you there?'

'Until 1928 – I moved to the Royals then, when I got promoted.' He paused, as if reflecting on those past times. 'In fact, you might say I've worked my way up through the ranks as I worked my way down the river.'

'You mean only Tilbury dock left now?'

Burton gave a short, bitter laugh.

'Yes, that's right. But I can't see myself making it to Detective Chief Inspector – as far as the job's concerned, it looks like this is literally the end of the river for me.'

Jago caught the expression in Burton's eyes. It reminded him of a few cocky men he'd charged over the years, whose air of confident defiance had suddenly turned to something more like a muted appeal for pity. He returned to Burton's question.

'I'm not saying Danbury was necessarily responsible for the thefts,' he continued. 'It's quite possible someone stole his car. But having said that, I wouldn't necessarily rule it out – he seems to have been in need of extra cash to pay for his daughter's legal training, for a start, so a bit of private enterprise on the side might've been his idea of a solution.'

'So are we going to question him?' asked Cradock.

'We certainly are. But there's something I'd like to find out first, and that's to do with where this booze was heading. The amount of Scotch in that car wasn't just what you'd need to keep a few pals happy for the night. I'm thinking about those bottle parties up in the West End, and I'd like to make one or two phone calls first. Perhaps you could take DI Burton off for a cup of tea while I do that, Peter, and bring one back for me when you've finished.'

'Will there be time for a bite to eat too, sir?'

'Yes, if you must, but don't be all day.'

Cradock took Burton away for their refreshments. When they returned, they found Jago already off the phone. The bottle of Mortlach whisky he had removed from the car stood on the desk in front of him. Cradock deposited a mug of tea on the desk next to it, together with a cake on a small plate.

'I brought a rock cake for you too, sir, in case you

were peckish. Did you get through?'

'Yes, I did,' said Jago, taking a sip of tea and eyeing the rock cake for size. 'A most fruitful call, in fact. I spoke to the sub-divisional inspector at Marlborough Street – he's the head of their bottle-party squad, and I asked him if they'd done any raids recently. It turned out they had, so I said I was particularly interested to know whether they'd come across any quantities of pure-malt whisky with a mark etched on the bottles, like this one.'

He passed the bottle to Burton.

'Do you know anything about marks etched onto whisky bottles?'

Burton glanced at it.

'No, I don't.'

'Well, it turned out the bottle-party squad did, and they'd been in touch with their colleagues in Scotland to find out what this particular etching meant. Apparently it's the mark the distillery uses to show the bottles are part of a consignment for export to the USA – they said it's a requirement under American law.'

'So it was stolen, then?' said Cradock.

'Without a doubt.'

Jago looked at Burton with eyebrows raised to invite an opinion, but his fellow officer seemed disinclined to venture one.

'Where was the club they raided?' Cradock asked.

'In Albemarle Street,' Jago replied. 'Seems the air raids have put a lot of people off the idea of nightclubbing, but there are still some bottle parties going on – and this particular club's in the basement of a big concrete building, so it's a very popular night-time haunt. They charge people seven and six to get in, two shillings for a sandwich, and double the lawful price for ordinary blended whisky, so you can imagine what they'd be making on a bottle of pure malt.'

'Did they pick up the owner?'

'Oh, yes. The proprietor and the manager have both been up before the magistrates and fined a hundred pounds each for permitting dancing and selling intoxicating liquor without a licence. They'd also been providing what the Defence Regulations call "demoralising entertainment" involving young ladies disrobing.'

'I've never been invited to a party like that.'

'I should hope not, Peter.'

'So did the Marlborough Street blokes find out where the club had got the whisky from?'

'No. Neither the owner nor the manager was forthcoming, and the sub-divisional inspector thought they were quite possibly just dummies put up by the real men behind the business. I did find out something else interesting, though.'

'Yes, sir?'

'I asked him whether they'd taken the names and addresses of everyone attending, as usual, and he said yes. He said they were an interesting bunch too – a viscount, a minor film star, and no end of officers and gentlemen, plus their ladies of course. Definitely the crème de la crème, as you might expect at a club in Mayfair. No charges were brought against any of the guests, but I asked him to check whether the list included anyone with an address in Forest Gate. And guess who he found.'

'A certain distinguished major, retired?'

'Spot on. A Major Royston Danbury and his good wife. Apparently he'd been very insistent on telling the constable his rank.'

'If they'd already nicked a viscount he should've known it wasn't worth playing that card. I'd say he's been well and truly caught out.'

'Well, at the very least it's a remarkable coincidence that the major and the whisky we found in the trunk on his car should've gone to the same party. I think we need to have a word with the gallant gentleman.'

'Right away, sir?'

'Right away. And ask the sergeant here if we can borrow some handcuffs. I have a feeling we may need them today.'

CHAPTER THIRTY-EIGHT

'After you,' said Jago, holding the car door open for Burton.

'You sure you need me to come along?' said Burton. 'I don't think I'll have anything to contribute.'

'If that whisky was pinched, it happened in the Royal Albert Dock, on your manor, so it's only right you should be there. Besides, something might crop up that you know more about than we do. I'd be obliged.'

'Very well, then.'

Burton edged himself carefully into the back seat, and Cradock settled into his customary place in the front. Jago took the wheel and set off eastwards along Albert Road, past the long row of terraced houses that backed onto the northern edge of the Royal Victoria Gardens. After skirting the eastern end of the docks he headed north through East Ham towards Forest Gate, and within half an hour they had pulled up outside Danbury's house.

Jago and Cradock strode up to the front door, with Burton hanging back a little behind them. Jago rang the doorbell, and it was opened by a maid: he inferred from her presence that the Danburys' domestic staff crisis had passed. She showed them into the house, and a few moments later Mrs Danbury joined them.

'Good morning, Mrs Danbury,' said Jago. 'Is your husband in?'

'Yes, he's in the drawing room. Shall I fetch him?'

'Perhaps you could take us to him. I need to talk to him.'

'Of course. Follow me.'

She led them to the drawing room, where Danbury was sitting with his daughter. He rose when they entered the room.

'Good morning, gentlemen. To what do we owe this visit?'

'Good morning, Major Danbury. I'm sorry to disturb you, but there's something I must ask you. This is Detective Inspector Burton, by the way. He's from the PLA Police.'

'Really?' said Danbury, taking a closer look at him. 'Ah, yes. You're the fellow I met in the dock on Tuesday morning when that body had been found, aren't you?'

'I believe we met very briefly,' Burton replied, 'but that was all.'

Burton made no further comment, and Jago continued.

'And this is Detective Constable Cradock, who was with me last time we met.'

'Of course.'

'Shall I leave you to talk to these gentlemen, Daddy?'

said Evelyn, half rising from her seat.

'No, no, you stay, my dear,' said Danbury.

She sat down again and positioned herself demurely on the sofa, next to her mother.

'So,' said Danbury to Jago, 'how can I help you? I should mention that I'm rather busy today, so I'd appreciate it if you could be brief. Is it to do with that burglary we had?'

'No, it's a different matter. We have reason to believe you recently attended a bottle party in Mayfair where stolen liquor was being served. Is that true?'

'Bottle party? No, I don't recall that at all.'

'It was at a club in Albemarle Street.'

'No, there must be some mistake.'

'Major Danbury, perhaps I could remind you that my colleagues from C Division of the Metropolitan Police not only raided that party but also took the names and addresses of those present. Your name and that of your wife were on that list. Now do you remember?'

Mrs Danbury stared silently at the floor. Meanwhile, her husband's face suggested that he'd suddenly recalled something so trivial that without prompting he'd have forgotten it for ever.

'And before you answer that question, Major Danbury,' said Jago, 'I must advise you that you're not obliged to say anything, but anything you say may be given in evidence.'

'What?' said Danbury. 'That sounds rather official. What's this all about?'

Jago was now beginning to feel irritated by his own willingness to pander to Danbury's insistence on being addressed by his military rank.

'Just tell me please, if you will, Mr Danbury. Do you remember being at that bottle party?'

'Why, I, er – yes, of course, now I do. We were at an establishment that the police visited, but I don't recall the address. Some friends took us there, you see – invited us to go along with them. It's not something we normally do.'

'I'm sure you don't.'

'It was just innocent fun, a light-hearted evening out with friends to take our minds off this ghastly war.'

'And we certainly had no idea there was anything dubious about the drinks they were serving,' added Mrs Danbury with an air of innocence. 'In any case, no action was taken against us. We didn't break any laws.'

'No, but the people running that club did.'

Jago turned back to her husband.

'Now, Mr Danbury,' he said. Danbury opened his mouth as if to remind Jago to call him Major, but seemed to think better of the idea. He closed his mouth and looked attentive. 'What really interests me,' Jago continued, 'is this – what connection is there between you and the stolen goods being sold at that club?'

'Connection? What on earth do you mean? Are you seriously suggesting that I'm involved in any way with stolen whisky being served in a London club?'

'Very perceptive of you to discern that it was whisky

I was talking about, Mr Danbury.'

'Well, I just assumed—'

'In that case you assumed correctly. Some very fine whisky too, as I'm sure you're aware.'

'I don't know what you're talking about.'

'All right, how about this, then? Can you tell me where your car is – that nice old Armstrong Siddeley of yours?'

Danbury looked uncertain how to reply.

'Well, er, actually it's missing.'

'Missing?'

'Yes. I was on duty last night in the docks, and when I came out this morning and went to where we'd left it parked, it had disappeared. My wife and daughter can confirm that – they were with me. It was very difficult for us too – we had to go home on the bus.'

My heart bleeds for you, thought Jago. He didn't imagine they'd have been thrown off the bus for smelling foul.

'So the car was gone,' he continued. 'What did you think? That someone had stolen it?'

'Well, yes, I suppose I did.'

'Suppose? Did you report it to the police?'

'Not yet. I was going to, but my first priority was to get my wife and daughter safely home, and then I had some urgent Home Guard matters to attend to.'

'Really?' Jago had his own ideas about why Danbury might not have reported the loss of his car immediately, but he decided to play along for the time being.

'I see. Well, I hope it'll reassure you to know that my

colleagues at North Woolwich police station have already located the missing vehicle and have it in safe keeping.'

'Oh – that's, er, good news,' said Danbury, looking a little disconcerted.

'Now, when you were at that bottle party, I don't suppose you noticed whether they were selling any Mortlach whisky, did you? It's a particularly fine pure malt, made in Morayshire, I believe.'

'No, I didn't. I don't drink whisky.'

'Really? Well, in that case could you explain why my colleagues found rather a large quantity of whisky in the trunk on the back of your car last night – of Mortlach pure malt, to be precise. It's just that DI Burton and I have heard reports of whisky being stolen in Scotland and finding its way to the London docks, haven't we, DI Burton?'

Burton looked uncertain whether to get involved in the conversation, but said, 'Yes, that's right.'

'And the whisky we found in your car this morning is part of the same consignment as was being sold at that club,' Jago continued.

'Then I can only imagine that whoever stole that whisky also stole my car to transport it somewhere,' said Danbury. 'It's nothing to do with me.'

'I'm sorry, Mr Danbury, but I don't believe you. I think it's everything to do with you. You've been stealing whisky from the docks and on at least one occasion you've supplied it to a bottle party for illegal sale at an extortionate price. If your plan had not been disrupted overnight you'd have supplied them with some more today. That's right, isn't it? You stole it.'

'No. I, I . . .'

Danbury's voice trailed away as the explanation he was looking for would not come. When at last he spoke he sounded like a cornered man, defeated.

'Please, Inspector,' he pleaded. His eyes scoured the room as if in search of someone to vindicate him. 'You have to believe me. I didn't steal anything.'

'That won't wash, Mr Danbury. I'll ask you again. If you didn't steal that whisky, what was it doing in your car?'

Danbury sank back in his seat and let out a sharp breath, like a suddenly deflating balloon.

'All right. Yes, I knew it would be in my car, but I didn't put it there, and I didn't steal it. I was forced into it, and that's the truth.'

'Forced by whom?'

'By the people who stole it, of course. I can tell you how they did it.'

The once-confident officer now looked different. There was something verging on the pathetic in his apparent desire to please.

'All right,' said Jago diffidently. 'You can tell me.'

He watched as Danbury struggled to compose himself. It seemed that the man was ashamed, perhaps, of having been seen in a moment of weakness.

The major cleared his throat.

'I'll tell you everything I know, Inspector,' he said.

'I hope then you'll see what kind of people I've been dealing with. They're out-and-out criminals, and once they'd got their claws into me there was nothing I could do.'

'So tell me how the whisky was stolen. Help me to understand.'

'Of course.' Danbury's spirits seemed to revive now that he could slip into the role of responsible citizen assisting the police. 'I don't know how much you know about the docks, Inspector, but the fact is that a certain amount of cargo gets lost or damaged. Fragile goods like bottles, for example, are vulnerable to what's known as "breakage".'

'I think I can understand what the term refers to.'

'Of course, yes. Well, it can happen if a ship runs into rough seas, especially if the cargo hasn't been loaded properly, but there are also accidents. A case slips as it's being unloaded from the ship, for example. It hits the ground and one bottle of the twelve in it is smashed, but the whole case is written off.'

'Very convenient. And what happens to the other eleven bottles?'

'Well, people do say some dockers often go home with a smile on their faces. Whisky's particularly vulnerable to so-called breakage, apparently – I've heard that when it's being shipped to America up to a third can be lost in transit, as much of it to thirsty dockers as to bad seas.'

'So was this how those bottles ended up in your car instead of with their rightful owners?'

'I don't know the whole story, but I believe the whisky in question was bound for export from Scotland to the USA. There's a lot of paperwork at both ends, with plenty of points where errors can creep into the record-keeping, intentional as well as unintentional, and sometimes the owners just have to accept the discrepancies. That's the case at the best of times, and now things are even worse, because the war means the Clyde docks are having to handle a lot more shipping than they used to. I'm told things are in turmoil up there.'

'DI Burton tells me some dockers from down here have been sent up to Clydebank to help. Are they mixed up in this racket?'

'I don't know. I'm not involved personally, but I've heard things.'

'So tell me what you've heard.'

'Well, I was told that when some of the men up there are loading cases of pure-malt whisky onto ships bound for America, they'll report that they've loaded, say, twenty cases more than they actually have, and hide the twenty somewhere in the dock. Then they pay off a crew member so that when the ship arrives in America he'll say those cases were lost due to breakage. Meanwhile, some of those London dockers who've been sent up there are helping to move cargo onto coasters for transhipment to London and other ports, which means that later the cases can be stowed away in a hiding place on a coaster without being recorded, and then delivered to the Royal Docks.'

'Where some other enterprising colleagues of theirs can get them over the fence and into a waiting vehicle, presumably under cover of the blackout.'

'That's it.'

'So the waiting vehicle was your car, and you then delivered the goods to the club in Albemarle Street?'

'Yes.'

'But I thought you didn't drive at night.'

'Who told you that?'

'I believe it was your daughter. Isn't that correct, Miss Danbury?'

'Not exactly,' said Evelyn. 'He does drive at night sometimes. I think I said his eyes aren't too good for night driving, so I like to drive him if I can, and on this particular occasion, as it happens, I did.'

'So you were at this bottle party too?'

'Me? My goodness, no. I had no desire to go to their stuffy old party with all those boring people – I left them there with the car and met up with a university friend instead. She's considerably wealthier than I am and has a flat of her own in Soho, so I walked over there, then when Mummy and Daddy had finished they phoned me there and I went back and drove them home.'

'Were you aware of what was in the trunk when you drove them to the party?'

'Definitely not. I had no reason to open it, and certainly no reason to ask my parents whether they were carrying illicit alcohol.'

'Thank you,' said Jago. 'And Mr Danbury, what was

your cut for providing this transport service?'

'Cut?' Danbury gave a dismissive laugh. 'You don't think I got anything out of it, do you? Someone obviously did – I heard the man at the club say he'd send the cash over as usual – but it wasn't me. None of his money came to my house. I've told you already, Inspector, I wasn't part of this. I had no choice – they forced me.'

'Indeed you have, but you haven't told me who forced you. Who was it?'

Danbury hesitated, as if he had several potential replies in mind and couldn't choose which one to use.

'It was as I said – the people who stole that whisky.'

'Why would they force you to provide their transport?'

'I think they were afraid I'd report them. My car would be useful to them, and if they could force me to get involved I'd be in no position to go to the police.'

'So who were they? Who stole that whisky, if it wasn't you?'

'Dockers,' he said, spitting out the word as if it was distasteful in his mouth. 'Just a pack of dockers. And don't ask me for names – I don't know who they are, and I don't want to know.'

'You surprise me,' said Jago. 'An officer and gentleman like you? I wouldn't have thought you'd take orders from people like that.'

'Like what?'

'Your subordinates. And criminals too. What power did they have over you that would make you do their bidding?'

Danbury fell silent again, his eyes fixed on the carpet

at his feet. When he looked up again there was anger in his face.

'That's just it. They're criminals, and they used me, not simply because I have a car but because they said I was the class of person to have contacts in the West End who'd take the whisky. But there was more to it than that, of course. It was clear to me that if I was the one who supplied the whisky to the clubs, I was also the one who'd be sent down if anything went wrong. One of them used a vulgar American expression from those dreadful gangster films – he said if there was any trouble with the police I could "take the rap". And he was right, wasn't he? I'm sitting here taking the rap, while he's not.'

'These dockers, Mr Danbury, how did they get to you? Were they members of your Home Guard platoon?'

'One or two, maybe. I told you I don't know all the names.'

'But you know the names of the men in your platoon, don't you?'

'Yes.'

'Was one of this gang of thieves called Lambert?'

'Yes,' said Danbury, his voice almost a whisper. 'He was one of them.'

CHAPTER THIRTY-NINE

Evelyn Danbury moved to her father's side and took his hand in hers, glaring at Jago, Cradock and Burton in turn.

'Can I get you a drink, Daddy?' she said.

'No, thank you, my dear.'

She turned to Louise Danbury.

'For you, Mummy?'

'No, thank you, darling.'

Evelyn pointedly declined to extend the same offer to the three police officers and sat down again.

'So,' said Jago, resuming his questioning of Danbury, 'how did a man like Lambert manage to call the tune so easily?'

The memory of this experience seemed to spark Danbury back into anger.

'I made a mistake – all right? Everyone's allowed to make a mistake or two in their life – except me, it seems.'

'Tell me about it, please, Mr Danbury.'

'All right, I will. But before I do, you need to

understand the circumstances. You were an officer on the Western Front, weren't you? You know what happens in war. Those smart alecs who stay at home think it's some kind of game, like a glorified rugby match, but it's not, is it? Their cosy rules don't apply.'

'So this is to do with something that happened during the last war?'

'Not quite. But it was a kind of war – it was that time I told you about when I was serving in India, those riots in Amritsar.'

'Yes?'

'Well, that's where I made . . . a mistake. The authorities were worried the riots might get out of hand, so they sent us – the troops, that is – to pacify them. The whole future of British rule in India was at risk. It was a very complicated situation and it wasn't what we were used to. We'd just spent four years fighting a modern war with tanks and machine guns, first against the Germans and then the Turks. You knew who the enemy were – they wore uniforms and you met them in battle. But now it was on our home territory, in a town in India. We couldn't tell who were the political agitators and revolutionaries and who were just ordinary passers-by – they all looked the same. We weren't ready for policing crowds of civilians.'

Danbury hesitated: he seemed to be trying to calm himself.

'Go on,' said Jago.

'I . . . I saw a man who I thought was up to no good

and pulled him out of the crowd. I took him away to one side to question him. He stared at me like a maniac – I could see real hatred in his eyes, and then he screamed some abuse at me in a language I couldn't understand and spat on my uniform – on the king's uniform. Then I, I . . . I don't really know what happened next. It was just too much. After all those years fighting, to have one of our own people, one of the king's subjects, spit on my uniform – something just snapped. I pulled out my revolver and shot him. He was the enemy. I threw him to one side and went back into the square. No one knew what I'd done, no one had seen me, but for twenty-one years that man's face has haunted me. I knew what I'd done was wrong, but I also knew I had to keep it secret.'

'But there was one person who saw you, wasn't there?'

Danbury nodded silently, his head down.

'And that man was Lambert?'

'Yes. I had no idea until he approached me one day at the docks.'

'Was this when you were still working in the Royal Albert?'

'No. For all I know he may have seen me or heard of me at some point in those days, but I never consciously met him.'

'So when did he approach you?'

'It was just after the Local Defence Volunteers were set up, so probably sometime in late May of this year. That brought me back into the docks, of course, but this time I was wearing my old army uniform. I think I mentioned before that some of us did that in the early days of the LDVs, especially former officers – we even wore our old regimental insignia. I don't know whether that's what made Lambert recognise me, but he joined the LDVs too and became part of my platoon. One day soon after that he came to me and said he knew me from India. I didn't recognise him, of course. As I told you the other day, he couldn't have been in my regiment, because the men who served as other ranks were all natives.'

'You also told me Lambert had never said anything to you about India during the time you'd been his commander in the Home Guard. But that clearly wasn't true, was it?'

Danbury cleared his throat nervously.

'Er, no. But the fact remains that when he approached me I had no idea who he was. To me he was just another docker. But then he said it.'

'Said what?'

'Just one word – "Amritsar". When I heard it, that incident I've just described to you came rushing back to me. He said he'd been there and he knew what I'd done – he was an eyewitness. He'd even found out the man's name.'

'Could you tell me that name, please?'

'Yes.' Danbury hesitated, then added quietly, 'He said it was Dayabir Singh.'

'I see. Carry on.'

'I asked him how he could claim to have seen me,

341

and he said he was in one of the armoured cars that our commanding officer had ordered to the square. He accused me of murdering the man, but that wasn't fair. I'd shot him because I believed he was an agitator, and the riot he and his kind had whipped up was a threat to law and order in the whole of India. The brigadier-general had made it quite clear – if the rioters didn't disperse quietly he planned to open fire with the machine guns mounted on those armoured cars. It was only the fact that the cars were too wide to get onto the square that stopped that, otherwise Lambert himself would have been the one who killed that man – yes, and many others besides. What right did he have to judge me? I was just doing my duty.'

'But there was an official enquiry, wasn't there?'

'Into my actions? No, there wasn't.'

'I'm talking about a government enquiry into the whole incident at Amritsar.'

'Ah, the Hunter Committee's report, you mean? Yes. They had the temerity to criticise my commanding officer's actions, but it's easy to condemn in hindsight from the comfort of a committee room. Those people weren't there – they didn't know the pressure we were under. How can they say they wouldn't have done the same thing if they'd been in our shoes? The whole exercise was a betrayal by a government that wanted to placate the Indian nationalists and save their own necks.'

'And what about Lambert? What did he want from you?'

'What do his sort always want? Money, of course.

He tried to blackmail me.'

'And did he succeed?'

'No. I don't take orders from riff-raff like that. And even if I did, I wouldn't give him money – my daughter's future was at stake.' He glanced in the direction of Evelyn, who smiled at him encouragingly. 'She's training for the law, and I would have spent every penny I had if it would help her fulfil her dream.'

'So what did you do?'

'I told Lambert he was an impudent upstart and a scoundrel and sent him packing.'

'But that wasn't the end of it?'

'No. Then he mentioned Sir Michael O'Dwyer, the former lieutenant-governor of the Punjab, the poor fellow who was assassinated in London in March. You remember?'

'Yes – at Caxton Hall in Westminster.'

'In that case you may also recall that he was shot dead by an Indian from the Punjab. It was because Sir Michael had always supported the action my commanding officer took that day in Amritsar, and his enemies said that as lieutenant-governor he was responsible for what happened. It was a murder of revenge.'

'What religion was the assassin?'

'I'm not sure – it was rather confusing. He wore western dress and gave his name as Mahomed Singh Azad, so of course people thought with a name like Mahomed he must be a Muslim, but on the other hand "Singh" suggested he was a Sikh.'

'As was Dayabir Singh, the man you killed?'

'I think so, yes.'

'What else did Lambert say?'

'He said if I didn't start paying up he knew how to get my name into the hands of people like the man who'd murdered O'Dwyer, and he was sure there'd be plenty of others like him who'd be only too glad to do the same to me. I could see no alternative, so I paid him.'

'But there's never a final payment, is there?'

'No,' said Danbury through gritted teeth. 'There isn't. He thought he'd got me by the throat and he wasn't going to give up lightly. I think he'd even joined the Home Guard just so he could get close to me and taunt me. He had that Indian's name written on a piece of paper, and he used to get some evil satisfaction out of taking it from his pocket and waving it in front of me whenever we were together in private – just to remind me of our arrangement, he said. Forcing me to be part of that shameful business with the whisky and using my car was just a small part of it. He did his best to torment and humiliate me.'

'You didn't think of reporting this to the police?'

'No. I had too much to lose – it had to remain secret.'

'Did anyone else apart from Lambert know about it? Other men connected with the docks, for example?'

'I don't know. He didn't say.'

'And did you tell anyone else yourself?'

'Only my wife. I have no secrets from her, and she had to know, because we couldn't spend money as we used to.'

'And you continued paying?'

'What else could I do? It wasn't just the risk of losing my good name – now my very life was at stake.'

'I see. And so you killed him. You waited until you thought the blackout would cover you, and you stabbed him – and you used an Indian knife. Was that some kind of historical irony for you, or did you want to implicate that lascar on the ship?'

Danbury looked up at Jago with pleading eyes.

'No! I didn't kill him, I swear I didn't. Look, I've told you, I don't possess such a knife. I used to have one, but it was stolen in that burglary. Yes, I heartily wished Lambert could die – I hoped he'd be killed some night by a bomb and I'd be finished with him. But I didn't kill him, I tell you.'

Jago turned to Danbury's wife.

'So, Mrs Danbury, the question is, is your husband lying?'

She looked confused, uncertain how to reply.

'N-no,' she stuttered. 'Of course he's not. My husband is an honourable man, Inspector, a man of integrity. He's never lied to me.'

'Well, he says you're the only person he's ever told about this, so if he's telling the truth, that leaves only you.'

Mrs Danbury jumped to her feet. Jago heard a gasp behind his back and turned to see it had come from Burton. Jago waited for him to speak, but his colleague merely shook his head and made a quick dismissive motion with his hand.

'Mrs Danbury,' Jago continued, turning back to face

her. 'You knew about Lambert and you were there in the dock that night. Did you kill him?'

Louise Danbury's eyes widened and her mouth moved in a silent expression of horror as she backed away. It seemed an age before she willed herself to speak.

'Me? You can't be serious. How could I kill a man? Tell them, Royston – help me.'

She took another step back and stopped as she came up against the wall. She looked around helplessly at her family and then back at Jago. In the brief moment of silence Evelyn Danbury got slowly out of her chair and cast a condescending glance in Jago's direction.

'It wasn't her, Inspector,' she said, her voice languid. She slowly lit a cigarette and blew a cloud of blue smoke across the room. 'I knew too. My mother told me, you see. She was so worried about Daddy, she had to tell someone, and I was the only person she knew she could trust. It was all quite straightforward, really. I decided Lambert had gone too far, and someone had to deal with him.'

'No!' cried her mother. 'Don't listen to her.'

'Don't worry, Mummy. I know what I'm doing.'

She turned back to Jago.

'I thought it was quite plausible that if Lambert had been in India he might have made an enemy, and a Sikh knife would be a sure indication of an Indian taking revenge on him for the very kind of accident that has haunted my father all these years. So I removed my father's memento and one or two other trinkets and broke a window to make it look like a burglary in the blackout. You see, my father is an officer and a gentleman who has served his king and country all his life, and people here look up to him and respect him. It was bad enough to think he might forfeit his good name just because a common thief of no value wanted to disgrace him, but when that man threatened to put him at the mercy of some bloodthirsty foreign assassins I could not stand idly by. Lambert was a horrid little man, a degenerate, typical of his class. He's the sort that our society shouldn't breed in the first place, and that we'd be better off without. You might call it a crime, but I call it playing my small part in purifying our race.'

She drew on her cigarette again and gave Jago a defiant look as he stepped towards her.

'But there, Inspector, my mouth's running away with me. Actually I need to make something else clear. It was self-defence. I only intended to threaten him, to frighten him enough to make him leave my father alone. But before I could do that, he caught me alone on the quayside and attacked me in the dark. He was like a fiend, grabbing me and holding me to him, trying to pull me down to the ground, and I had no other recourse but to get that knife out of my pocket. It was the only way I could defend my honour. It was an act of desperation by a virtuous young woman, as I'm sure any jury will accept. That's all I have to say.'

'We'll see about that,' said Jago grimly. 'You're under arrest.'

CHAPTER FORTY

Jago beckoned Cradock, who produced two sets of handcuffs from his pockets. Evelyn Danbury made no response, but gazed at him like a disinterested observer. Drawing impassively one last time on her cigarette, she deposited it carefully in an ashtray before offering up her wrists to Cradock. He applied one set of handcuffs to her while Jago put the other on her father.

'What am I charged with, Detective Inspector?' said Evelyn, her voice cool and composed.

'You're not charged with anything yet,' said Jago. 'But you're under arrest on suspicion of murder, so you're coming to West Ham police station with us.'

Her father stood in silence, looking stunned by what had happened in the preceding few minutes.

'And me?' he said finally, his voice fragile. 'What have I done? I'm a victim, not a criminal. I had no part in stealing those things.'

'You're under arrest too, Mr Danbury. In your case it's on suspicion of receiving property, knowing it to have been stolen. Larceny Act, 1916, section 33. Receiving is as serious a crime as stealing.'

Danbury's shoulders slumped in resignation, his habitual military bearing seemingly now abandoned. He stood meekly, as if waiting for Jago's next order, and made no further comment.

Detective Inspector Burton too seemed to have nothing to say and followed silently behind Jago and Cradock as they escorted Danbury and his daughter to the car. Once the two prisoners were installed in the back seat, Cradock took the one at the front, from where he could keep an eye on them.

'Looks like there's no room for me, then,' said Burton, a barely concealed tinge of bitterness in his voice.

'I'm sorry about that,' said Jago. 'Shall I phone the station and get one of our lads to come and pick you up?'

'No, I'm sure your men have better things to do. Besides, I don't really think you need me now – I'm just part of the scenery in this case. What the film people call a walk-on part, isn't it? I'll get the train back to my office – the railway station's only round the corner, isn't it?'

'Yes, but are the trains still running as far as the docks? I heard the lines down there were out of action because of the bombing.'

'Last I heard they were – as far as Albert Dock Junction, at least, but that'll do for me. I'll be fine – I'll run along now and leave you two ace detectives to tie up the loose ends.'

'Very well.' Jago tried to read Burton's face, but it was a mask. 'There is something I'd like to ask you, though, before you go. Just now, when I was questioning Mrs Danbury, I thought I heard you make what sounded like a gasping noise behind me. Were you going to say something?'

Burton hesitated, as if trying to recall the moment to which Jago was referring.

'No,' he replied. 'Nothing in particular. I think I was just surprised when you suddenly turned on her. I wasn't expecting it. I suppose I'm just not used to these big murder enquiries.'

'I see,' said Jago, still uncertain about him.

Burton was about to go when Jago added, as an afterthought, 'Tell me – you mentioned when I first met you that you'd served in the Indian Imperial Police after the war. You didn't by any chance happen to meet Mr and Mrs Danbury then, did you?'

'No, of course not,' said Burton. 'It's a big place, you know, India.'

'Of course. Well, thank you for your help.'

'Any time,' said Burton. 'I look forward to working with you again.'

He turned away abruptly and set off in the direction of Forest Gate station. Jago watched him until he turned the corner at the end of Claremont Road and was lost from sight.

CHAPTER FORTY-ONE

Jago remained where he was for a few moments, pondering what Burton had said, then shook his head silently and turned back to join Cradock in the car.

'Right, Peter,' he said, 'let's get these two back to the nick.'

The two handcuffed passengers in the back of the Riley said not a word as they drove to the police station, and the two men in front maintained a similar silence. On arriving at the station, they walked Danbury and his daughter in and handed them over to Tompkins.

'Put these two in the cells, please, Frank,' said Jago. 'We'll be charging them later.'

'Very well, sir,' said Tompkins. 'By the way, there's a couple of gentlemen wanting to speak to you. Will you see them now, while I take care of this other pair?'

'Yes, I will.'

Jago and Cradock made their way to the interview

room, where they found their two visitors waiting. Jago recognised the lascar from the *Magnolia* accompanied by Hibbert, the man he had met at the Coloured Men's Institute. He strode over to them.

'Ah, Mr Jamal,' he said, 'I'm very pleased to see you. We'd heard you'd gone missing and were worried about you.' He turned to Hibbert. 'And you, sir, thank you for passing on our message to Mr Jamal.'

'I assured him that you'd said he wasn't in any trouble,' Hibbert replied, 'and he said he was willing to speak to you, so I phoned your colleagues here this morning and they suggested we come in to see you.'

'Thank you. I appreciate your help.'

'I should mention that I've also assured Mr Jamal that you only want to speak to him as a witness. I trust that if he has anything to answer for he will be treated with the best of British justice.'

'Mr Jamal has nothing to fear here.'

'I should certainly hope not. And if you don't mind, I would like to stay here while you talk to Mr Jamal.'

'By all means.'

Jago turned to Jamal, who had been listening to their conversation nervously, sitting with his hands clasped together between his knees.

'Now, Mr Jamal,' he said. 'I understand you left the SS *Magnolia* sometime on Wednesday night. Is that correct?'

'Who told you that?'

'It was reported to the Port of London Authority

Police, and Detective Inspector Burton passed it on to me. Is it correct?'

'Yes,' Jamal replied, his voice subdued.

'And I also understand that you left the ship without permission. Correct?'

'Yes, I'm sorry. I should not have done that.'

'It's not a very sensible thing to run away during a murder investigation, is it?'

'I know, but please believe me – I had no choice.'

'Why's that?'

'Will I get in trouble if I tell you?'

'That rather depends on what you say. You'll only be in trouble with me if you've broken the law. I suggest you just listen to my questions carefully and answer them truthfully – starting with explaining to me why you ran away.'

'It's not what you're thinking. I had to get away. There were bad things happening, and I thought I was in danger.'

'What bad things?'

'Things on the ship. Things were being stolen, and I thought I would be the one who was blamed for it. It's easy to blame the foreigners for everything. I thought if someone said I was the thief you would believe them.'

'What kind of things were being stolen?'

'Food, and also drink. Bad drink – alcohol. In my religion we do not drink it, but I have seen how men love it here, and how it makes them fight. If anyone accused me of stealing it I would feel ashamed.'

'So who was doing the stealing?'

'I'm sorry, Inspector, I cannot tell you.'

'Look, Mr Jamal, I want to catch whoever did this and put them behind bars. You knew what was happening and you knew it was a crime. Did you report them to the master?'

'No, I tried to, but he was not there when I went to look for him.'

'The mate then?'

Jamal looked down into his lap and fell silent.

Jago waited for an answer, but none came.

'Was it him?' he asked. 'Was it Mr Carlisle who was doing it?'

Hibbert placed a hand on Jamal's shoulder.

'I think you'd better tell the inspector, Abdul,' he said gently.

Jamal nodded without looking up. When he spoke, his voice was barely audible.

'Yes,' he said. 'I could not report it to Mr Carlisle, because I knew he was doing the stealing – I had seen him. And then he came looking for me. He said there were men who wanted to hurt me because I had spoken to you as a witness when you asked about the man who was murdered. He said they might even want to kill me, so I should save my life by running away. I do not like him, but I believed him, so I ran, and I never want to return to that ship. Now, please, do not ask me any more questions – I cannot help you. I am afraid.'

'Very well,' said Jago. 'I suggest you go back with Mr

Hibbert for now – I'm sure he'll look after you. But don't leave this area until I say you can. We may need you to give evidence.'

Jamal looked more nervous than before but nodded quickly.

'Is it all right if I help him try to find work on a different ship?' asked Hibbert.

'Yes,' Jago replied. 'As long as he doesn't disappear again without asking me first. As far as I'm concerned, no one's going to force him to go back to the *Magnolia*.'

CHAPTER FORTY-TWO

'Any more of what DI Burton calls loose ends to tie up, guv'nor? Apart from Carlisle, of course – what Jamal said was pretty damning, wasn't it?'

'Yes, it was. There might be one or two other matters to tidy up, I think, but first things first. Jamal may not be returning to that ship, but we are. We're going straight down to the Albert Dock for a word with Mr Duncan Carlisle about stolen whisky.'

Jago and Cradock went out of the police station's back door into the yard, where the car was parked, and set off down West Ham Lane, heading south. Traffic on the road was light, and occasional shafts of autumn sunlight broke through the cloud as if to defy the gloom of war and destruction that surrounded them. Cradock appeared to be thinking quietly to himself, his eyes closed and his brow furrowed. Jago was enjoying both the absence of noise and the thought that the case was almost wrapped up.

It was Cradock who broke the silence first.

'I've been thinking, sir,' he said.

'Not again,' said Jago. 'If you're not careful, this is going to become a habit. What've you been thinking about this time?'

'Well, it was all a bit complicated, wasn't it? Why Ray Lambert ended up getting murdered, I mean.'

Jago nodded, keeping his eyes on the road ahead.

'I suppose it was, yes,' he replied. 'Lambert was killed because he was blackmailing Danbury, and Danbury was blackmailed because he'd murdered a man called Dayabir Singh thousands of miles away in India, and Singh was murdered because a British brigadier-general ordered his troops to open fire on a crowd of civilians . . .'

'Exactly. It makes you wonder where it all started, doesn't it? I mean, whose fault was it all in the first place?'

'I think that depends on how far back you go. Someone does something bad to someone else, and that means they want to get their own back. It can go on for centuries.'

'Is that why we had the war to end all wars and now we're having another one?'

'Some people would say so. It's not just an ordinary person who might want to get their own back. Sometimes a whole country wants to, and then it starts all over again. It's called a vicious circle, and the trick is how to break it.'

'Lambert didn't manage to, did he?'

'No. You thought it might be a revenge killing, and you were right. All anyone can hope is that in this case, at least, we've seen the last round.'

They drove on in silence. This talk of endless cycles of revenge had made Jago feel strangely weary, and by the time they reached the SS *Magnolia* he found himself hoping never to see it again. He focused his mind on confronting Carlisle.

They found him on board and went with him to his cabin.

'I'll come straight to the point, Mr Carlisle,' Jago began. 'I have a few questions to ask you. You're not obliged to say anything, but anything you say may be given in evidence.'

Carlisle looked at him warily but said nothing.

'Now,' Jago continued, 'I'm aware that you called West Ham police station early yesterday morning and withdrew your earlier statement about having a drink with Charlie Bell on your ship – in fact, you went so far as to say you'd lied. But Mr Bell said you did invite him on board for a drink, so you can't both be right. I want to know which of the two stories you've told us is true.'

'What?' said Carlisle. 'Why are you still pestering me like this? Surely it's not that important?'

'A man was murdered that night, so that makes everything that happened or didn't happen important.'

'You're not suggesting I killed that man? That's preposterous, it's ridiculous. Why would I do that?'

'It's all right, Mr Carlisle, you don't need to get het up about it. As a matter of fact I'm pretty sure you didn't.'

'Really? Oh, well, thank you, I mean, I'm sorry, but I was worried you—'

He sank back in his chair with a loud sigh. Jago took it to be one of relief.

'Yes, well, you can stop worrying, but I do want to know the truth. The thing is, you may not be a murderer, but you have been involved in stealing whisky and other goods, and supplying them illegally to third parties. Now that is true, isn't it?'

'You what?' Carlisle began, half rising from the chair, but then he stopped and slumped back again. He looked like a boxer who'd retired to his corner and lost the will to fight.

'All right,' he said. 'Yes, it is. But I wasn't doing any harm to anyone. Think about it – all that whisky being shipped off to America while no one in this country can get a decent dram, shops with no food worth buying. I was just diverting a little of it to people in this country who need it.'

'Very noble. And lining your own pocket into the bargain.'

Carlisle gave no reply.

'Is that why you tried to incriminate Bell?' Jago continued. 'What was going on?'

'He'd threatened me – he'd found out about the racket from Lambert and wanted a share of the spoils. I was already having to pay off the other men involved, so I couldn't afford to lose more.'

'Who were these other men? And no nonsense now.'

'All right. It was some of the dockers up in Scotland, Lambert and a couple of other men from the docks down here, and two of the *Magnolia*'s crew – the cook and one of the firemen.'

'You mean the lascar?'

'No, this fireman's English, from Yorkshire – we didn't involve any foreigners.'

'So you were the ringleader, the mastermind of this operation?'

'Aye, and Bell wanted to muscle in on it. He's a strong man, aggressive, and with his sort you can't assume what he says is just idle threats. I certainly wasn't going to be able to frighten him off myself. I needed to get him out of the way, even if it was only for a few days, and destroying his alibi for that murder was the only thing I could think of. I never thought you'd hang him, but I reckoned it might be enough to make you hold him for a while and that'd give me time to get away. I'm not a violent man, Inspector.'

'And what about Mr Jamal? You frightened him, didn't you? Why was that?'

'You mean the lascar?'

'Yes. I mean Mr Jamal. Why did you want to scare him?'

'He said he knew I'd stolen whisky and food from the ship, and that I was a bad man, because it's always people like him who get blamed for things like that. I didn't ask him how he knew – I didn't want to have him trying to blackmail me too – but I couldn't let him stay here and tell someone like you. I didn't want to hurt him, so I decided just to put the wind up him – told him that because he'd come forward as a witness to the murder there were men who were planning to kill him, and he'd better run away while he could. I laid it on a bit thick, but it worked. He was off this ship within the hour.'

'And you didn't care that if he fled we might think he was the murderer?'

'No, he was down in the boiler room all night, so I didn't think he'd done it and I reckoned you wouldn't either. He hasn't come to any harm, has he?'

'No, he hasn't, but it's no thanks to you.'

'I'm glad to hear that. I'm not a bad man, Inspector, just a tired man who's had enough of war and enough of the sea.'

'Well, I think it's likely you'll be having a break from seafaring pretty soon. You may've seen your economic enterprise as philanthropy, but the law calls it larceny. The courts don't like that sort of thing, even in peacetime – and in time of war they take an even stronger view of it. You're under arrest, Mr Carlisle.'

CHAPTER FORTY-THREE

By Cradock's reckoning it was past lunchtime, but with a prisoner to take back to the station he tried to put all thought of food from his mind, at least for the time being. With a bit of luck, he thought, by half past two they should have got shot of Carlisle and be tucking into something hot and filling in the station canteen. He put Carlisle in the back of the Riley and was about to get in with him when Jago restrained him.

'There's just one other person I want to see on our way back to the station,' said Jago. 'While we're down here, I'd like to call on Brenda Lambert and let her know we've arrested someone in connection with her husband's death.'

Cradock did his best to conceal his disappointment.

'Righto, guv'nor,' he said.

'It shouldn't take long, if she's in. I'll just pop in for a moment while you stay in the car with Carlisle and make sure he doesn't try to make a run for it.'

They drove round from the dock to her home,

where Jago got out and knocked on the door. It was opened, however, not by Mrs Lambert but by a young man in battledress.

'Ah, good afternoon, Mr Lightfoot,' said Jago. 'Is your mother at home?'

'Why do you want to know?' said Lightfoot.

'I'd just like a quick word with her. It's to do with your stepfather's death – I wanted to let her know we've made an arrest. Can I come in?'

Lightfoot looked slightly distracted, but opened the door wider and let him in.

'Come through to the kitchen,' he said.

Jago followed him into the small, dingy room. It was chillier than on his last visit: he suspected that the fire in the range had gone out.

'She's not here,' said Lightfoot.

'I see,' Jago replied. 'Do you know when she'll be back?'

'No – she didn't say. I don't know where she is, or how long she's gone for. She's just gone. I must've only just missed her myself. The thing is, I'm due back at Deal tomorrow – I told you I was on embarkation leave, didn't I?'

'Yes, you did.'

'Well, I was out with some mates last night having a bit of a farewell drink, and I ended up staying the night over in Canning Town to sleep it off. I came back about half an hour ago to get my kit and say goodbye to Mum, but there was nobody here. Then I found this.'

He pulled a crumpled envelope from his pocket and

opened it to remove a single sheet of paper.

'It's a note, from her to me.'

He straightened the notepaper and began to read.

'"Dear Tommy," she says – she always calls me Tommy, just like when I was a kid – "dear Tommy, just a quick line to say I'm sorry I won't be here when you get back, but I've got to go. You know I love you, and I'll be thinking of you all the time when you're back with the Marines, wherever you are. But I've just had a visit from a policeman – Detective Inspector Burton, from the dock police – and he said they've found out who killed your stepdad and arrested them. He wouldn't say who it was, but he said it wasn't you. I asked, you see, not that I ever thought it was you. I've been planning to go ever since he died, but I thought it might make them think I'd done it if I just disappeared, and besides, I couldn't go while you were home on leave. You've always been my lovely boy, and you always will be."'

He stopped to rub his nose, running his finger across his eye as he did so as if to hide what might have been a tear. He coughed and continued reading.

'"But like I said, I've got to go. I'm not running off with a man, though, in case you were wondering – I've had enough of men for the time being. The thing is, I've come into some money. I had another visit a couple of days ago, from a bloke I didn't know. He turned up at the front door with some cash in an envelope and said it was for the last job Ray had done for him. I said what job was that, and he just said, 'Ask me no questions,

I'll tell you no lies,' then sort of winked at me and went on his way. All very mysterious, but it reminded me of another little mystery. Ray had this suitcase that he kept locked, and he always said no one was allowed to open it – he said if he ever caught me trying to, he'd kill me. Well, you know what he was like, so I never chanced it. But with him gone, I took the poker to it and forced it open. There was quite a lot of money in it. I knew he was mixed up in something dodgy, and now I think I know what it was. There was a little cash book in the case, and it looked like he must've written down all the stuff he'd nicked from the docks and what he'd sold it for. All very neat and tidy it was, but then our Ray always was very good with figures, wasn't he? Didn't miss a trick. Anyway, to cut a long story short, for the first time in my life I've got a bit of cash, so I'm going away – I need to get away from this house, from Silvertown, from these damned bombs. If I don't, I think I'll go mad. All my love for ever, Mum."'

He stopped reading and handed the note to Jago, who ran his eye quickly over it.

'I see,' he said. 'I called in to let your mother know that we've arrested someone in connection with your stepfather's murder, but it looks as though she's already heard that news from DI Burton.'

'Yes, well, thanks anyway,' said Lightfoot.

'And I see there's a PS here,' Jago continued, reading from the notepaper. '"I can't tell you where I'm going, because I don't know. Besides, it's better for you not to know in case the police come asking. I'm just going to get on a train and go somewhere – anywhere – that's better than this place. But I'll let you know where I end up. I'll write to you on your ship and you'll get it sometime – hopefully the navy'll know where you are, even if I don't.'"

A smile began to cross Lightfoot's face.

'All things come to those who wait, I suppose,' he said. 'That's what they say, isn't it? She deserves a bit of good luck for a change. The only thing she's ever done wrong in her life is probably trying to love a man, so I say good luck to her. Or will you be launching a nationwide manhunt for her, Inspector?'

Jago's recent conversation with Dorothy about vengeance, mercy and justice drifted through his mind. Perhaps life had already taken enough revenge on Brenda.

'Police resources are under considerable strain at the moment, Mr Lightfoot,' he said. 'But I'll be keeping this information on file.'

CHAPTER FORTY-FOUR

Jago got off the Tube at Piccadilly Circus and walked eastwards in the direction of Leicester Square. The Guinness clock on the north side of the circus, no longer illuminated but still readable by day, said ten past four, and while the place was not as busy as he recalled from peacetime, a stream of buses, lorries, cars and horse-drawn carts still swarmed round the Shaftesbury Memorial Fountain on its island at the centre of the circus. The famous fountain was now present only in the visitor's imagination: the figure of Eros had been removed to a safer home shortly after war broke out, leaving just the dome of protective hoarding that covered its base as a reminder.

It was Dorothy who'd suggested they meet for tea at the Lyons Corner House: the big one on the corner of Coventry Street and Rupert Street, only a hundred yards or so from the station. He was ten minutes late, but with his two prisoners charged and put safely under lock and key, he could now clear his mind and concentrate on matters other than crime in the Royal Docks. Before leaving the police station, he'd taken Cradock to the canteen and bought him a mug of tea and a substantial helping of fruit cake, confident that as long as he fed the boy he could abandon him with a clear conscience.

When he got to the Corner House he saw Dorothy sitting at a small table, studying a menu. To his relief, she looked up and greeted him with a smile.

'I'm sorry I'm late,' he said contritely as he took the seat opposite her. 'I had a few loose ends to tie up and couldn't get away until I'd finished.'

'Don't worry,' she replied. 'I was a couple of minutes late myself.'

'Have you been busy?'

'Nothing too demanding – you remember I told Rita the other day I was writing a piece about what people in Britain are eating?'

'Yes.'

'Well, today I was researching how the upper crust are getting by on the food front. I went to Fortnum and Mason's in Piccadilly and discovered you can order Filet de Sole Polignac and have it delivered to your home, so things aren't too bad, at least for some.'

'A bit out of Rita's league, but then she has a different clientele – people like me.'

'And like me too – I may be living at the Savoy Hotel, but believe me, it'd be a very different story if the *Post* wasn't paying for it. But anyway, how about your day? If you've finished tying up those loose ends, does it mean you've got your case all sewn up?'

'I certainly hope so, and right now I feel in need of a break – I've spent enough time in those docks this week to last me a lifetime. It's like a world within a world down there, behind those walls and fences – different rules, different traditions, different ways of doing things, everything different to the outside. But I feel like I've escaped now, and I'm back in my own world. As for the case, it's all sewn up for a few days at least, I think – at any rate, I've got three people to take before the magistrates next week. One's a minor matter, illegal trading, but the others are more serious – one for larceny and one for murder.'

A nippy dressed in the distinctive Lyons uniform of black dress, white apron and starched cap came to their table, pad and pencil poised, and took their order. When she had gone, Dorothy looked round the room and lowered her voice a little so as not to be overheard.

'Larceny and murder, you say. Were the two crimes connected?'

'I suppose the answer's yes and no,' said Jago. 'There were some men stealing whisky from ships in Scotland – whisky that was supposed to be exported to your country – and they were sending it down to London to sell it on the black market. The Home Guard volunteer who was murdered was involved in the racket, although it turned out that wasn't why he was killed.'

'And you say you've charged someone.'

'Yes, we have, but I think she's going to plead self-defence. If the court accepts her plea she could walk out a free woman, although given that she was carrying a dagger while on voluntary duty with a mobile canteen she might find it difficult to persuade a jury there was no malice aforethought. There were no witnesses to support the idea of self-defence either, but that's not prevented juries returning a verdict of not guilty in the past when the accused was a young woman.'

'Will you be disappointed if she's cleared?'

'That's not for me to say. It's a jury's responsibility to make that decision, not mine. My job's just to bring her to court.'

'Of course.'

'It's quite an ironic case, really. It seems she wanted to protect her father from public shame, which sounds like a noble intention, but she ended up taking the law into her own hands. She had big plans for a career in law and said she even wanted to be a judge someday, but instead she set herself up as judge, jury and executioner.'

The nippy returned with a tray bearing plates of bread and butter, cucumber salad and Dundee cake for both of them, then brought cups and saucers and a china teapot, set them out carefully on the neat white tablecloth, and left.

'Shall I be mother?' said Jago, picking up the teapot.

'I've heard someone say that before,' said Dorothy. 'Do you British people always say that when you pour the tea?'

'I suppose we do, yes.'

'OK, then – yes, please.'

Jago poured two cups and they began to eat in silence.

'Oh, by the way,' said Dorothy, as if suddenly

remembering, 'I heard something this morning that you may think is good news.'

Jago waited for her to expand on this announcement, but all she did was fix him with what he thought was a curious gaze.

'Well?' he said. 'What good news is that?'

'It's about my colleague Philip Eliot. Seems he's got a new job, back in the States, so you may not be seeing him again.'

'Really? Give him my congratulations, then, if he can remember who I am.'

Dorothy couldn't fail to detect the note of sarcasm in Jago's voice.

'You don't like him, do you?' she said with a mischievous smile.

'It's not that. It's just – well, he's not my kind of man.'

'What's wrong with him?'

'I don't know. Maybe he's a little too comfortable, too healthy, too sure of himself.'

'Is that all?'

'I'm sorry. I shouldn't talk about your friend like that.'

'Don't worry – we're not that close.'

'Good. The thing is, I suppose he struck me as one of those men whose life seems to glide along from one success to another, probably because he was born with a silver spoon in his mouth.'

'I do believe you're jealous of him.'

'Perhaps I am. Perhaps if I'd been born rich I could've

sailed through life as a perpetual glamour boy too.'

'Glamour boy? Don't you think it might be a little unfair to decide that's what he is when you've only known him five minutes?'

Jago didn't reply. He had remembered where he'd last heard the phrase 'glamour boy' and the ease with which he had diagnosed its use by DI Burton as evidence of jealousy. She was right: he was jealous.

'I'm sorry,' he said. 'It's not fair, and I apologise. I don't like to appear jealous of anyone, but I think I am.'

'Why would you need to be jealous of Philip?'

'Do you want the truth?'

'Yes, please.'

Jago replied gently. He realised the problem was in his own mind and he didn't want to sound combative when talking to Dorothy.

'I think it's just because he's everything I'm not. He's wealthy, educated and sophisticated. There'll be doors that open to him that I wouldn't even presume to knock on. But mostly it's because he's from a different world to me, and it's your world too. I love . . . I love being with you, spending time together. I feel happy and at home when I'm with you. But when someone like him comes along, I suddenly feel like an intruder, an inferior – and I think that makes me feel jealous.'

'I guess you're right – he is educated and sophisticated, and probably wealthy too. He's what we call a Boston Brahmin, which means for an American, he's got breeding – he can trace his family back to the days when we were still a colony. But I can tell you this – he's got one big fault that as far as I'm concerned means you put him in the shade.'

'Really?'

'Yes, really. Not to put too fine a point upon it, the fact is he's not honest, especially about himself. That business about him being wounded in Spain, for example. It's not true. He and I were in Madrid together in thirty-seven during the Spanish Civil War, when Franco was bombarding the city. We were based at the Hotel Florida with most of the other foreign journalists – a bit like the Savoy here, but without the nice food. There was Ernest Hemingway, Martha Gellhorn, Sefton Delmer, who writes for your *Daily Express* – although we called him Tom – and lots of others. I think Eliot borrowed the story of his leg wound from Hemingway. Ernest got a shrapnel wound in the leg in 1918 when he was in Italy with the Red Cross ambulance service – when Italy was on our side against the Austrians – and even he's been known to exaggerate, but in Eliot's case I happen to know that he fell down a hole in the road in the dark during the attack and had to be evacuated on a stretcher with his leg in plaster. He's embellished the tale since, and I think he may even believe it himself now. It wasn't a real wound, but he boasts about it, whereas you're the opposite. You're quiet about your time in that war. I only found out you'd got the Military Cross when I saw it in the newspaper.'

'You don't believe what you read in the papers, do you?'

'Not necessarily, but I checked it out. I'm a journalist, remember – I'm paid to ask people questions and not necessarily believe what they tell me. You're just the same, aren't you?'

'Yes, I suppose I am.'

'So, I looked you up in the *London Gazette*. I found the citation, and it said you'd got it for conspicuous gallantry and devotion to duty, and that you'd displayed great coolness and courage under heavy shellfire on many occasions. That rings true for me, from what I know of you.'

'That was a long time ago,' said Jago. 'So you really checked up on me?'

'Of course I did. I've met a lot of liars in my time, and I wanted to know whether it was true. It was, and so I trust you. Eliot may be a charming friend and colleague, but I can't say I trust him. When you talk to me, it feels like the truth, and I like that.'

Jago knew he should feel pleased that she saw him as a man who told her the truth, but instead her words only troubled him more. He remembered talking to Dorothy at another time, in another place: on the steps of St Martin-in-the-Fields, where he'd admitted to himself, but not to her, that for twenty years he'd allowed no one into his life and yet he'd yearned to have someone who knew him truly and deeply. And that was the problem – to be known in that way meant telling someone what he'd never said to anyone. Perhaps there'd never been anyone to tell, no one he could trust enough to reveal his deepest and darkest secrets, but Dorothy was someone he could trust, so what excuse did he have now?

He needed time to think.

CHAPTER FORTY-FIVE

There was a silence while they both finished their tea. Jago glanced across at Dorothy's plate and saw that it was empty.

'Do you fancy some fresh air?' he said, draining his cup. 'I thought maybe I could walk you back to your hotel before the blackout.'

'Sure,' she said. 'I'd like that.'

He paid the bill, and they left the cafe. They walked back the way he'd come, towards Piccadilly Circus, but then turned left down Haymarket. A year or so ago at this time of the evening the street would have been filling with elegantly dressed people on their way to its theatres, but not now: all such entertainments had been closed down by the government.

They continued into Cockspur Street, past the Admiralty Arch and on into Northumberland Avenue, a wide, tree-lined street with grand stone buildings that rose on either side like the cliffs of a canyon, making the cabmen's shelter at its southern end look like a ramshackle garden shed in comparison. A few yards more and they were crossing the Victoria Embankment to the river, with trains rumbling in and out of Charing Cross station on the Hungerford Bridge above their heads.

Dorothy stopped by the stone balustrade that ran along the edge of the embankment and leant on it, facing the water. Jago joined her, still wrestling in his mind with what to say. Looking downstream to where the Thames curled away to the right, they could see in the distance the new Waterloo Bridge, still being built, and beyond it the dome of St Paul's Cathedral towering over the jumble of riverside wharves and warehouses.

'I like watching the river,' said Dorothy. 'There's something very calming about it – as if no matter what terrible things we people may do to each other, it just rolls along day by day, year by year, always the same.'

Jago said nothing. He found the sight far from calming: it reminded him again of the face he'd seen, the face that haunted him. He broke away.

'What's the matter?' said Dorothy.

'I need to sit down,' he replied. 'Let's go further along – the Victoria Embankment Gardens are just down here. They back onto the Savoy, so we can sit there for a while and then I can escort you right to the door.'

They walked on silently towards Cleopatra's Needle and entered the gardens. These were a narrow strip of trees and neatly trimmed grass, no more than two hundred yards at their widest and laid out with paths, flower beds and statues, between the embankment and the grand buildings that lined the southern side of the Strand. The gardens were deserted and quiet, with only a faint rumble of distant traffic in the background. They found a bench and sat on it, side by side. Jago still didn't know how to begin.

'I've been thinking about what you said the day before yesterday,' he said at last, 'when we were in that bar in Maiden Lane – about tempering justice with mercy.'

'Yes?'

'I think you're right, but it's something I find difficult to do – it just doesn't seem to come naturally to me.'

'Anyone can do it, John. You just have to decide.'

'But that's it. I don't think I can decide.'

'I don't understand.'

He felt as though he was walking into a trap that he'd deliberately constructed for himself. He wanted to have no way of escape, otherwise he would never say what he knew he must.

'Do you remember when we sat on the steps outside that church – St Martin-in-the-Fields?' he began.

'Yes, I do.'

'You said something like we all want to be known by someone.'

'That's right – known, accepted and understood.'

'When you said that, I thought that's what I want, but I don't think I've got that kind of relationship with anyone.' He paused. 'I hope you don't mind me saying this, but if there's one person I'd like to know me and understand me, I think it's . . . well, I think it's you.'

The sound of these words coming from his own mouth

brought him to a halt again. Dorothy was silent, but it seemed to him a warm and patient silence, encouraging him to go on.

'The thing is,' he continued, 'if I want you to know me, I need you to know me as I really am, and that's what I find difficult. I was brought up to be strong, never to admit weakness – that's what men were supposed to be like. I don't know quite how to put it.'

'You don't need fancy words, John. Just say it. I said back in the cafe that I like the fact that you tell me the truth, and I mean it.'

'OK,' he said, drawing a deep breath to steady his nerves. 'Here's a piece of the truth about me, then. It's something I was thinking about just now, when we were standing by the river. I was doing the same thing on Wednesday, down in North Woolwich, staring into the Thames. I thought I could see something in the water – a face. Just my imagination, of course, but it's a face I've seen again and again over the last twenty years and more. It's the face of a German soldier. I was in the front line for the first time, and we were ordered to advance. We came under fire – machine guns. I dived into a shell hole, and that's where I met him. He was crouching with his bayonet pointed at me, and we stood there, face-to-face. It seemed like for ever, but it must've been just seconds. My mind was racing.'

'You thought he was going to kill you?'

'Yes – or that I was going to kill him. I'd never been that close to the enemy before. It's one thing when you're firing a rifle at them from hundreds of yards away, but another when you're just a few feet apart. When I think about it now, it feels as though I had two duties – a military duty to kill the king's enemy and a moral duty not to take another man's life in cold blood. But all I could think then was that I had to make a choice, and I didn't know what to do.'

'Some people might say you had no choice.'

'And maybe they're right. It's fine to talk about seasoning your justice with mercy when you're on a stage in a play, but real life's not like that. How can you be merciful in a war, when you've been put in a brown uniform and some other poor soul's been put in grey? You've never met before, you've got nothing against each other, but it's your duty to kill each other.'

His voice broke off. She could see this wasn't just a rhetorical question: it was an expression of some deeper pain.

'I'm not sure I know the answer to that,' she said gently. 'I've been in a war. I saw what it does to people when I was in Spain, but I was only watching it, not fighting it. I haven't been in your shoes – only you can find an answer to that.'

They were both silent.

She was right, Jago thought. Only he could find an answer, but he needed her help. He thought of what he'd said in the Corner House about the docks – a world within a world. The experience he was trying to tell her about was his own world within a world: a separate place deep within him barred by security gates that let nothing in or out. Only he could break those gates open.

'So what happened?' said Dorothy, her voice almost a whisper.

He steeled himself to speak, doing his best to look her in the eye.

'In the end,' he said, 'I made my choice. I remember standing there, waiting for him to move, wondering if I was about to die. Then suddenly he threw himself towards me, rifle and bayonet pushed out in front of him. He slipped in the mud and stumbled, and I dodged the blade. He was trying to get up. Maybe I could've escaped, maybe I could've let him do the same – some people might even say I should've taken him prisoner. But I didn't. Instead, before he could get to his feet I clubbed him on the side of his head with the butt of my rifle. He fell to the ground and didn't move.'

'He was dead?'

Jago slowly nodded his head.

'I think so, yes,' he replied, his voice as quiet as hers. 'For a moment I was frozen, but then I bent down and rolled him over, and I saw his face. He was young. He looked just like me. I didn't know what to do – I just got away as fast as I could.' He paused. 'So that's it. That's what I wanted you to know about me – that I could take a man's life just like that. I've never forgotten it.'

Jago waited for Dorothy to say something, anything, but there was nothing. He searched her face for an answer but found none. All he could see was a dampness in her eyes that slowly grew until it brimmed over into a tear and rolled gently, silently, down her cheek.

ACKNOWLEDGEMENTS

When I was a boy I learnt that people who worked in the London docks had ways of obtaining things. Quite what things, and how, were a mystery to me, but then the docks were a mysterious place, sealed off from the outside world by forbidding walls, fences and gates, a place that operated by its own rules. As Jago reflects in this story, they were a world within a world – and one that is now gone for ever, the railway lines pulled up and the transit sheds torn down.

The strip of land on which once stood the southern quay of the Royal Albert Dock, where the murder victim's body was discovered at the start of this story, is now the runway of London City Airport. Where in November 1940 the SS *Magnolia* had moored after its voyage from Scotland, today every few minutes jet airliners land from all over Europe.

As I have tried to recreate the world of London's Royal Docks for this book, I've drawn on a wide range of sources. I'm grateful in particular to the archives of the Museum of London Docklands, who showed me numerous historical maps and documents, and the Museum of London, who let me listen to their oral history interviews with dockers and Port of London Authority Police officers of the 1930s and 1940s. A. E. Smith's book *London's Royal Docks in the 1950s* was also a fascinating source of historical information.

I'd like to thank Sarabjeet Singh for his advice on Sikh names, and Faisal Shaikh and Nurul Hoque for theirs on Muslim names. Thanks are due as always to Roy Ingleton for his expertise on wartime policing and to Rudy Mitchell for his help with American English matters, and also to Dr David Love for his guidance on knife wounds. I have benefitted greatly from the advice of my old friend Captain Dennis Barber, who has drawn on his fifty-four years of experience in the Merchant Navy and the shipping industry to help me navigate my way round the life, language and practices of mercantile shipping.

Lastly, thanks to my editor Kelly Smith and all her colleagues at Allison & Busby for their commitment to these books, and to Margaret, Catherine and David for their unfailing patience, wisdom and encouragement.

MIKE HOLLOW was born in West Ham, on the eastern edge of London, and grew up in Romford, Essex. He studied Russian and French at the University of Cambridge and then worked for the BBC and later Tearfund. In 2002 he went freelance as a copywriter, journalist, editor and translator, but now gives all his time to writing the Blitz Detective books.

blitzdetective.com   @MikeHollowBlitz